"Is there anything else you wanted to say?"

Amanda snapped, glaring at Chance's smiling face.

"You don't like me, do you?" he asked with a chuckle.

"No, I don't."

Chance's smile broadened at her words. "Would you care to tell me why?"

"You remind me of my father," she blurted out, unable to stop herself.

"In looks or character?"

"What difference does it make? You're nothing but a drifter, just like him."

Amanda sucked in her breath as Chance reached out and ran a finger down the side of her cheek. "I'm not such a bad guy when you get to know me. And you do present an awfully tempting package...."

Dear Reader,

From a haunted ghost town to a widower with five daughters, there is something for everyone in our titles for December.

There is trouble brewing in DeLoras Scott's *Springtown,* and Chance Doyer and Amanda Bradshaw are right in the middle of it. This intriguing tale is sure to delight DeLoras Scott fans who have been patiently waiting for her next book.

British spy Anne Hargraves is on a mission to expose Queen Victoria's would-be assassin, when she finds herself falling for one of her prime suspects in *Dangerous Deceptions* by Erin Yorke.

Promises To Keep from Nina Beaumont is the sequel to *Sapphire Magic.* In this tale of an American woman's journey to unravel the mystery of her birth, the heroine returns to Vienna at a time of political turmoil.

Amity Becker is a mail-order bride in Lynda Trent's *Beloved Wife,* the story of a young woman who is overwhelmed by her handsome new husband and his five unruly daughters.

We hope you enjoy this month's selection, and, from all of us at Harlequin Historicals, we would like to wish you and your family the very best of the season.

Sincerely,

Tracy Farrell
Senior Editor

Springtown

DeLoras Scott

Harlequin Books

TORONTO • NEW YORK • LONDON
AMSTERDAM • PARIS • SYDNEY • HAMBURG
STOCKHOLM • ATHENS • TOKYO • MILAN
MADRID • WARSAW • BUDAPEST • AUCKLAND

Harlequin Historicals first edition December 1992

ISBN 0-373-28751-8

SPRINGTOWN

Books by DeLoras Scott

Harlequin Historicals

Bittersweet #12
Fire and Ice #42
The Miss and the Maverick #52
Rogue's Honor #123
Springtown #151

Harlequin Books

Historical Christmas Stories 1991
''Fortune's Gift''

DELORAS SCOTT

was raised in Sutter's Mill, California—an area steeped in history. At one time it was gold country, and the legacy of wagon trains, cowboys and miners has remained. It's no wonder she enjoys writing about a chapter of history referred to as the Old West.

Prologue

California, 1856

As the sun slowly disappeared behind the mountain peaks, the digger pines, cliffs and rocks began to look like nothing more than dark shadows to the solitary rider. Still, Chance Doyer continued to move his mount at a leisurely pace. For the past year, he had traveled across the great mother-lode country, from one mining town to another, searching. He released a tired sigh. There was no longer any reason to continue.

Spotting a campfire about half a mile down the hillside, Chance brought his big buckskin, Cactus, to a halt. Having someone to converse with suddenly appealed to him. Maybe being a loner and drifter was beginning to wear thin, although he still couldn't rid himself of the gut-wrenched hate he felt toward Logan and Patricia, even though he now knew they'd been killed. That was something he'd planned on doing, savoring, himself. He'd been so close. But, less than a week ago, someone had cheated him of the pleasure.

Chance glanced up at the sky, already dotted with a few stars, then back down at the campfire. Two shadowy figures moved back and forth in front of the orange flames. Cautious by nature, he palmed the pistol resting in his holster. Satisfied, he nudged his horse forward, making sure the men would hear his approach.

"Pa, how much money you reckon they're keepin' in that Wells Fargo office in Columbia?" Vern asked excitedly.

"Keep your damn voice down, boy! You never know who's ridin' around these parts. And I've told you before, I ain't got no idea how much money they got, so stop askin'!" The grizzled old man shifted his rear to a more comfortable position on the bedroll. The heat of the fire was the only thing that seemed to alleviate the aching in his joints. "Fred, how much longer is it gonna be before we eat?"

"It's ready, Pa." Fred was about to spoon some of the rabbit stew onto a tin plate when he heard a rider approaching. He glanced at the other two men. His father was sliding a shotgun to his side, and his brother stood rigid, his hand close to his pistol.

"Keep sloppin' that food in the plate, Fred," Gus Himple ordered softly, "and act like nothin's wrong. Damn it, Vern, look busy!"

When the stranger rode into view, the three men stared openly. They watched the tall man dismount with the litheness of a cat. His short beard was the same sandy color as the long hair that hung well past the collar of his brown coat. His hat was pulled low, hiding his eyes. As he stepped forward into the firelight, his smile did nothing to ease the hardness of his face.

One look at the dirty threesome changed Chance's mind about remaining the night. "Name's Chance. Thought you might be willing to share a cup of coffee with a weary traveler.''

"Chance?" Fred laughed nervously. "Where the hell did you come by a name like that?"

"My pa was a gambler."

"Come join us," Gus has hospitably. "Fred, dish our visitor up a plate of stew. I'll bet he's right hungry."

"That's mighty kind of you." Chance wasn't about to turn down a free meal, even though he had a hunch the trio spelled big trouble. He accepted the plate Fred handed him before squatting on his heels.

"My name's Gus, and these here are my two boys, Vern and Fred."

Chance acknowledged them with a nod, then took a bite of the savory stew.

"Where you headed?" the old man asked.

"Thought I'd pull up at Angels Camp and see if there's any gold left."

"Hell, you should ride to Columbia with us. I been told there's still plenty of gold there."

While enjoying the tasty meal, Chance observed the men busily slurping down their own food. They were a grubby lot, with their full beards, grimy clothes and sweat-stained floppy hats. They didn't smell any better than they looked, especially the old man. Of course, if he hadn't spent last night at a hotel, he wouldn't have looked much better.

Chance guessed Gus to be at least in his sixties. The old man's gray hair was straggly, a red bulbous nose dominated his weathered face, and his front teeth were missing. But he was big, a bull of a man. In contrast, the sons were short and rail-thin. Each looked as if he'd kill a man just for the pleasure of it. But was he any different? Over the years, only his fast draw and fists had kept Chance from lying dead in some unmarked grave.

All in all, the group proved to be friendly enough, but as soon as he'd finished his meal, Chance stood, ready to leave. Whether he was holed up at Angels Camp or Columbia really made no difference. "Thanks for the food, but I think I'd best be moseying on. I still want to cover some distance before I call it a night." He was about to mount his horse when he felt the end of a steel barrel jammed into his back. "What the hell's going on?" he demanded.

"Nothin' you gotta worry about," Gus replied amicably. "We're just goin' to relieve you of your belongings. Now pull that pistol out real slow and drop it on the ground, or Fred's gonna kill you."

"I've taken a likin' to that pretty pearl handle," Fred stated excitedly.

"And I've taken a likin' to your buckskin horse," Gus added. "Sure as hell beats that piebald nag of mine. What's his name?"

"Cactus," Chance answered sharply.

Gus scratched his chin. "Why would you name him that?"

"You'll find out if you try riding him."

"Never saw a horse I couldn't ride. Now step away and drop that damn gun!"

Chance clenched his teeth. He was furious at the thought of losing his pistol. It was the only thing he had left of his brother's, and it was the possession he cherished the most. As he slipped the gun from his holster, he suddenly jerked around and planted a fist squarely on Fred's jaw. Fred crumpled to the ground, unconscious. Chance heard a shot fired, and a burning pain ripped through his shoulder. He turned, ready to take on the other two, but it was too late. Vern brought the butt end of his gun down hard on Chance's head. Chance felt himself falling, and then everything went black.

Chapter One

Columbia, California

"You did what?" Amanda Bradshaw straightened, the skirt she'd been washing dangling from her hand.

"You heard me, girl. I've arranged for you to marry Lester Adam."

Amanda waved a wet fist at her father. "You really have lost your mind this time! I wouldn't marry that sickly toad if it meant my life! Good Lord! He's even two years younger than I am!" Considering the conversation closed, she leaned over the large copper tub again, then slapped the skirt onto the washboard. The steam drifting up from the hot water caused short, straggly hairs to cling tenaciously to the sides of her reddened cheeks.

"It's your duty!" Ben Bradshaw persisted, pulling a handkerchief from his pocket to mop his forehead.

"How could you even consider such a thing, Pa? If I wanted to marry, I could have my pick of men in this town!"

"Amanda, come into the house and let's at least talk about it," Ben pleaded.

"No. There's nothing to talk about."

"What are you going to do? Spend the rest of your life doing people's laundry? You're not getting any younger. You're twenty, girl! And look at your hands. All red and chapped from lye soap. All you do is work, work, work!"

"Which is more than I can say for you." Amanda wiped her hands on her soiled apron. "You'll do anything to get your hands on money, short of work or landing in jail. It's my laundry that keeps food on the table and a roof over our heads!"

Ben threw his hand across his chest. "You know I haven't gotten over your mother leaving me," he whined.

"Don't give me that, Pa. You bought her a ticket on the Wells Fargo stage just to get rid of her."

"And you should be grateful. She wasn't a fittin' mother. But it's because you don't have a mother to guide you that it becomes my responsibility to see you properly married."

Amanda brushed past him and entered the lean-to shack. Ben followed right behind her.

After pouring a drink of water, Amanda turned and looked suspiciously at her father. "What's in this for you?"

"What's in it for me?" Ben flopped down on one of the rough-hewn chairs. "How could you even think such a thing?" He removed his dusty old derby and mopped his bald head. "I'm giving you a chance to live like a lady. You'll have a fine house and never have to scrub clothes again."

"I don't believe you. You wouldn't be about to get rid of me if there wasn't money in it. And speaking of money, I don't have to ask what you did with the money you stole from me. I can smell your breath."

"You have no right to keep money from your father."

"I have every right. That money was mine. I was saving it for some material to make a dress. I only have two, and both of them are practically rags. Not that you care."

"That's exactly my point. You wouldn't have to worry about such things if you'd only marry Lester."

Fire danced in Amanda's brown eyes. "You can go tell Henry Adam that I'm not going to marry his son!" She left the shack and returned to her washing.

"Damn!" Ben muttered. Thinking about the gold that was quickly slipping from his hands made him all the more determined. After all, a man had to look after his own well-being! And even though Henry Adam had more money than was humanly decent, it had taken a lot of bickering to get him to bargain away a healthy sum plus a percentage of his mine! Henry wanted a grandson before Lester was too sick to produce one. Ben stuffed his handkerchief back in his pocket and looked at the clean but sparsely furnished room. What furniture they did have, Amanda had taken in trade for washing. If this deal went through, he would be financially set for life. There had to be a way to get Amanda to agree to a wedding.

An hour later, Ben had a solution.

Amanda wiped her face with her apron and watched her father head back toward town. A slow smile spread across her full lips. The one thing she'd learned from her father was how to be wily. She'd deliberately left a small amount of money in the cookie canister, knowing that when he found it, he wouldn't look any further. The rest of her stash was safely hidden under her straw mattress. Before too much longer, she'd have saved enough for the stage fare to Sacramento, plus some left over for food and lodging until she could find work. One way or another, she was leaving this damn mining town. The big fire in '55 had scared the living tar out of her. And just last week there'd been twelve murders. Not surprising, since there were over thirty rip-roaring saloons scattered about. She tossed more clothes into the large vat. Once she left, she'd never look back.

That night, Amanda went to bed early, dead-tired, as usual. Tomorrow was another long day, and she had to rise at daybreak to pick up and deliver laundry.

Amanda was having a wonderful dream about being kidnapped by a handsome stranger who was taking her away from a life of slavery. But he insisted on tying her wrists, even though she assured him she wouldn't try to escape. Amanda awoke with a start. Still a bit disoriented, she wondered who had lit the lantern. Then she saw her father standing beside the bed, holding a rope. When she tried to sit up, she was shocked to discover that her hands had been tied. "What in God's name are you doing?" she demanded, anger darkening her eyes almost to black. Too late, she started to swing her legs off the bed, only to have them grabbed. Her father made short work of tying her ankles.

"You're going to regret this." She knew this had something to do with her marrying Lester Adam.

"Now, Amanda," Ben said, grinning down at his daughter, "there's no need for you to get upset. I'm only thinkin' of your future."

"Pa, you untie me right now!"

"I'm afraid I can't do that, girl. Since you refused to marry Lester, I realized I had to take matters into my own hands."

"You can't make me marry him!"

"We'll see. Stop struggling. I don't want your intended to see bruises."

"I'll struggle all I want! I'm warning you, take these ropes off of me or you'll never see a scrap of food on your table again."

"I'm sorry, Amanda, but with all your carrying on, I have no choice but to gag you."

Amanda began releasing one ear-splitting scream after another, while at the same time kicking and thrashing her head back and forth, but it was all to no avail.

When he'd completed the seemingly impossible task of gagging her, Ben's face was bathed in perspiration. But at least he'd finally stopped that confounded noise. Though she'd become silent, her flashing eyes made Ben leery. He cursed aloud when suddenly she again managed a hard kick to his thigh. As he stepped away to prevent any more damage to his body, she slid off the bed, landing on the floor with a thud.

"Damn it, Amanda, quit fighting me. I'm your father. You're not supposed to fight your father!" Ben considered his daughter a moment. Though both he and Amanda were slight of build, Amanda was still half a head taller, and as strong as an ox. Getting her into the small delivery wagon wasn't going to be easy. She was already inching her way across the floor toward the door. At least her actions were of some help. He wouldn't have to carry her.

When Amanda had made it to the front doorway, Ben came up behind her and placed his hands beneath her arms. She struggled with the might of a captured bear, and Ben was sweating profusely by the time he succeeded in dragging her to the wagon. Once he managed to get her over his shoulder, he wasn't sure he could stand. Expelling a loud grunt, he forced his body upward, staggered, then leaned forward and dumped Amanda into the back of the delivery wagon. Holding his aching back, he stumbled around to the front. He scrambled up onto the seat, then slapped the reins over the horse's rump before Amanda could work her way out of the wagon. He was already worn out, and he still had over two miles to go before he reached Henry Adam's house.

Amanda could not remember ever being so furious with her father. He'd pulled many stunts over the years, but this one beat them all. To top it off, he was moving the horse at a fast pace. Every time she tried sitting up, a wheel would hit a rock, knocking her down again. Finally, she just gave up, telling herself that Henry Adam would never go along with this, and she'd be damned if she'd say "I do" to some preacher!

Ben expelled a heavy sigh of relief when he finally brought the horse to a halt in front of Henry's fine two-story house. He jumped down from the wagon, scurried up the three steps, then pounded his fist several times on the door. After what seemed like an hour, the door swung open. Dressed in his nightshirt and holding a candle, the big, barrel-chested Henry Adam filled the doorway.

"What the hell are you doing here this time of night?" Henry roared.

"I've brought Amanda," Ben replied meekly. Suddenly he wasn't so sure of his plan.

Henry glanced around. When he saw no one else, his eyes focused on Ben again.

"She's tied up in the wagon." Ben blessed the fact that Henry was a widower.

"What the hell—"

"Now, Henry, you've obviously given a lot of thought to this marriage, and you must want it pretty bad, or you wouldn't have made that deal with me. I have an idea that'll satisfy us both, but we need to talk. Why don't you help me get Amanda into the house so we can discuss it?"

"All right, bring her in."

"I'm not getting any younger, Henry, and since this was your idea, why don't you do the carrying?"

Disgruntled, Henry handed Ben the candle. Walking to the back of the wagon, he scooped Amanda up in his arms. "I don't know what your problem is. She's as light as a feather."

Ben scowled at Henry's broad back as he followed the man inside.

Once Amanda was deposited on a brocade divan, the two men entered the small library, closing the door firmly behind them.

"Start talking," Henry stated menacingly as he dropped onto a deep leather chair.

Ben locked his hands behind him and looked Henry straight in the eye. "It's like this, Henry. My little Amanda doesn't know how to use the sense she was born with. I couldn't believe how dead set she was against marrying such a fine, upstanding boy as Lester. Thank the good Lord that I'm here to properly guide her."

"Just get on with it, Ben."

"Because Amanda was so adamant, I realized there was only one way to get her married. It would have to be by that traveling preacher...." Ben scratched the back of his head. "Hanson! That's his name."

"How are we gonna get Amanda to agree?"

"That's the easy part." Ben pulled a vial from his pocket before sitting in the chair across from Henry. "You keep Amanda locked in a room, and in a couple of days, when that preacher comes through, I'll give her some of this." He held up the vial. "She'll be so groggy she won't know what she's agreeing to. I know my daughter, Henry, and when she realizes she's married, she'll settle right down and make you a good daughter-in-law and Lester a good wife. She loves children.''

Henry broke out laughing. "Hell, Ben, that doesn't sound like such a bad idea!''

Ben closed his eyes in relief. This hadn't been an easy night for him, but at least this part of the plan was over.

The men had just gone into the library when Lester made his way down the stairs, wondering what all the commotion was about. As he entered the foyer, he was shocked to see Amanda Bradshaw hopping toward the door, her ankles bound with rope. He moved quietly behind her. "Amanda?'' When she jerked around, he gasped at seeing that her hands were also tied and she had been gagged. Her already large eyes became the size of two moons when he reached toward her. "I'm only going to remove your gag,'' he said gently.

Amanda nodded, then turned her head so that he could undo the knot. "I'm not going to marry you, Lester,'' she declared as soon as moisture had returned to her mouth.

"What are you talking about?''

Amanda stared at the thin young man, whose face was nearly as white as alabaster. She wasn't even sure he'd reached eighteen yet. "You mean you know nothing about this?''

"That's right. Here, I'll untie you and you can tell me what this is about.'' He broke into a coughing fit.

To Amanda's exasperation, he doubled over and leaned against the door to support himself, preventing her escape. Hearing him wheeze between bouts, she felt sorry for Lester. But she was suffering from a far more pressing problem. Had he blocked the door on purpose so that she couldn't get away? Maybe he was in cahoots with her father. Time was running out, and she had to escape! She was thinking about shoving him aside when the coughing stopped and he straightened up. She held her hands out, praying he'd untie the rope. "Neither you or anyone else can make me marry you, Lester. Now if you don't turn me loose, I guarantee you'll live to regret it!"

"Not until you tell me what this is all about."

"As if you don't already know that your pa and mine are planning on us getting married," Amanda said sarcastically. She was surprised to see Lester's face turning red with anger.

"I should have known Pa would try to keep me away from Polly O'Neil," Lester grumbled as he untied the knot. "He's furious because I told him I was going to marry a dance hall girl. Well, they're not going to get away with it. We'll make our own plans."

They both heard the door to the library creak open. Amanda groaned. She'd waited too long.

"Listen, Amanda," Lester whispered. "I can get us out of this, but you have to help. You have to pretend you're willing to go along with the wedding."

Amanda was horrified.

"You don't know my pa. Once he sets his mind to something, nothing stands in his way. You gotta trust me. We have to stall them. They're coming."

Amanda vacillated between hopping out the door and doing what Lester said. The decision was taken from her when she saw the two men enter the foyer. In a moment of sheer desperation, she threw her arms around Lester's neck. If nothing else, the rash action would give her time to plan an escape.

"Amanda," Lester murmured in her ear, "I want to leave as bad as you do. You have to take me with you."

"What's going on here?" Henry demanded.

Lester turned, a weak smile spreading across his pale lips. "Thank you, Pa. I never thought Amanda would get over that argument we had. When did you discover how we felt about each other?"

The two men looked at one another then back at the young couple.

"What's he saying, girl?" Ben asked suspiciously, his brow deeply furrowed.

Deciding she had nothing to lose, Amanda forced a bright smile. "He's saying he has talked me into marrying him. We've been in love since we were children. I'll have a fine wedding dress, won't I?"

"Indeed you will," Henry assured her.

Ben didn't know what the pair was trying to pull, but he wasn't about to ask any questions. Not in front of Henry. "Then there's no need to delay. We can go wake up the preacher!"

"But—but I need at least a couple of days to prepare." Amanda glanced at Lester. Seeing his slight nod, she continued. "And what about my trousseau?"

Henry stepped up and gave Amanda a bear hug. "We'll have the wedding one week from today," he proclaimed as he stepped away.

"I think we should do it tonight," Ben stated anxiously.

"No, Amanda is right." Henry said. "She should have a trousseau. In fact, she'll stay right here under this roof so she can start getting used to us."

Amanda bit the inside of her lip. "But what will people think? It wouldn't be proper to remain under the same roof until *after* the wedding."

"That's no problem. Ben will stay here, too. Now it's late, and I need my sleep. Follow me. I'll show you to your adjoining rooms. Lester, you go to bed."

Ben was convinced Amanda was up to something, and he didn't like the delay one bit. But at least he could keep a close eye on her.

Feeling momentarily defeated and worn out, Amanda went with Henry up the stairs. Her father was right behind her, and she knew he wasn't about to let her out of his sight.

Their escape took place two days later. It was pitch-dark when Lester and Amanda left the house and made their way to the corral. Amanda wasn't the least bit worried about her father waking up and finding them gone. While hanging up his coat the other night, she'd found a bottle of laudanum in his pocket. She'd slipped some in his whiskey before he'd gone to bed.

Lester quickly saddled a horse. Riding double, they headed for town. When they arrived at the livery stable, Polly O'Neil was sitting on the seat of a wagon. Although Amanda had protested her joining them, Lester had insisted. Two sturdy horses had already been hitched up, and everything was in readiness for their departure.

"What took you so long, Lester?" Polly demanded. "I've been here for over an hour. Hell, we could have been halfway to Sacramento by now! Well, are you going to get off that nag and onto the wagon?"

The moon was only a sliver, and Amanda couldn't see the other woman's features clearly. But she could certainly hear Polly's grating voice. As Lester helped her down from the horse, Amanda was already having second thoughts about their journey. At least one good thing had come out of all this. During one of his trips to town, Lester had stopped by her house and procured her money from beneath the mattress. She wasn't about to let her father enjoy it.

Chapter Two

Faces sunburnt and gingham bodices soaked with perspiration, the two women stared at the mound of dirt and rock.

"How could Lester have the nerve to up and die?" Polly complained peevishly. Impatiently she brushed back the tuft of bright red hair hanging in her face. "Now what are we goin' to do?"

Amanda leaned on the shovel handle, as exhausted as Polly. Though she'd been brought up to act like a lady, Amanda had been around miners for a good many years. There was little she hadn't heard—including some tales about the ladies of the night. She didn't approve of Polly, but she was trying awfully hard to maintain some respect for the dead. "I guess we should say some kind of prayer."

"You say a prayer. I'm going back to the wagon." Polly started up the hill. "Lester's coughin' fit wasn't any worse than the others he'd had, so I don't see why he had to let this one kill him!"

Amanda hastily said, "Rest with God," then ran after Polly. They hadn't gotten along since leaving Columbia almost two weeks before, and she'd had enough of Polly's constant complaining. Now that Lester was dead, there was nothing stopping her from giving the hussy a piece of her mind.

As soon as Amanda caught up with Polly, she grabbed the buxom woman's arm and spun her around. "I've had enough of your attitude. Lester was a good-hearted boy, and he deserved a lot better than you. If you didn't care about him, why did you bother coming along?"

Polly placed her hands on her well-rounded hips and glared at the smaller woman. "Why do you think? Someday he was goin' to inherit his pa's mine. Now I've got nothin'! And if that isn't bad enough, we can't even return to Columbia, 'cause his old man would have us both hangin' from a tree once he found out his son was dead!"

"That's the most selfish, cold-blooded thing I've ever heard. But what could I expect from a dance hall girl?"

"Ha! You think you're better? You're white trash who takes in laundry and has a good-for-nothing father who probably never worked a day in his life! He was always tryin' to get one of the girls to give him a free—"

"At least I didn't sleep with every man who had a little gold in his pocket!" She started on up the hill, ignoring Polly's guttural snarl.

The moment Amanda passed in front of her, Polly grabbed a handful of Amanda's black hair and yanked, sending Amanda sprawling to the ground. Suddenly Polly felt Amanda grab her legs, and before she could do anything, she was shoved to the ground with Amanda on top of her.

The two women rolled down the hill, biting, scratching, pulling hair, socking and screaming. It was the mound they'd buried Lester under that stopped their downward progress. In horror, the women immediately stopped fighting, sat up and scooted away.

"It's an omen," Polly whispered.

"No, it's Lester." Trying to catch her breath, Amanda stared down at her skirts. They were gathered around her hips and covered with dirt. Gently she reached up and touched her eye.

"You're gonna have a real shiner," Polly said proudly, her breathing as labored as Amanda's.

Amanda looked sideways at Polly. Her hair was in wild disarray, and the paint on her face was now smeared and mixed with dirt. Seeing the puffiness beneath one eye, Amanda managed a smile. "Don't act so smug. You're going to have one, too." Realizing she had to look every bit as bad as her traveling companion, Amanda suddenly broke out laughing. It deepened the pain in her already tight chest. "You know, Polly, after... burying Lester and... tussling with you... I don't think I can make it back up the hill." She collapsed back onto the ground.

For a good ten minutes, the two women lay in silence, staring up at the blue sky, catching their breath and contemplating their fate.

"What are we goin' to do now?" Polly finally asked.

"I guess we have no choice but to keep going. I don't know how Lester could have been so positive we'd make it to Sacramento. Scarecrow Jackson was probably dead drunk when he drew that map. The least Lester could have done was take a good look at it before we left. No one would be able to follow all those squiggly lines."

"So we're lost."

"I think we were lost from the time we crossed the Stanislaus River." Amanda pulled herself to her feet and looked up. They were in a forest of giant redwood trees that reminded her of sentinels touching the sky. The huge trunks were larger than a house, and rays of sunlight filtered through the treetops, making her think of God. For a moment she expected to hear a voice booming down from the sky.

"Are we gonna die?"

Polly's words snapped Amanda back to reality. "Not if I can help it. All we have to do is find a town. I know Lester wanted to throw his father off our trail, but I don't know why he kept insisting we head north. I used to do one of the stagecoach drivers' laundry, and he told me Sacramento was west." She reached down and helped Polly up.

"Well," Polly said as she tried dusting off her skirt, "at least we have a couple of things goin' for us. The water barrels are full, and we still have some supplies."

Amanda stared at her traveling companion, unable to believe the sudden determination in Polly's voice. "Does this mean you're finally going to stop your confounded complaining and be of some help?"

Polly smiled. "I'm tired of eatin' beans."

Amanda laughed. "So am I."

They walked back up the hill. Once they were settled on the wagon seat, Amanda flicked the reins and started the team forward. She was surprised to see Polly take a last glance at Lester's grave, and there was even a hint of sadness in her eyes. For the first time, Amanda felt she might have misjudged Polly. "We sure look a mess," she said, trying to sound lighthearted.

"Maybe a good fight was just what we needed to clear the air."

"Maybe so." After a pause, she asked, "Where are your parents, Polly?"

"My ma died of the pox, and I never knew who my pa was. I took up with a gambler and followed him around from one minin' camp to another. Then he ran off and left me high and dry. What happened to your ma? I know she left town about a year ago, but your old man stayed.''

"She went back to her family."

"You plannin' to get in touch with her?"

"No."

"Lester told me about that weddin' arrangement. I can't blame you for wantin' to get out of Columbia."

Amanda laughed softly. "I planned on leaving anyway. It just came a little sooner than expected."

Polly fell silent, and Amanda's thoughts drifted to her past. For as long as she could remember, she'd been told her parents had both come from wealthy families. They had been so incompatible that Amanda could never understand why they had even married in the first place. As far as she knew, Ben had never done a lick of work in his life, had been the black sheep of the family—according to her mother, Constance—and had always suffered from wanderlust.

After going through what money he had, plus Constance's dowry, Ben had moved his family to Columbia to restore their wealth. From what he'd heard, there was gold laying around everywhere, just waiting to be picked up. But once he'd realized actual work was required, he had quickly given up any ideas of mining. Since they had little money to live on, he'd begun looking for easy ways to line his pockets. It was Amanda's mother who'd came up with the idea of Amanda taking in laundry. Constance, a lazy woman by nature, had counted every penny Amanda's labors brought. At the same time, she'd continually nagged, given orders and informed everyone that she came from a prominent, wealthy family. She'd excused her worthlessness by stating that Amanda and Ben owed it to her to try to keep her in the style she was accustomed to.

Though Constance had never shown any affection, she felt she had three parental obligations. To teach her daughter to hold herself proudly, to teach her to read and write, and, most importantly, to explain the evil ways of men.

Ben had been gone most of the time. Therefore, it came as a surprise when one afternoon he arrived at the shack they called home and flashed a stagecoach ticket to San Francisco. Constance couldn't have been happier. She'd left two days later without saying goodbye.

Never having received affection from either parent, Amanda hadn't expected it. At times she'd felt lonely upon seeing how the other parents treated their children, but, on the whole, she'd been content. She liked no longer having to answer to her mother's demands. She liked doing what she wanted, when she wanted. However, she didn't like having to put up with all her father's schemes. So she'd tucked money away, waiting for the day when she, too, could leave Columbia. Who would have thought that once she did get away she'd end up in the middle of nowhere with a dance hall girl? But, even though things weren't looking exactly rosy, she was free, and it felt wonderful.

Late afternoon, they came upon what looked like an old road, and Amanda and Polly laughed with jubilation. Even though the way was partially covered with grass and young shrubs, it was the first sign of civilization they'd seen.

The next day, the road forked. They decided to take the path to the right, because it appeared to be a mite more traveled and it headed west.

For two more days they continued on, never seeing a soul. The road now looked considerably more traveled, and their hopes of meeting someone who could point them toward Sacramento escalated. Live oak, blue oak and even white-leaf manzanita were scattered across the mountainous area. The rolling slopes covered with orange poppies would have delighted Amanda under normal circumstances, but her thoughts were on more pressing matters. The sun was blistering, and their food supply was becoming dangerously low. Lester had put in only enough provisions for three weeks.

It was Polly who spied what looked like a town in the distance, nestled at the rocky base of a cliff. Amanda was tempted to urge the horses to a faster pace. However, they could ill afford to tire the animals any more than necessary should it turn out to be some sort of mirage. Time seemed to crawl by; both women were afraid to express the excitement that continued to grow within them.

As they reached the edge of the main street, Amanda brought the horses to a halt. She and Polly stared ahead in disbelief. On either side of the narrow road were stores and a hotel. Farther on they could see well-kept houses, with large oaks offering tempting shade. In the center of town stood a community well built of stone. But other than the spotted dog running toward them barking, and a burro moving slowly down the street clipping the grass that had grown along the boarded walks, there was no sign of life. A rough sign sat off to one side.

Welcome to Springtown

"I don't like it," Polly said in a hushed voice.

"At least we'll have a place to rest up."

"There's nobody here, and it's creepy. I told you when we rolled against Lester's grave it was an omen."

"Don't be silly, Polly. Maybe everyone has gone to a picnic somewhere near. We need food. A pot of stew sounds awfully good to me." Amanda raised her hand to release the brake.

"Wait!" Polly barked out.

"Now what's wrong?"

"I say we turn around and keep goin'. It could be Lester's curse on us."

"I can't believe you're acting this way." Seeing the fear in Polly's green eyes, Amanda released a heavy sigh. "If I go check out the place and prove there is nothing to fear, would you be willing to stay a couple of days?"

Polly hesitated. "What if somethin' happens to you?"

"I've had enough of this foolishness." Amanda hiked her skirt up and climbed off the wagon. "Just don't drive off without me."

"Amanda, why would people up and leave a place like this?"

"It's probably an old mining town. It will still give us a place to rest up. I'll be back shortly."

Polly scooted over to the driver's seat, her eyes never leaving Amanda as she walked toward the town. "If you get into any kind of trouble, holler!" she called. Amanda's steps didn't falter. "I'll drive the team forward, you hop in, and then we'll get the hell out of here!"

Amanda smiled over her shoulder, but she wasn't feeling nearly as confident as she was acting. Polly's concern had brushed off on her. Even the spotted dog had disappeared, and the burro made sure a good distance remained between them. A light breeze suddenly kicked up dust from the road, and a wooden shutter banged, causing Amanda to jump. She stopped and took several deep breaths, chastising herself for being so skittish.

Amanda walked down the middle of the road and stood by the well, her palms already damp. Polly's warning of doom was having its effect. She had to force herself to take a good look around. Some of the shutters hung by one hinge, but on the whole, the clapboard stores were in surprisingly good condition. Not knowing what to expect, she cautiously stepped onto the boarded walk, opened the door to the general store and entered.

After she came in from the sunlight, it took a moment for Amanda's eyes to adjust to the dark room. As everything came into focus, the corners of her lips curved upward into a smile of disbelief. There were glass cases, candy bins, rifles, pistols, material, ready-made dresses, barrels of beans, tins of food, sacks of flour, and anything else a soul could possibly want. Realizing she and Polly had found a haven, she broke into hoots of laughter. There were cobwebs everywhere, which meant no one had been there in months. Maybe even years! Her excitement growing, she ran back outside, then entered the hotel next door.

By the time Amanda had looked in quite a few stores, she was overwhelmed with delight. She returned to the middle of the road and stared at all the houses on down the way.

"What's the matter with you?" Polly called impatiently. "Why are you laughin'? Are you finally ready to leave?"

Amanda turned and looked at her companion. "Leave? Everything we could possibly want is right here! Polly, we've found a home! Bring the wagon."

"I think *you* should come here so *we* can get the hell out of this place."

"The town's deserted, Polly. It's all ours. And there's food! I'm going to look in a couple of the houses."

"My grandmother back in West Virginia warned me from the time I was a child about the devil's—" Polly didn't finish what she'd started to say. Amanda was already headed down the street. Torn with indecision, Polly dropped the reins and wiped at the beads of perspiration on her forehead. Admittedly, the sky was clear, and nothing looked spooky. What kind of food was Amanda talking about? Curiosity getting the better of her, she picked the reins up and released the brake. As the team moved forward, her eyes were constantly darting from one direction to the other.

Chapter Three

Though they'd only been in Springtown a week, both Amanda and Polly were quite content to stay put—at least until someone rode through and gave them directions to Sacramento. Neither woman could understand why a townful of people would just take off leaving everything behind, but they weren't about to begrudge their good fortune. There were even overgrown gardens where potatoes and other vegetables had managed to survive. The houses were completely stocked and, except for the dust and cobwebs, looked as though the inhabitants had only stepped out for a short time.

Polly had found a few brightly colored gowns in the saloon, but had chosen to emulate Amanda's more modest attire. It made her feel as if, wearing different clothes, she could become a different person. Her pride and joy, however, was a diamond necklace she'd found in one of the houses, and she wore it constantly, even to bed. Never having a place of her own, Polly wanted to claim one of the houses. But because she was still afraid of the night, she opted to stay in the hotel with Amanda.

Having had only two much-mended dresses for more years than she cared to count, Amanda was enthralled with the clothes. And staying at the hotel, with its fancy rooms and fine feather mattresses, was like living in a castle. Though Polly stuck to one room, Amanda couldn't resist sleeping in a different room each night.

It was Amanda's idea that they use the closest house to town to fix their meals. Because Polly wanted to do the cooking, Amanda reciprocated by making sure the kitchen was well stocked with fresh vegetables from the garden.

Between feeding the two horses, caring for the garden and cleaning, Polly and Amanda were kept busy.

It was early morning when Polly finally located Amanda. She'd already searched through four rooms. Polly sat on one of the small chairs and watched Amanda make up the bed she'd slept in the night before. "You know, we could be here for months before we'd ever be able to go through everything," she stated happily. She fingered her necklace. "I wonder if there's other jewelry sittin' around, waitin' to be discovered?"

Amanda laughed and looked at her companion. Surprisingly, she'd become quite fond of the redhead. Now that Polly no longer wore paint, she was even more beautiful than before. Her face and skin reminded Amanda of a china doll, while her own skin had been darkened from spending so much time in the sun. Polly's rosebud lips, green eyes and curly red hair were decidedly more fetching than her too-full mouth, brown eyes and straight black hair. And while Amanda was slender, Polly was downright curvaceous. That was the type of figure men were drawn to. "What are you going to do with a lot of jewelry?"

"Hoard it. I've never had anythin' to speak of, and if need be, I can sell it in Sacramento."

Amanda picked up a brush and began drawing it through her thick hair. "What will you do when we get there, Polly?"

Polly frowned. "Go back to workin' in a saloon, I reckon. What are you goin' to do?"

"I don't know, but I've been giving it a lot of thought. You know, with Lester's money, plus any money we might collect around here, we could probably set up some kind of business of our own." In case anything went wrong, or Polly tried to claim Lester's money for herself, Amanda had deliberately not mentioned her own stash.

Polly's eyes lit up with delight. "We could have our own saloon!"

"I was thinking more in terms of—" Amanda became very still. Was that voices she heard outside?

Polly jumped to her feet and ran to the window. "By damn, we got company!" She was about to head for the door when, to her surprise, Amanda grabbed her arm.

"Shh!" Amanda whispered. "Let's see who they are first."

"What difference does it make?"

Amanda went to the window. Standing to the side so as not to be seen, she looked down on the street below.

"There's just three of them."

Amanda jumped, not realizing Polly had come up behind her. "And I don't remember ever seeing a meaner-looking bunch, especially that old buzzard. Looks as if he hasn't washed since he was born."

"They're just men, Amanda. I can handle them. And they might be able to tell us how to get to Sacramento." Again she started for the door.

"Polly!" Amanda kept her voice hushed. "We don't know who they are. What if they want nothing more than to rape, steal and kill? And that necklace you're wearing could be temptation enough.''

Polly fondled her precious possession. ''I didn't think of that.''

''Let's just wait and see what they're up to. The horses are in the barn, so they won't know we're here. Now be quiet. Maybe we can hear what they're saying.''

The riders pulled their horses to a halt by the well, then sat quietly staring at their surroundings.

''Damn, Pa,'' Vern said excitedly, ''we can hole up here. Delayin' ain't gonna make any difference. That Wells Fargo office ain't goin' nowhere. We can rob it whenever we please.''

''I wonder if anything was left behind in this place,'' Fred added.

''Stop lickin' your chops, boys. When folks leave a town, they take all their belongings with 'em.'' Gus shifted uncomfortably in his saddle. '' 'Sides,'' he mumbled, ''this place gives me the willies. 'Specially after seein' that whitewash sign with them big letters Vern said spelled 'Yellow Fever.' ''

''Damn it, Pa, maybe there's a bed somewhere. Hell, I ain't laid on no bed for months! And what if there's gold around here?''

''Shut your mouth, Vern. If there was still gold, there'd still be folks. We'll rest up by that creek we been followin'. My legs are botherin' me, and it's fixin' to rain.''

To Amanda's relief, the rough-looking men rode out of town. Rain indeed. There wasn't a cloud to be seen. ''Did you hear that, Polly? They're robbers.''

Polly released a wistful sigh. ''Too bad. One of them was right cute.''

''How can you even think of such thing at a time like this?''

"You never had a man trail his hands over your body while sayin' how pretty you are and how he can't get enough of you. Or them special ones that *you* can't get enough of."

"You don't know that's so," Amanda said defensively. "Why, I've had all kinds of men pay attention to me."

"Havin' men just pay attention to you ain't what I was talkin' about."

Not liking the turn the conversation was taking, Amanda left the window and headed for the door. "I think we'd best keep our eyes open and stay hidden. One of those men might take it into his head to return."

"Amanda, what about that sign they was talkin' about. Maybe that's why everyone left. We could die from it!"

"Calm down, Polly. We didn't see any sign like that, did we? I doubt if that man can even read. Besides, how can we get it if there's no one to catch it from?"

For the rest of the day, they moved about cautiously, in case the men returned.

By nightfall, Amanda's concern finally faded. "I'm sure the crooks are gone, and it's doubtful they'll return," she told Polly as they stood in the hotel hallway. "At least if they came through Springtown, there's bound to be others. Before long, we're going to be on our way to Sacramento."

Polly giggled, and they parted to go to their separate rooms.

Dressed in a white nightgown, Amanda fingered the delicate lace intertwined with pink ribbons that adorned the yoke and the bottom of the long sleeves. She smiled, pleased at the feel of the soft cotton material against her bare skin. She'd never had anything so lovely to wear to bed. In fact, she'd never had so many clothes. Being able to put on a different dress every day made her feel like a princess living in fairyland. She'd already made up her mind that while they were stranded in Springtown she'd collect all the clothes that fitted her and store them in one of the houses. Then, when she and Polly were finally able to leave, she could carefully transfer them to the wagon. She wasn't about to leave such treasures behind!

Amanda climbed into bed, enjoying the crisp sheets and the feel of the large, comfortable bed. She had truly found heaven. She lifted up on one elbow, and blew out the candle on the bedside table. A quick fluff of the pillows was all that was needed to complete her comfort.

As Amanda stared into the enveloping darkness, her thoughts drifted to the men who had ridden into town that morning. She had spent a lot of time wondering why the inhabitants had left town, and if there truly was a sign telling of yellow fever, at least it put an end to her questions. Maybe she *was* in heaven, because someone must have been watching over her and Polly. If they hadn't slept late, those ruffians would have caught them wandering about the town. But why think about it? They were gone, and good riddance. She closed her eyes, ready to call it a night.

"The men are camped just outside of town."

Amanda's eyelids flew open. Except for her hand sliding under the pillow and gripping the pistol, she didn't dare move until she could at least determine where the man was hiding in her room. The seconds passed at a snail's pace, but Amanda remained still, listening. She couldn't hear a thing. Could she have been dreaming? Feeling like a fool, she pulled the blanket up to her chin to ward off the sudden chill in the room. Of course. She must have been dreaming.

"They're dangerous. Remain hidden."

Terrified, Amanda jerked up to a sitting position. With the gun held in her shaking hand and her chin quivering, her gaze darted around the dark room, searching for any signs of movement. Then, to her horror, a white fog began to form at the end of the bed—and yet she could see right through it. "I'm dreaming. I know I'm dreaming!" she repeated to herself.

Amanda released a bloodcurdling scream as she fell out of bed. Her first instinct was to climb under the bed so that the witches of the night wouldn't find her. Instead, she forced herself to her feet. She tried lighting the candle, but she couldn't hold her hand still enough to accomplish the task. The door suddenly flew open, and Polly bounded into the room. "What happened?"

"Polly...we...we have to get out of here!" Amanda whispered, enveloping her friend in her arms.

"Why?"

Amanda couldn't stop trembling. "A ghost. I swear I saw a ghost. Hurry! We'll get the horses from the barn and hitch them to the wagon."

"But if we leave the room, they might find us!"

"Who?"

"The ghosts, damn it!"

Amanda turned loose of Polly, trying to think what she should do next. "There was only one."

"How can you be sure?"

Amanda's nerves were already at the breaking point. "You'll find out if we just keep standing here." She forced herself to peek out the doorway. She could see nothing. "Come on, we have to get away."

"Lester's returned."

"Polly, it wasn't even Lester's voice! Now come on!"

"Oh, blessed saints!"

Amanda turned and saw, to her horror, that Polly had plopped down on the edge of the bed, holding her head in her hands. "What are you doing?" she gasped.

"You mean he talked to you? He's trying to possess your soul!"

In an effort to get control of herself, Amanda leaned against the wall and took several deep breaths. "Well, he's going to succeed if you're going to just sit there."

Polly jumped to her feet and grabbed the lantern from the bedside table. A moment later they were running down the hall to the stairs.

By the time the women had made it out of the hotel, Amanda's mind was beginning to function. Feeling the dirt beneath her bare feet brought forth realizations. She grabbed Polly's arm. "Stop!"

"What do you mean stop!"

Amanda stood gasping for breath. "We—we can't leave like this. We're still in our nightgowns. We have no clothes or shoes. We can't just get in the wagon and take off."

Polly spun around. She was holding up the lantern she'd brought from her room, and she suddenly realized it wasn't lit. "Why not?"

"We need food, clothes, water..."

"Are you suggesting we stay?"

"No. I'm saying we hitch up the wagon, then take it around and stock it. *If* what I saw was a ghost, we're probably safe as long as we don't go back in the hotel."

Polly raised an eyebrow. "*If* what you saw was a ghost?"

"Now that I can think about it, maybe one of those crooks came back to warn us. I was asleep, so it could have seemed like a ghost. And with all the carrying-on you've been doing about monsters of the night, I was letting my imagination get the better of me."

A heavy rumble of thunder made them glance up at the sky.

"Great," Polly moaned. "Now we'll probably have rain on top of everything else. Oh! Damn! I just stepped on a big pebble! Are we leaving or not?"

Still upset, Amanda had no desire to remain, even if it had been one of the crooks who had spoken to her. "Yes. We'll get shoes when we stock the wagon." Amanda headed for the livery stable, with Polly hobbling behind her. "I hope you brought some matches for that lantern."

"I did, and if you'll wait up a minute, I'll light it!"

As soon as the lantern was lit, they hurried on to the livery stable. When they entered, there was a strong smell of hay and oats, but there were no horses.

"I thought you told me you'd put the horses in here," Polly complained.

"I did. Maybe they got loose and went to the back." Amanda took the lantern from Polly and started walking between the stalls, glancing to either side. "I don't understand. They're gone!"

"Maybe they got out the door," Polly said despondently.

"How? I latched the paddock doors." Amanda wiped her dry lips with the back of her hand, trying to think. "Unless . . . unless those men that rode through here this morning! I'll bet one of them snuck back and stole them. That's probably who frightened me."

Polly moaned loudly. "What are we going to do now?"

Amanda settled down on a bale of hay. "The man in the hotel said they were camped just outside of town. We can steal the horses back."

Polly tossed her hands in the air in frustration. "First you say we shouldn't have anything to do with them because they're robbers, and now you want us to go find them and steal our horses back! What if they catch us?''

''I don't like the idea any better than you do, but what choice do we have? If we get the horses, we can be gone by the time they find out. If we don't, we have no idea how long we could be stuck here.''

Hearing raindrops hitting the roof, Polly groaned, already resigned to her fate. The loud clap of thunder directly overhead added to her dread.

''At least the storm will cover any noise we make,'' Amanda said encouragingly. ''Let's hurry. We'll stop at the house and get dressed.''

Convinced she was about to go to her death, Polly reluctantly followed.

Using the night to hide his position, Chance remained squatted on the hill. He was holding a heavy stick, his eyes were narrowed, and his jaw was set. The three men he'd been tracking had set up camp by the stream below. They'd fashioned themselves a shelter with *his* oilskin, but the campfire still allowed him a perfect view of what was going on.

A short distance away, their horses were tethered to a line stretched between two cottonwoods. Vern was already asleep, the sound of his snoring drifting through the night air. The other two were huddled around the fire. For the past hour they'd continued guzzling whiskey, and Chance could only hope it wouldn't be much longer before they passed out.

Paying scant attention to the rain that had begun to fall, Chance kept his thoughts centered on the pain he'd suffered at the hands of these men. The bullet had miraculously gone straight through his shoulder, but fever and loss of blood had disabled him for a while. Doggedly he'd followed their trail, sleeping only when he couldn't go a step farther. The only thing that had kept him going was his deadly determination to get back Cactus and his pistol, then wreak his revenge on the three scavengers who had left him for dead. At last the time had come to settle the score. But because he didn't have a gun, he was forced to wait until he got one of them alone or until they passed out.

A grin spread across his cracked lips. Gus and his boys had made a big mistake by spending more time camping than traveling. With each new campsite Chance had come to, he'd known he was getting closer. Had the men bothered to search him, they would have found the small bag of gold hidden in the side of his boot. but again they'd made a fateful error. That was how he'd been able to pay a doctor in Hangtown and purchase provisions. He hadn't had enough to buy a horse, too, so he'd stolen one.

The rain grew heavier. Chance pulled his hat lower and continued waiting. The thunder was louder now, and the streaks of lightning seemed to be getting closer.

"Damn it!" Gus roared. "Didn't I say it was gonna rain? How the hell can Vern sleep with that damn thunder?"

"Hell, Pa, you know he can't hold his liquor."

One of the horses nickered, then another.

"Fred, go see what's the matter with them critters," Gus ordered.

"It's pourin' rain, Pa. I don't want to go out in it."

"And you ain't gonna want to walk if one of them gets loose!" Gus picked up a rock and threw it at his son. "Now get your ass up!"

Grumbling, Fred crawled out from under the oilskin and stood. The sudden movement caused his head to spin, and he had to stand still a moment to clear his blurry vision.

"Damn it, what are you waitin' for?" Gus asked angrily.

"I'm goin', I'm goin'...."

As Fred staggered toward the horses, the hard, cold rain impeded his vision but caused him to sober a bit. It wasn't until lightning flashed again that he saw two women untying the buckskin plus his pa's mount. Smiling, he pulled the pearl-handled pistol from his holster. "Well, now, just look what the good Lord done delivered."

Soaking wet and each holding a lead rope to a horse, Polly and Amanda stared at the man who had caught them. Having discovered that their horses were nowhere around, Amanda had concluded that they had no choice but to take two that belonged to the men. Now, neither woman could think of a plausible excuse or a way out of their predicament. Horse stealing was a hanging offense.

"Oo-ee! Pa, me and Vern is gonna have one hell of a night with you two!"

A bolt of lightning struck just feet away, followed by another. The second one hit a thick limb just above Fred's head. Scared out of their wits, Polly and Amanda jumped backward, but the man looked up in disbelief instead of moving away. The thick limb made a loud cracking, splintering noise, then crashed down, knocking him to the ground, its branches covering his body like a shroud.

Neither woman knew if the bushy-faced man was dead or not, but they weren't about to hang around and find out. Without thinking, Amanda reached down and grabbed the pistol that had fallen from the man's hand, then took off running after Polly. At least now they had the horses they needed to get away.

Chance had already been moving down the hill to take care of Fred when he'd spotted the women. Though he hadn't been able to get a good look at them, their long dresses made their sex apparent. When Fred had drawn the gun, Chance had had no doubts as to whose pistol it was. Still too far away to take advantage of the situation, he'd cursed silently when he saw the tree limb fall on top of the man, and one of the women pick up his pistol. He wouldn't have seen any of it had it not been for the continual lightning. To add to his problems, they had also taken his horse.

Angered that his opportune moment had gone astray, Chance looked back at the makeshift shelter. The old man was still sitting there, unaware of what had happened to Fred. There wasn't any doubt in Chance's mind that Gus was well armed. Even drunk, the bastard was dangerous. Chance knew exactly the type of man Gus was. He'd spent years riding with gangs a lot tougher than Gus and his boys.

The rain had become a steady drizzle, but rather than stand beneath a tree to ward off the wetness, Chance started walking toward Springtown. He had no choice but to follow the women. He'd thought the town was deserted. Obviously he was wrong. Once he had retrieved his horse and pistol, he'd return for Gus and Vern.

Chance yanked off his hat and slapped it against the leg of his jeans to knock off what water he could, then jammed it back on his head. At least one thing was in his favor. He wouldn't have to take on a group of men to get his belongings back.

It wasn't until they were walking back down the main street in town that Amanda and Polly's breathing returned to normal.

"We did it," Polly said in awe. "We actually did it!"

"Yes, but we've wasted too much time," Amanda replied worriedly. "We're going to have to hurry like the devil to get the horses hitched up, load the wagon and get out of here. We don't even know if these beasts can pull a wagon properly."

As they neared the livery stable, a hard wind suddenly kicked up, and deafening thunder cracked overhead. The ball-eyed horses began backing away and nervously tugging at the ropes. Polly and Amanda held tight, but the wind grew stronger, driving piercing rain into their faces and making it impossible for them to see. The animals reared and snorted, and then, as if someone had prodded them with a pitchfork, they jerked free.

As quickly as it had started, the wind died down. Heartbroken, Amanda could only stand in the middle of the muddy road and watch the horses gallop away.

"Now what?" Polly asked.

Amanda brushed the tears and rain from her face. She felt as dejected as Polly, but they didn't have the time to bemoan their fate. Nor could she allow Polly to become hysterical. "We load guns and wait. Those men are going to come looking for their mounts."

Chance made a wide circle, then stealthily worked his way around the clapboard houses at the edge of town. Finally he caught a glimpse of light emanating from the back window of one of the houses.

Moving with the silence of a cat, he carefully entered through the front door. Thankfully, it didn't squeak. He stood silently, listening. Someone was busy in the kitchen. He moved forward.

Satisfied she'd collected enough food to last the day, Polly twisted the end of the flour sack. She knew Amanda was going to be angry that she'd sneaked out of her hiding place in the old barn, but the possibility of spending an entire day without something to eat was carrying things too far. She looked longingly at the cured ham she'd left on the counter. Had she taken enough? As far as she was concerned, Amanda was being overly cautious. If those men were coming, they would have already been here.

Needing to hurry back to the barn, Polly raised the candle, turned, and dropped the flour sack. A tall, broad-shouldered man filled the doorway, preventing her escape. His wet hat was pulled low, but she could clearly see his half-cocked grin.

Chance leaned a shoulder against the doorjamb, his gaze taking in the woman's fine female qualities, and the diamond necklace she wore. "I hadn't expected to find such an appealing creature in the middle of nowhere. What's your name, honey?"

Polly felt both fear and desire working its way up her spine at the sound of his deep, husky voice. Even with the full blond beard, the man was magnificent. His deep, husky voice only added to his appeal. "Polly. Polly O'Neil."

"Well, Polly, why don't you tell me what you did with the horses?"

Polly gulped. "Horses? What horses?"

"They escaped before we could get them tied down." Amanda answered from behind him.

Chance spun around. The other woman had found him. She was wearing a hat and standing outside the light of the candle, so he couldn't get a good look at her face. But her wet dress clung to her body. She was smaller than the redhead, and she had quite a figure. Unfortunately, his pearl-handled pistol was clutched in her hand, and she had it pointed at his chest.

"Put your hands in the air and step into the parlor," Amanda ordered. She had a quick, too-vivid image of herself hanging from a tree for horse-stealing.

"I'm sure we both know that if you pull that trigger those men by the stream are going to come running. All I want is my horse and that gun you're holding."

"You're crazy if you think I'd do something that foolish. Now move!"

Taking his time, Chance did as she ordered. He was furious at having been caught off guard. Especially by a woman. "If you let me go, I'll make sure those men don't bother you. I have a score to settle with them. They left me for dead."

"Sure. And I'm the queen of England," Amanda retorted.

"You're making a big mistake!"

"Polly, get some rope."

Chance realized he might be able to turn the situation to his advantage. Time was wasting, and he didn't want to lose his edge of surprise over Gus and his boy. "What are you going to do when those men come looking for their horses?"

Amanda watched Polly enter the kitchen. "Don't bother with false concern. It won't work." Her eyes almost popped out when she saw Polly reappear. Instead of rope, she was clutching the handle of an iron skillet. She raised it in the air as she walked up behind the stranger. Amanda scrunched her face as Polly brought it down hard on the back of the man's head. He immediately slumped to the floor.

Polly dropped the skillet. "Did I kill him?" she asked as she stared at the still figure.

Amanda leaned down to place two fingers on his neck. "No, you just knocked him out." She straightened up, still astonished at what Polly had done.

"As big as he is, I got to thinkin' he could easily overpower us."

Amanda laughed with delight. "Polly, you amaze me."

"What are we going to do with him?"

"I haven't the slightest idea. He's too big for us to take him anywhere." Amanda glanced back down at the man sprawled on the floor. "I guess we can put him on the bed and tie him to the posts. Then we'll have to gag him so he can't yell for his friends. Can you think of anything better?"

Polly shook her head.

"All right, then, I'll take his hands, you take his feet."

Lifting the man proved to be impossible. Amanda tried pulling, but he didn't budge.

"Here," Polly said as she dropped his feet, "let me try." She grabbed each wrist and managed to move him a few inches.

"Wait a minute, Polly. At this rate he'll be awake before we can even move him. You take one wrist and I'll take the other. At the count of three, pull. One . . . two . . . three! All right, let's do it again, but this time, when we start moving, keep going until we get him inside the bedroom."

Both women were panting by the time they finally dropped the man's arms. Polly looked at the bed, at the man, then at the bed again. "It was all we could do just to get him in here, so how we gonna get him on the bed?"

"You grab him under the left arm, and I'll get the right one."

After much tugging and struggling, they had the man's head and torso on the bed. Amanda hiked up her skirts, straddled his waist and placed both arms beneath his. "Polly, you go around the bed, take his wrists and pull."

Polly hurried to the other side. She tugged, and Amanda tried lifting, but it quickly became obvious they were getting nowhere. Polly looked at Amanda questioningly.

"There has to be a way of doing this. All right, here's what we're going to do. We'll turn him on his side, then I'll sit on him so he won't slide back onto the floor. You go around and see if you can lift his legs onto the bed."

Once they had his long legs up, the rest was easy. Amanda hurried to retrieve the gun so that she could keep it pointed at him while Polly collected the rope and rags.

When Polly returned, they made quick work of tying the man to the bedposts and gagging him. Satisfied, they stood back and looked at their handiwork.

Amanda was feeling quite pleased with the way she'd handled such a harrowing night. Years of outwitting her father had developed not only a strong backbone, but dogged determination, as well. Thinking about her father, she asked, "Polly, did you say anything to that man about us hiding in the barn?"

"I don't remember. I was so shocked to see him. . . ."

Amanda groaned. Like her father, Polly thought of nothing except the present. "We're going to have to find a different place to hide," she stated worriedly. "I saw an old mine as we were bringing the horses back. We'll hide in there. If those others return and find this one, they'll know we're here. Let's hurry. This one could come to any moment." Amanda was so tired she wasn't even sure she could make it to the mine.

Polly grabbed the flour sack full of food, and they scurried out of the house. "Amanda, maybe that feller was telling the truth. He could even be the one that warned you about those men at the stream.''

Amanda's smile was faint. "Before long it will be daylight, and after what we've been through, I'm too worn-out to even care.''

"Amanda, we're still stuck in Springtown.''

"I know. Maybe someone else will ride through soon.''

"You think those men are still goin' to come lookin' for their horses?''

"I'm sure of it. Now hurry so we can get hidden.''

Chapter Four

"Someone's done took off with our horses!"

Gus opened his eyes and saw Vern hurrying toward him. "What the hell you talkin' 'bout?" he snapped.

"Two of our horses is gone, Pa! That buckskin and yours. And where's Fred? He ain't even got coffee started."

"He's probably taking a piss." Gus was slow getting off his bedroll. His head was throbbing from the whiskey he'd drunk. "Now what's this about missing horses?" He waddled over to the line rope. "Damn it! Vern, mount up and find them horses! They can't of gone far."

Vern was about to go back for his saddle when he and Gus heard a loud groan.

"Fred?" Gus called, his hand now resting on the butt of his pistol.

"Pa! Get me out from under this damn tree!"

Gus and Vern rushed forward. Using his bull strength, Gus raised the end of the heavy limb while Vern pulled Fred from beneath it. When Fred was on his feet and it was obvious there was nothing wrong with him except for the lump on his head, Gus raised a big fist and socked him, sending him back to the ground.

Fred shook his head to clear his vision. "What did you go do that for, Pa?" he whined.

"Cause you let them horses get away!"

"It weren't me, it was them two women."

"Two women, hell. You was so drunk you wouldn't know a woman from a tree. You never did have smarts. Now get up and go with your brother to find them horses."

Fred pulled himself up, making sure he kept a safe distance from his father, then headed back to camp with Vern to get the saddles. After thinking about it, Fred concluded his pa was probably right. He must have made them women up in his head. But they sure was purty.

It didn't take long to locate the horses a short distance away, peacefully munching grass. Vern rode up to Gus's piebald and slipped a rope over his head. But try as they might, they couldn't catch the buckskin stallion. He was too fast. Vern and Fred finally brought their mounts to a halt, then sat and watched the buckskin disappear over a hill.

"Pa ain't gonna be happy about this," Fred mumbled as he rubbed his sore jaw.

"Pa couldn't even ride the ornery critter."

"Yeah, but he planned on gettin' a good price for him in Columbia."

Amanda was laughing as she approached the mine entrance. "The men are gone!" she called to Polly. "You can come out now. They located their horses, and I watched them ride off not more than fifteen minutes ago. We're safe!"

Giggling, Polly ran out into the sunlight. "I'm sure glad to be out of that mine. I could just picture us havin' to go in deeper and deeper, then not bein' able to find our way out. Did they ride through town?''

"No, I guess they circled it."

"Now that they're taken care of, what are we gonna do with the one we tied up? Kill him?"

Amanda frowned. "Are you saying you could just walk into the house and shoot him?"

Polly looked shocked. "Lord, no. I figured you'd take care of it."

"I've never killed a man in my life!"

"Well, neither have I. So, like I asked, what are we gonna do with him?"

Amanda tried brushing back the long strands of hair that kept falling in her face. She glanced at Polly, thinking they looked worse than they had when they'd first come to Springtown. Their hair hung in tangled disarray, and their once crisp dresses were wrinkled, limp, and caked with mud. "I'm going to heat some water, get these damp things off, bathe and put on fresh clothes." She looked up at the clear blue sky. "Thank heavens that storm passed so quickly."

"But what about the man?"

"We didn't invite him here, Polly!" Amanda tugged at the waist of her dress, which had shrunk from the rain. "We'll just have to keep him tied and fed until I can think of something." She shifted her gaze to the hotel. Even though she was positive one of the three men had spoken to her—maybe even the one they'd tied up—and that the foggy haze had been a figment of her imagination, she still felt queasy about going inside. She took a deep breath, determined not to let her imagination play tricks on her again. "I'm going to the hotel. Are you coming?"

"Not me," Polly stated flatly. "I don't want no part of that place. From now on, I'm staying in the house we've been using to do our cooking. I'm still not convinced Lester didn't pay you a visit.''

Amanda nodded, already sorry she'd been so hasty. Not having Polly in the hotel made her even more leery, but she refused to let her doubts show. ''Well, like I said, I'm going to get cleaned up.''

Chance relaxed his taut muscles and forced himself to lie quietly on the bed. His splitting headache was made worse by the sun shining though the window onto his face, which in turn increased his already surly disposition. This was the second time he'd been struck on the head in a matter of weeks, and he was getting damn tired of it. On top of everything else, if Gus and his boys had gotten away, he'd have to track them down again.

Chance rotated his hands to get the circulation in them again. At least he didn't have to worry about getting free. The women had bound his wrists and ankles to the bedposts, but the knots were poorly tied. The looseness allowed him to bend his hands forward and work at the knots with his fingers a few minutes at a time. He'd been at it most of the night, but one more time should do it. He'd thought the women had hightailed it out of town, taking his pistol and horse with them. However, half an hour ago the redhead had peeked in to check on him.

Chance was about to tackle the knots again when he heard footsteps, and the two women's voices. ''I'll go check on the man. He's awake, but I didn't remove his gag.''

''No, you start breakfast and coffee. I'll check on him,'' the other one replied.

Chance remained perfectly still, waiting for her to make an appearance.

Chance's anger lessened somewhat when he saw the woman step into the bedroom doorway. He could forgive a beautiful lady for *almost* anything, and this one was indeed magnificent. A floppy hat covered most of her glossy black hair. She had finely arched brows, a flawless complexion, high cheekbones with a natural pink blush, and wide, full lips that would make any man stare in appreciation. But combine all that with a long, slender neck, a full, ripe bosom—pressed enticingly against the bodice of her green shirt—and a tiny waist, and it was enough to cause a man's britches to tighten. He could even smell the pleasing scent of her perfume.

Keep away from her, Doyer, he told himself. He knew she was trouble, and trouble had always drawn him like a magnet. On the other hand, maybe he could turn this to his advantage, even if she did have his pistol tucked in the waistband of her paisley skirt. It had been a long time since he'd had a woman, and he was in the company of two very appealing ones. His horse had to be nearby, and at the rate Gus and his boys were traveling, he could always catch up with them in Columbia.

Amanda glanced at the ropes to make sure he was still tied before going over and removing his gag. "The other men have left, so if you want to yell, go right ahead."

Now that she was close, Chance could see that her eyes were the color of fine whiskey. "Just what do you plan on doing with me?" Because of his size, he was intimidating to most men. Yet this slip of a woman stared down at him unflinchingly. Of course, she was the one with a gun, he reminded himself, and she undoubtedly thought she was safe.

"I haven't decided. Maybe we'll kill you. I suggest you don't try giving us any trouble." She was pleased at the way his eyes narrowed. She'd gotten her point across, and he believed her. My goodness, she thought, I hadn't realized he was such a handsome devil. "How come you didn't ride through town with your friends?"

"They aren't my friends. A few weeks back those men took everything I owned, with the exception of the clothes on my back. Then they shot me and left me for dead. I was fixing to get even when you and your friend Polly fouled up everything by stealing the horses and tying me to this damn bed! It'll be hell catching them now. I'm not your enemy, lady, so how about letting me go?"

"How come you know Polly's name?"

"She told me."

Though Amanda was listening to what he said, her attention was focused on his body sprawled out on the bed. He was broad-shouldered, and his height was such that the soles of his boots hung well past the end of the bed. Tufts of sandy-blond hair rested against his forehead, and he had a full, untrimmed beard. She had to admit that, in all her twenty years, she'd never seen a more fetching man. Yet there was something about him that reminded her of a coiled snake waiting to strike, and though she didn't let it show, he frightened her. "What's your name?"

"Chance Doyer."

"You made that up. Nobody has a name like that." Amanda turned on her heel and left the room.

"Wait a minute," Chance called. "Aren't you going to untie me?"

Amanda didn't bother to reply. Once outside the room, the lump in her throat went away. No doubt about it, she thought, Polly and I have a big problem on our hands.

Polly looked up from her cooking as Amanda entered the kitchen. "Is he awake?"

"He's awake." Needing something strong, Amanda poured coffee into a delicate china cup.

"Is he all right?"

"Quite well, considering how hard you hit him with that iron skillet." Before sitting down, Amanda pulled the pistol from her waistband and placed it on the table.

"You know, Amanda, that's a mighty fine-lookin' man in there. I say we let him go. He might even know the way to Sacramento, but he's not gonna tell us if we keep him tied up."

"Looks aren't everything." Amanda almost choked on her coffee when she said it. Even she had just been admiring the man. "And what good is knowing how to get to Sacramento if we have no way of going?"

"But we'd at least know which direction to take when we can leave. We might even be close enough to some town that we could walk." Satisfied that the canned meat and potatoes she'd fried were ready, Polly spooned some onto two plates.

Amanda toyed with her fork. "Polly, there's a coldness about him that..." She couldn't find the words to express how she felt. "I know we can't leave him tied up, but it seems to me we should find out something about him first. How do we know he's trustworthy, or that he won't try to harm us?"

Polly giggled as she set the plate in front of Amanda. "I'll bet I could calm him down real fast. And there's something else I was wonderin' about. If we keep him tied to the bed, how's he gonna get to the outhouse?"

Amanda's fork stopped in midair. "I hadn't thought about that."

Polly pulled out a chair and joined Amanda at the table. "See, we have no choice but to let him go."

"Unless…" Amanda's lips spread into a smile. "I have the answer. I saw shackles in the blacksmith's shop. We could shackle his ankle to the leg of the bed. There would be enough chain for him to move around, but not escape! Then we'd put a chamber pot in there."

"Then all I'd have to do is lift the end of the bed and I'd be free."

Both women jerked around to find their prisoner standing directly behind them. Amanda grabbed the pistol off the table and pointed at him. "Get back in that bedroom!"

"No way, lady. I'm not about to let you tie me up again, so if you're going to pull the trigger, you'd better do it now."

Polly sucked in her breath.

Amanda's hand started shaking. His face looked as if it were cast in stone. Yet she couldn't kill anyone in cold blood, and he was calling her bluff.

"Perhaps you'd prefer shooting me in the back." Chance turned and waited. There had been no cruelty in her eyes, just confusion and indecision. Slowly he turned around again. "I believe we've come to an understanding."

Seeing the smug look on his face, Amanda knew she couldn't let him know how intimidated she felt. She shoved her chair back and rose, still keeping the gun pointed at him. "I may not kill you, but I won't hesitate shooting you in the leg. How did you get loose?" she demanded.

"If you're real sweet and tell me where my horse is, maybe I'll show you how to tie a decent knot."

"We don't have your horse," Polly whispered.

"Come, come, you really don't expect me to believe that? I watched you take off with him. Mine was the buckskin."

Polly slowly rose from her chair, then inched her way to Amanda's side. "It's the truth. They got away from us during the storm, then this morning those other men caught them and rode away."

Thinking back, Amanda suddenly realized that when the robbers had left they hadn't had the buckskin with them. She wasn't about to inform this man, or Polly, of her discovery. Polly talked too much. If the horse was free and could be caught, she and Polly would have a means of escape.

Chance had been watching Amanda closely, and the moment she glanced at Polly he reached over and twisted the pistol from her hand. "Now, ladies, the shoe is on the other foot."

Furious at allowing him to outsmart her once again, Amanda made a dash for the doorway. She felt the breath knocked out of her when a strong arm wrapped around her waist and pulled her back into the room. It took some fast footwork to keep from falling. "I knew you were a snake," she hissed. "What do you intend to do with us?"

"Polly," Chance said casually, "why don't you pour me a cup of that coffee I've been smelling? And while you're at it, I'll take a plate of those potatoes."

"Polly, don't you move an inch," Amanda ordered. "He can fix his own food."

"B-but..." Polly stammered

"If he's going to shoot us, he'll do it whether we wait on him or not!"

Chance grinned at the dark-headed one's show of bravery. She had her chin jutted out in defiance, all but daring him to pull the trigger. At least he'd found out one thing—they didn't have the guts to kill him. "What's your name?"

"Amanda," Polly quickly replied for her friend.

Chance pursed his lips as if he were in deep thought. "Well, Amanda, as I see it, it would be perfectly fitting to show you the same hospitality you've shown me. With the possible exception of knocking you over the head." He glanced at Polly, then returned his gaze to Amanda. "In fact, the thought of having two lovely women tied down on a bed certainly isn't without appeal." He leaned his back against the wall, enjoying the horrified expression on Amanda's face. "Why are you women living in this deserted town?" Seeing that Amanda had her mouth clamped shut, he looked at Polly. She was obviously the more talkative of the two. "Maybe you'll be a little wiser and answer my question."

To Chance's amazement, Polly started rattling off something about fathers, riding off in the dead of night, Sacramento, someone named Lester dying, a grave being a curse, trees, food getting short, and finally how she and Amanda had accidentally arrived at Springtown.

Polly ended with "And, as if all that wasn't bad enough, I thought Lester's ghost had followed us here!"

Aside from the part about accidentally finding this town, Chance had absolutely no idea what the woman had been jabbering about. He glanced at Amanda, who simply shrugged her shoulders and continued staring at him. Her aloofness was beginning to appeal to him. Besides being such a beauty, she piqued his curiosity. The absurdity of his situation suddenly tickled his funny bone, and, for the first time in months, he broke out laughing.

Amanda was convinced they had an insane man to deal with. Why else would he laugh at such a situation? Because he continued to block the only way out of the kitchen, she was beginning to panic. She tried to appear calm. The only possible chance for freedom was for Polly and her to humor him. "All right, I'll get you a cup of coffee and a plate of food." When he made no protest, she cautiously moved toward the stove.

"It's like this, ladies," Chance finally said, when his laughter had subsided. "Because you've left me with no means of transportation, you might as well get used to having me around for a while." Taking his time, he studied each woman. "Like I said, I just want my horse and pistol. I got the pistol, now where's the horse? Give me that, and after a few days' rest, I'll be on my way."

Amanda slammed his plate down on the table, causing the fork to bounce off it. "As much as we'd like you to leave, we can't produce something we don't have. Polly told you the truth. The storm scared the horses away!"

Chance became serious. "And do you agree with that, Polly?"

Polly nodded.

"Well, then, since you insist on sticking to your story, I guess I might as well pick out a house. Are there other folks around here?"

Polly shook her head.

"Don't look so worried, ladies. If you leave me alone, I'll leave you alone. However, I would suggest you don't try anything foolish again." He took the few steps to the table and picked up his plate. "Thanks for the meal."

In a state of stupefaction, Amanda watched him leave.

"What do we do now?" Polly kept her fingers busy twisting the material of her skirt. "I just know he's gonna want to get even with me for hittin' him with that skillet. Did you see the way he looked at me?"

Amanda stared at the open doorway. "We could be in even deeper trouble than you realize. I think he's addle-pated."

"You do?" Polly gasped. "Why?"

"Didn't you notice his quick change of moods? Anger, meanness, laughter, then threatening? There was a woman in Columbia that was the same way. Crazy as a jumping bean."

"Are you making up one of your stories?" Polly asked suspiciously.

"No, of course not! I knew a lot of people. I think we should stay at the hotel so we can keep an eye on him. We'll keep loaded pistols with us at all times, and stick together if we have to leave the hotel."

"He said he wasn't goin' to harm us if we left him alone," Polly whispered.

"And you believe that? Why didn't we shackle him while we had the chance?"

Polly stared, wide-eyed, at the smaller woman. "You're not plannin' on trying to capture him again?"

Amanda thought about that for a moment. "No, he'll be on his guard," she finally answered. "He's so big even the two of us couldn't take him down. But if he tries anything, I won't hesitate to shoot him next time."

"What a shame. He's so damn beautiful, and even charming."

"There was also a man in Columbia who could charm a snake, and from what I heard, he was the meanest man that God ever put on this earth."

"Damn!" Polly exclaimed.

Chance leaned against the community well and looked up and down the dusty main street. By tying him up, the women had not only allowed Gus and his boys to get away, they'd also left him without any means of going after them! He'd returned to where he'd left the stolen nag tethered last night, but the animal was gone, too. Either he'd pulled the reins loose during the storm, or someone had found him.

After several hours of checking the livery stable, barns, sheds, and anything else that could house a horse, Chance was still on foot. It appeared the women were telling the truth. On the other hand, they'd had plenty of time to hide the animals while he'd been tied to the bed. The only problem was that he had absolutely no idea where that hiding place could be.

Chance looked down the well, wondering if it was dry. The rope didn't look old. During his search, he'd entered several of the houses and shops and had been surprised to find them fully stocked. As he'd returned from the creek, he'd seen a sign warning of yellow fever, which would explain why the town was deserted, but not how Polly and Amanda had managed to survive. Still, he found it difficult to believe the other residents would have left *everything* behind. And, since the people had apparently taken off in a hurry, where were the dead bodies? Surely the women hadn't buried them. On the other hand, maybe everyone hadn't left at once. Nothing made sense. Surely others must have ridden through Springtown. So why had only two pretty women chosen to remain?

He went around to the hand crank and began turning it. When the bucket of water came into view, he secured the handle, then removed the dipper hanging from a nail at the side. After dipping it into the bucket, he smelled the water to make sure it wasn't poisoned. Still not satisfied, he stuck his finger in it, then licked it. Even though he couldn't be sure the water was safe, he took a long, appreciative drink, then hung the dipper up again.

Chance rubbed his hairy chin, wondering what he was going to do now. Go after Gus and his boys on foot again? The idea had no appeal. He was tired of being a hunter. The time had come to put some normalcy back into his life. Tracking Gus and his boys just wasn't worth it, even though it singed his britches to know they'd get away with horse-stealing. Gus and his boys had to have found their mounts, or they would have scoured the town by now. He'd never see Cactus again—unless the women had him hid somewhere. And at this point, that didn't seem likely.

Chance's gaze traveled from the hotel to the general store, and then to the barbershop. Some clean clothes, a shave, and a bath in the creek sounded good. When that was accomplished, he'd select a house that had a comfortable bed. Though he was worn out, he knew a good night's sleep just wasn't in the cards. He had to be ready for whatever the *ladies* decided to try next. After seeing scatterguns, rifles and pistols in the general store, he had no doubt in his mind that the women were well armed. Squinting, he looked up at one of the windows on the second floor of the hotel and doffed his hat before heading back to the general store.

"Did you see that?" Polly exclaimed. "He knew all along that we were watchin' him." She pressed her cheek against the window, trying to see where he'd disappeared to. "Where's he goin' now?"

"How would I know? Maybe he went into one of the stores. You can see just as much as I can. And you don't have to whisper. He may have seen us, but he can't hear us talking." Amanda went over and sat on the edge of the bed.

"You don't have to snap at me, Amanda. It ain't my fault the way things turned out."

Amanda sighed. "I know. I'm just tired. At least *you* got some sleep in the mine."

"There he is again. He's got denim britches and a shirt draped over his arm. He must've gone in the general store, 'cause he's also got a rifle and a gun belt for his pistol. Now he's disappeared again."

"Polly there's no use—"

"I see him! There's something in his hand, but I can't make out what it is. He's cutting through the houses. Looks like he's headed back toward the creek again. That's the second time. I wonder what he finds so interestin' there?"

"Maybe he's decided to leave." Amanda's eyes narrowed, and then she shook her head. "No, we couldn't be that lucky."

Polly collapsed in the armchair next to the window. "Maybe we're wrong about him," she commented. Emulating Amanda, she straightened her back. "Maybe he told the truth about chasin' them robbers."

"And maybe he was one of them!" Amanda wearily got to her feet and returned to the window. For a good fifteen minutes she waited, but Chance didn't return. "Polly, I'm going to find out what that man's up to."

"Amanda! He could catch you and—"

"We have to know what he's up to."

"You're right. I'll go with you."

"No, you wait here. I can make faster time by myself, and move a lot quieter."

"What about us not going anywhere alone?"

"He won't even know I'm around. Maybe he lied about not having a horse and he's really decided to leave. When I come back, I'll get some sleep while you keep watch. It would be just like him to attack while we're asleep. I heard tell of a man in Columbia that did that. Killed the entire family."

"Amanda, if he wanted to harm us, why didn't he do it before?"

"Because he's nutty," Amanda mumbled. She picked up her pistol and checked to see that it was ready to fire. "He's probably a predator."

"Predator?"

"An animal who hunts prey. Like a big cat."

"A mountain lion?"

"Exactly."

"You gotta admit, he's one mighty fine-looking mountain lion."

"That's a matter of opinion," Amanda said over her shoulder as she headed for the door. "He's not anyone I'd be interested in." Her curiosity, like Polly's, getting the better of her. What was it the man found so interesting by the creek?

Polly stared at the empty doorway. Maybe Amanda had lived in a mining town too long. At times she sounded like the miners who had come into the saloon. They could weave a tale about anything, none of it bearing a grain of truth.

Silently, cautiously, pistol ready, Amanda worked her way between the thick shrubs as she headed toward the creek. Taking the path would have been a lot faster and easier, but she was relying on the tall shrubs to hide her presence. Having seen neither hide nor hair of the man, she was beginning to believe he really had left.

Feeling a tug on her skirt, Amanda stopped and looked down. Somehow she'd managed to get it tangled on a stiff branch. She gave the skirt a gentle tug, but it refused to budge. That was followed with a hard yank. The branch snapped, and the material ripped. Aggravated, she gathered her skirt in front of her and continued on. She could only hope Chance wasn't close enough to have heard the noise.

Amanda hadn't taken more than a dozen steps when she saw what looked like a small lake up ahead. She couldn't be sure, because of the many trees and the curve in the shoreline. Excited about her discovery, she started up the steep incline, feeling considerably more relaxed. The rocks were covered with lichen, and thick vines and ferns were everywhere. Some even traveled up tree trunks and hung from limbs. Amanda was grateful that she'd never had a reaction from the poison oak that was scattered throughout the foothills.

As she rounded the bend, Amanda came to an abrupt halt. There was indeed a lake, and someone was standing in the shallow part. It looked like Chance, but with the sun glaring off the water, it was difficult to see. She inched forward and hid behind a tall, leafy bush.

Chance was standing waist-deep in the water. Soapy lather covered his body and hair, but he continued to scrub his chest. With a shock, Amanda realized he was naked. Her pa had always worn his long underwear, except when he was dead drunk. That was when she would strip him so that she could wash the filthy things.

Chance tossed the bar of soap onto a small, sandy bank. Until that moment, Amanda hadn't noticed his guns, boots and clothes in a pile near where the soap had landed. There was also a straight razor, and a mirror. Amanda told herself she should leave. After all, she had discovered what he was up to. Still, it was awfully tempting to steal his things and leave him naked as a newborn babe. Unfortunately, it would mean revealing herself, and he might easily reach her before she had time enough to snatch his things and get away. She didn't dare risk it.

Amanda glanced back at Chance, and was instantly mesmerized. While she'd been thinking about causing trouble, he had rinsed off. His wet, bronzed body glistened in the sunlight. Obviously he had spent a lot of time shirtless, and for some unknown reason, just the thought of it excited her. He shook his hair, and rivulets of water danced in the air. Her gaze traveled to the clean-shaven face, and she thought she'd swoon when she saw how devastatingly handsome he was. His muscled body reminded her of a sculpture she'd once seen, and his stomach was corded and flat. Even his . . .

Amanda's eyes widened. He was walking out of the water! She couldn't prevent her gaze from traveling down his body, amazed to see that he looked nothing like her father. Chance was much more . . . She gulped and quickly returned her gaze to his face. To her shock, he was standing in ankle-deep water, hands on slender hips, and staring in her direction. She was positive he couldn't see her, but she didn't dare move. She'd die of humiliation if he found out she'd been watching.

"I know you're there, Amanda," Chance said calmly. "You made enough noise to scare off a buffalo herd. Would you like me to turn so you can get a complete view?"

Mortified beyond words, Amanda turned and started running, trying not to think about the deep, rumbling laughter that followed her. Vines whipped across her face, twigs tore at her sleeves, and the rip in her skirt widened. Several times she tripped, landing hard on the ground, but each time she scrambled to her feet again, the echo of his mocking laughter driving her on.

* * *

Gasping for breath, Amanda entered the hotel and collapsed onto the wooden bench in the small waiting room. By the time her breathing had returned to normal, she had chastised herself a hundred times for the way she'd acted. If Chance had asked *Polly* if she'd seen enough, she'd probably have replied with a knowing "Yes," then calmly turned away. No. Polly would have joined him. Nevertheless, Amanda scolded herself, you didn't have to act like a scared ninny and run the entire distance back here! Well, what's done is done. As crazy as he is, he'll probably try using my reaction to his benefit.

She took a deep, stabilizing breath and stood, satisfied that she could now make it up the stairs. She was already anticipating a long sleep. "I thought I was tired before," she muttered, "but it's nothing compared to how I feel now."

When she entered the room, Amanda was shocked to see Polly asleep on the bed. The woman had already had enough sleep to last a lifetime! Amanda was sorely tempted to wake her. But Polly looked so peaceful, she couldn't do it. Left with no recourse, she shoved the heavy brocade chair to the window so that she could see out and at the same time keep an eye on the door to the room. At least she'd be comfortable during her vigil. Polly was probably right about her being overly cautious, but still, they knew *nothing* about Chance Doyer, and a little caution certainly wasn't going to hurt.

Amanda suddenly noticed that she was missing her pistol. Apparently she'd dropped it one of the times she'd fallen. She wanted to kick herself for being so careless. "At this rate, we won't have *anything* to protect ourselves with."

After taking Polly's gun from the bedside table, Amanda returned to the chair. Her clothes were filthy and torn, but she just couldn't dredge up the strength to change. Once settled, she placed the gun on her lap. Less than five minutes later, her eyelids became unbearably heavy. To remain awake, she tried concentrating on the mystery of Springtown. But her thoughts kept returning to the lake, and to the magnificent man she'd seen there. Just thinking about it made her heart pump faster. A few minutes later, she was sound asleep.

Polly awoke feeling refreshed and hungry. She stretched lazily, swung her legs over the edge of the bed and sat up. A rare twinge of guilt ran through her when she saw Amanda with her head slumped forward. All last night and today, Amanda had been the one who kept guard while she slept. It wasn't any wonder she'd dozed off. Polly suddenly noticed the woman's ripped skirt, the dirty smudges on her clothes and body, and last, but certainly not least, the scratches and dried blood on her arms and hands. Furious, Polly jumped off the bed and went to the dark-haired woman. Amanda not only reminded her of a graceful swan, she was also the first real friend she'd ever had. While she'd been sleeping, Amanda had been attacked by the stranger!

Convinced she was feeling the same pain Amanda must have experienced, Polly gently shook Amanda's slender shoulder. She jumped back when Amanda's head snapped up.

"Is he here?" Amanda asked, her head still foggy from her deep sleep.

"No," Polly replied softly. When she saw the scratches on Amanda's lovely face, it was as if a knife had pierced her heart. "You're safe. Amanda, you can talk to me. What did Chance do to you?"

"Go away. I need sleep."

"All right, honey. Here, let me help you over to the bed."

"You stand guard."

When Amanda stood, the pistol fell from her lap. Polly kicked it out of the way, then guided her none-too-steady friend to the bed. "Don't worry, Amanda. I'll make sure nothing like this happens to you again."

As soon as Amanda was stretched out comfortably, her long lashes fluttered, then came to rest peacefully on her cheeks.

Polly picked the gun up off the floor and left the room. She was going to shoot Chance Doyer right between the legs for what he'd done to Amanda.

Hungry and tired, Chance could think of nothing but the cured ham he'd seen in Polly's kitchen. Since it was the women who had detained him in this town, they could damn well feed him. Leaving the house he'd chosen as his own, he headed down the street.

Polly's place was well lit, so he knew someone was home. Without so much as a knock, he opened the front door and entered. As he walked down the hallway, Polly stepped out of the kitchen. Chance came to a quick halt. "Hell, not again," he groaned when he saw the pistol pointed at him. "Is that all you women can think of, or is it just me?" He looked up at the ceiling, trying to keep his temper under control. "Why am I going to be killed this time?"

"You know why, you bastard."

"Now I'm a bastard! It's not you that should be calling names, sweetie. I'm not exactly here of my own free will. Before I'm condemned and hung, would you mind telling me what this is all about?'' The way her hand was shaking, he doubted she'd hit him if she pulled the trigger.

"You raped Amanda!"

"I did what?" he asked in shock. "Did she tell you that?"

"You're not going to get out of this. I saw what condition she's in."

Chance looked back up at the ceiling. These women were lunatics! "And pray tell, just what condition was that?" he asked in disgust.

"Her torn, dirty clothes, and the scratches on her body! She didn't deserve that. She could have killed you, but she didn't. Well, I'm going to do it for her."

"Wait just one damn minute! She saw me bathing naked at the lake, and she took off running like the devil was chasing her. If anything happened, it was her fault, not mine. Now put that damn gun away. I just came here to get something to eat. I'm hungry and tired and I'm in no mood to put up with any more of this confounded foolishness!"

"You didn't do anything to her?"

"That's what I said. If she told you differently, she's lying."

Polly's determination wavered. If Amanda had been raped, wouldn't there have been bruises on her body and blood on her skirt? Chance brushed past her as he entered the kitchen, and she lowered the pistol. Maybe she had jumped to conclusions. Maybe Amanda had, too. The man wasn't in the best of moods, but he sure didn't appear deranged. And he certainly wasn't the type who would find it necessary to resort to rape to get what he wanted. Women probably searched him out. "All right," she said, joining him. "Maybe I was wrong."

"Maybe?"

Polly felt his sudden smile all the way down to her toes. This man was more normal than most of her former customers had been. "Let's talk this over. Sit down, and I'll fix us both something to eat."

For the next hour they ate and talked. It was plain to see that Chance was worn out, and by the time he left, Polly knew that the most dangerous thing about Chance Doyer was his charm. She was already excited about seeing him in the morning. She'd told him to come over and she'd fix him breakfast. Once he was well rested, she had every intention of finding out if he was as good in bed as she thought he'd be.

The voice seemed to persist, until Amanda slowly opened her eyes. Realizing she had been dreaming, she sat up and glanced around the pitch-dark room, surprised at how late it was. "Polly?" she called quietly. Receiving no answer, she called a bit louder. "Polly?"

"Your pleasingly plump friend is contentedly enjoying the cowpoke's company."

Amanda's heart began pounding against her chest as a white fog again formed at the end of the bed. She scooted backward until she was against the headboard, trying to get as far away as possible.

"You shouldn't be afraid of me. I would never let anything harm you."

The fog was starting to take shape. Consumed with fear, Amanda tried to scream, but no sound was forthcoming.

"To prove I'm your friend, I'll tell you a little secret. There is gold hidden in this town."

"G-gold?"

"That's right. Enough to make you rich for the rest of your life."

Amanda could see the outline of a man, but nothing more. "You...you don't mean me any harm?"

"Now why would I want to harm such a lovely creature?"

Amanda watched the glowing, outlined figure move to the window. "I don't believe in ghosts. This has to be a trick! What are you doing here?"

He laughed. "You're worried about the cowpoke named Chance. I wanted you to know he's a drifter but won't give you any trouble. However, you should try to make him leave. You don't need him."

The vision started to disintegrate. "Wait!" Amanda said as she leapt off the bed. "I want to know what this is all about! Don't leave! What about the gold?" But the ghostly figure had disappeared, and she was standing alone in the middle of the room. Still shaken by what she'd just experienced, Amanda started toward the bedside table to light the candle. A chill ran through her, and with each step she became more weighted down with fatigue. She collapsed onto the bed, telling herself she had to go find Polly and make sure she was all right.

Chapter Five

With a shotgun tucked under her arm, Amanda marched down the street in search of Polly. She had already looked in every room in the hotel, and she was racked with guilt for having slept so late. It would be her fault if anything had happened to her friend. She didn't care if she ran into Chance Doyer, either. She was looking forward to it. She was going to kill him.

As she neared the house where they had been doing their cooking, Amanda was surprised to hear Polly's laughter. Circling to the back, she found Polly and Chance standing in the shade of an oak tree. Polly's arms were wrapped around his neck, and the look on her face reminded Amanda of a child who has just been handed a lollipop.

"What's going on here?" Amanda demanded, even though she had a hunch she knew exactly what was going on.

"Amanda," Polly replied happily. "You're awake."

"You look like you've been through a briar patch," Chance commented. "Did something happen to you?"

Amanda bristled at his smug grin as he removed Polly's arms from around his neck. "Very funny," Amanda stated scornfully. "Now, if you don't mind, I'd like to speak to Polly alone." She was relieved when he walked away without an argument, though that grin was still plastered on his face. And he certainly took his own sweet time! As soon as he was out of hearing distance, she centered her attention on Polly. "I thought you were supposed to be protecting us!"

"I was. Amanda, there is nothin' wrong with Chance. He was angry 'cause of everythin' we did to him, and I can't say I blame him much. He'd almost caught the men that had left him to die! I think we should start actin' more decent to him, cause he's gonna be around for a while."

Amanda was stunned. She couldn't conjure up a respectable argument against Polly statement, because when it came to men, Polly had plenty of experience to draw upon. It galled Amanda to think that she might have jumped to conclusions about Chance, and she still intended to keep an eye on him. "How long is 'a while'?"

"I guess till he's ready to leave. What happened to your face and clothes?"

"Nothing. It doesn't matter." Amanda had just noticed that Polly's hair was done up in neat ringlets that had been piled on the top of her head. She was even wearing the beautiful green satin dress that Amanda had claimed as her own! Because Polly was heavier, her large bosom nearly spilled out over the low neckline, and the seams appeared to be ready to burst at any moment. "You consider slinking up to a man being protective? Polly, how could you have risked the possibility of him killing us? And just what are you doing wearing my dress?"

"I wanted to look pretty for Chance." She patted the back of her hair. "Besides, it's not as if it's the only dress you got. Amanda, I only fed him and we talked. I might have gotten further if you hadn't come along. But I got time."

"You've ruined my dress."

"Nonsense," Polly replied happily. "I can get a lot more wear out of it. I might just have to let the seams out a tad, though. Don't look so angry. You'll be happy to know I've got breakfast cooked."

Polly walked away, and Amanda had no choice but to follow her into the house. It bothered her that Polly and Chance had developed such a quick liking for one another. Of course, as pretty as Polly was, she could certainly understand Chance's attraction to the redhead. But that didn't mean she had to like it.

As soon as they were in the kitchen, Amanda asked, "Just what did Chance tell you?"

Polly ladled some mush into a bowl and handed it to Amanda. "He talked about different mining towns, and we swapped miners' tales. He also said you found him without clothes on. Is that how you got so scratched up and dirty?"

"I fell in some bushes."

Polly had to turn away to keep from laughing. Chance had been right. Amanda had panicked at seeing a naked man.

"What else did he say?"

"Not much more. Now that I think about it, he did more askin'. Anyways, I discovered he's just as nervous about us as we are about him. He said he keeps waitin' for you to come up behind him with a gun."

That caused a smile to toy at the corners of Amanda's mouth. Keeping him worried seemed like an excellent idea. But nervous? He hadn't struck her as being the least bit nervous when she'd seen him at the lake. She began eating her mush.

"So," Polly continued as she joined Amanda at the table, "I sort of told him what we're doin' here, and he settled right down." Again she reached up and patted the tight curls she'd worked so hard on that morning.

"Did you ask him where Sacramento is, or if there is a town nearby?"

"Yep, but he's never been to Sacramento. He came from the north. Said he hasn't seen a town since leavin' a place called Angels Camp over three months ago. The poor man's been in the saddle a mighty long time, and nary a woman to help satisfy his needs," Polly finished sadly. "That's terrible hard on a man, Amanda."

"Did he tell you that, or was it something contrived in your head?"

"He told me most of it, but I'm smart enough to know a man can get mighty gruff if he doesn't have a woman. What I'm sayin' is, we don't have to be on our guard, 'cause Chance is stayin' here."

"Why? Are you planning to keep him calmed down by making love to him? He's nothing but a drifter, Polly, looking for whatever he can get."

"That doesn't make him any different from other men."

Amanda smirked. "Did you ask if he'd help get us out of here, or help catch that burro to carry supplies so we can leave on our own?"

"Not really." Polly removed a piece of lint from the bodice of her dress. "I had other things on my mind."

Amanda's anger flared. Polly's lack of concern over their plight, her brazen attitude toward Chance, infuriated her. "Don't you think of anything other than yourself?" The legs of her chair scraped the floor as she shoved it back. "Go to him if you like, that's your business. But I would appreciate it if you'd find your own clothes to wear."

Amanda stormed out of the house, feeling suddenly alone. How could Polly be blinded by a handsome face? Well, she could have the good-for-nothing man! A dance hall girl with lust on her mind and a drifter who had the audacity to primp stark naked deserved each other.

Amanda stood in the middle of the road, trying to decide what she should do next. She wasn't about to leave Springtown until she got her hands on the gold. But how could she get it without Chance finding out? If Polly knew, she'd probably tell him. The horse! If she had the horse she could pack the gold on him and leave. Lifting her skirt, she took off in the same direction the crooks had come from when they'd located their horses, but as she passed the livery stable she suddenly realized she'd have to go inside for a rope. When the ghost told her the location of the gold, she was going to be ready.

As Amanda left town, she saw something on the road ahead, sparkling in the sunlight. Curious, she hurried forward. It was partially covered with dirt. When she picked it up, her laughter drifted in the air. It was a ring. A very beautiful ring. Feeling a bit light-headed, she dropped it in the pocket of her skirt and continued on. The day wasn't a disaster after all.

Having chosen one of the larger houses as his temporary residence, Chance proceeded to rummage through the place. When talking to Polly this morning, he'd found out that she and Amanda weren't the last residents of the town, as he'd suspected. In fact, they had been here but a short time, and had done very little searching of the homes or stores. He thought about the necklace Polly wore. Maybe he should do a little looking of his own. And what better place to start than this house?

It wasn't until Chance opened a trunk in one of the three bedrooms that his interest was truly piqued. At the bottom, hidden beneath blankets and baby clothes, he found two heavy pouches of gold.

Carrying both pouches, Chance sat on the rocking chair near the window and stared in disbelief at his find. Why would the owner of the house have left without them? Where had the gold come from? They were probably questions he'd never find the answers to. However, there were a couple of things he did know. This was gold country. Springtown was smack-dab in the Calaveras hills, right in line with the great mother lode. So the gold could have come from an abandoned mine nearby. Was it played out? He put the pouches back where he'd found them, then placed everything on top.

After combing the house from one end to the other and finding nothing more of value, Chance stood in the hallway and stared at the back door. He almost wished he hadn't found the gold. If he hadn't, he wouldn't be standing there trying to talk himself into checking out the food cellar. He had never been afraid of man or beast, but small underground rooms scared the hell out of him.

Even though he knew it was because of what had happened when he was a boy, he couldn't rid himself of the old fear. It had been late afternoon, and his mother had sent him to the store to purchase sewing shears. As was his habit, he'd cut across a graveyard to reduce the distance. On his way back, he'd come upon a freshly dug grave. Curious, he'd walked over and looked down. Chance shuddered, remembering how the edge had given way and he'd fallen inside. He'd panicked, yelled, screamed, jumped, scratched, and cried. But no one had come to his rescue until the next morning.

Chance shrugged his shoulders, as if to shake off the bad memories. This was ridiculous. He wasn't a child anymore. He was a grown man and had seen a hell of a lot worse than some damn food cellar. He picked up a candle and left the house.

When Chance pulled open the cellar door, his nerves were on edge. Staring into the dark hole, he was tempted to close the door and forget it. But he'd be damned if he was going to allow some foolish fear to get the better of him. He started down the wooden steps, counting each one and feeling as if he were entering the darkness of hell. Seven steps, then his feet were solidly planted on the hard-packed earth floor, with the musty smell of dirt permeating his nostrils. He suddenly realized he hadn't lit the candle.

Striking a match, he held the flame to the wick. The light fluttered, then came alive. There was little down there. Just canning jars—some full, some empty—and a few other things. All were covered with a thick layer of cobwebs. He forced himself to move forward. It would only take a moment to search the place, and surely he was man enough to do that. He began wiping away the cobwebs, wondering if he would meet up with a spider. When he found nothing, he hurried back up the stairs and into the open.

Amanda staggered into town, worn out and thirsty. She'd not only found horse droppings, she'd also located the horse. But he was smart. He'd wait until she was almost upon him, then scamper away, stop, and watch her. She'd chased the darn critter all over the foothills. When the afternoon heat had become unbearable, she'd given up. But she was determined to try again in the morning.

Eager for a drink of water, Amanda stopped at the well. She was about to draw up the bucket when she saw Chance walking toward her. As much as she wanted to dislike him, she had to admit that Polly's description was most appropriate. He was indeed tall and beautiful. She turned to leave.

"Wait up!" Chance called.

Not sure she was doing the right thing, Amanda waited.

"I thought we might have a talk," Chance said when he joined her.

"About what?"

"I wanted to tell you I believe you don't have my horse."

"Why? Because you've searched everywhere?"

"That's right."

Amanda had to steel herself to keep from reacting to his devastating smile. His even white teeth were a pleasing contrast to his sun-bronzed skin. A picture of his wet, naked body flashed across her mind. "Is there nothing else you wanted to say?" she snapped, refusing to let him cast a spell over her like he had Polly.

"You don't like me, do you?"

"No."

Chance's smile broadened. "Would you care to tell me why?"

"Not that it's any of your business, but you remind me a lot of my father."

"In looks or character?"

"What difference does it make? If you have nothing more to say, I'll be on my way."

"I assure you, I'm not a bad guy when you get to know me."

"Bears aren't bad, either, unless you get in their way. Now if you'll move—" She sucked in her breath when he ran a finger slowly down the side of her cheek.

"You're very beautiful, and very tempting."

Amanda slapped his hand away. "You might charm Polly, but it won't work on me."

"Why are you so nervous?"

"Because I don't trust you." She raised her chin in defiance. "I think you're nothing but a drifter who is too lazy to do a hard day's work."

"Is that what your father was?"

"I haven't finished. I also think that because you've found two women alone in a town you think you can . . ." Amanda couldn't think of the right words.

Chance chuckled. "Enjoy unrestrained pleasures?"

"Yes. Exactly. Well, I'm not that sort of woman, so I would appreciate it if you'd keep your distance."

Chance was totally amused. "Oh, there's no doubt in my mind that you aren't *that kind of woman.*"

"Good."

"However, you do present an awfully tempting package."

"How dare you say such a thing to me?"

"You'd better be careful, Amanda. The more prickly you get, the more curious I become. I always have liked a good challenge."

Amanda opened her mouth to say something scathing, but thought better of it. She gritted her teeth and smiled. "Then I'll simply have to be nice to you. Sir, if you would be ever so kind as to move, I shall be on my way."

Chance roared with laughter at her mock politesse. He moved, then made a dramatic wave of his hand to beckon her on. He laughed all the harder as he watched her march away, her back as stiff as a fence post.

When Amanda entered the hotel, she saw Polly waiting on the bench in the lobby. The redhead immediately jumped to her feet, and Amanda winced at hearing the back seams of the once beautiful dress rip. At the same time, she felt guilty when she saw the woebegone look on the buxom woman's face. Amanda had to admit she hadn't been exactly fair. After all, Polly really hadn't done anything wrong. She shouldn't have become so upset at finding Polly in Chance's arms. She decided to try to offer the proverbial olive branch. "I'm a pretty good seamstress, so why don't we find something that fits? If it's too big, I can always take it in."

"I'd be beholden," Polly replied dejectedly. "I've never had fine clothes."

Amanda smiled weakly. "Neither have I. I suppose that's why they're so important to me. I learned a long time ago that if you have fine clothes, people think you're somebody."

Amanda reached in her skirt pocket and pulled out a handkerchief to mop her forehead. She'd forgotten all about the ring until it hit the floor.

Polly leaned down to pick it up.

"I found it partially buried in the road."

"Don't make sense for me to try and hog all the jewelry," Polly said softly as she examined the ring. "It's got quite a few diamonds, but that big square green thing in the middle looks like glass."

She handed it back to Amanda, who stuck it in her pocket again.

"Amanda, do you still want us to go into business together when we reach Sacramento?"

Amanda smiled. "I don't know why not."

Polly released a heavy sigh. "I guess now I can tell you I was awfully worried about that when you left the house angry. I was thinkin' that if we're gonna have a business, maybe we should grab up all the money in the stores 'fore Chance gets his hands on it."

"Does this mean you're not going to have anything more to do with him?"

"Lord a-mercy," Polly declared with a wave of her hands. "Amanda, you may be smarter about a lot more things than I am, but when it comes to men, I swear I gotta be a hundred years older. Of course it don't mean I'm not goin' to have anything more to do with him. It also don't mean that I'm gonna make the mistake of spillin' all I know."

"Well then, why—?"

"I like men, and you gotta admit Chance is one mighty fine-looking feller. We're each on our own as far as he's concerned."

"Just what's that supposed to mean?"

"It means if you want him, you gotta go get him."

Amanda gasped. "Hasn't anything I've said had any meaning? I not only don't want him, I don't even want him in this town!"

"Amanda, people haven't exactly been flocking to Springtown. We need Chance to help us get away from here. Besides, he's such a big...toy."

"He thinks the same thing about us," Amanda said sarcastically. "If I tell you a secret, will you promise not to tell Chance?"

"I promise."

Amanda looked toward the door. "Let's go upstairs, where we can't be overheard. Besides, I'm dying of thirst."

After three glasses of water, Amanda sat on the side of the bed and looked at Polly, who was sitting properly on a high-backed wooden chair. Amanda could hardly wait to share her secret. "The ghost visited me again."

Polly's green eyes bulged. "But...but we decided it was one of those men who rode through that talked to you."

"I watched them ride off yesterday morning, and the ghost appeared to me again last night."

"It was a dream, or you're just making up another one of your stories. You were so tired you wouldn't know the difference." Polly started wringing her hands. "Or it was Chance." She stood and began pacing the floor. "Yes, that's it. He was the one in your room both times. At least that makes sense. I'll ask him."

"You can't do that. You promised! Polly, I was frightened to begin with, too, but I think the ghost is harmless. More importantly, he wants to help us."

"How?" Polly asked suspiciously.

Amanda leaned forward and whispered, "He told me there's gold hidden in this town."

"Gold?"

"Shh. Keep your voice down. Do you want Chance to hear?"

Polly stopped her pacing and stared at Amanda. "How do you know he's telling the truth?" she asked in an equally hushed voice, her excitement growing rapidly.

"I don't, but what if the ghost *is* telling the truth? Polly, do you realize how rich we would be? I'm willing to share with you, but not with Chance Doyer. The ghost said we should get him out of town."

"How?"

"I thought it all out while I was trying to catch Chance's horse."

"The crooks took off with his horse."

"When they left, they didn't have the buckskin with them. I didn't tell Chance, because we need that horse. We won't collect any more money around town. I've already raided all the stores. But maybe I'll return some. We'll let him find it. You can tell Chance about his horse—then he'll have no reason to stay. But after you've told him, I don't think you should have anything more to do with him."

A look of stubbornness tightened Polly's features. "Why?"

"Because it has to be the interest you've shown that's keeping him here! What other reason would he have to remain?"

"Then how are we going to get the gold out of here?"

Amanda smiled. "We'll use that burro that keeps coming into town. I saw him just this morning."

"But he always stays out of reach."

"So we put food out, then rope him."

"Where do we go when we leave?"

"Maybe the ghost can tell us."

"Oh, Amanda, you have to be very careful. He could be the devil."

Amanda laughed nervously. "I doubt that."

"Gold." Polly collapsed on the chair again, causing the side seam of her dress to tear. "Damn, that's a pretty word."

As much as she hated to admit it, Amanda could feel greed taking hold of her, too. "I'm hoping to see him again tonight."

"Amanda, I don't want him taking over my soul. But at the same time, I can't resist the possibility of being rich. So if you're willing to do this, I guess I gotta earn my share. I'll sleep with you tonight."

"Thank you, Polly. I know how frightening this must be for you, but when you see him, I think you'll change your mind. He has a most pleasing voice. Why don't you go see if you can find where Chance is staying, and accidentally let it slip about the money and his horse? While you're doing that, I'll return the money."

Polly giggled, already excited about their little conspiracy. "Believe me, it'll be my pleasure. And this time, don't come lookin' for me."

Amanda frowned.

"Meet me at the house about six for supper." Polly giggled again as she stood. "If I'm lucky enough to not be there, you'll have to fix your own meal. I know you told me to have nothin' to do with Chance, but just one time's not gonna hurt nothin'. And don't worry, my lips are sealed."

Amanda couldn't believe the envy she was suddenly feeling. What would it be like to have a man make love to her? Though she considered her thoughts to be wicked, it was something she'd wondered about for several years.

Polly turned slowly. "If he kills me, I'll have died from pleasure. That's a lotta man we got for a neighbor." She looked down at her dress, knowing it was destroyed. She didn't have the nerve to look at Amanda. "I'm gonna look for a dress that fits," she mumbled as she left the room.

Amanda fell back on the bed and rubbed her temples. Polly had no idea how much she appreciated not having to stay in a room alone tonight. She'd lied about not being afraid to see the ghost again. To deliberately wait for something inhuman to reappear scared her to death. Was she playing with the devil, or was all this really nothing more than dreams? She had to find out the truth.

If it really was a ghost and he had told the truth about the gold, she could hardly turn her back on something that would make her rich. Why, she could have all the things she'd always wanted. A fine house, clothes, and people looking up to her with respect. It seemed like she'd been working her fingers to the bones ever since she was a child. Now all that could change.

It occurred to Amanda that it wouldn't be wise to return *all* the money. After all, there wasn't that much. And what would she and Polly have if there proved to be no ghost or no gold? Instead, she'd only put a little back for Chance to find. She climbed off the bed and lifted the mattress.

Amanda slowly made her way down the boarded walk. She was in no hurry, and remaining cloistered in the hotel held no appeal. Especially not on such a lovely afternoon. Polly was probably in bed pleasuring Chance. That was something that still didn't sit well with her, but other than killing the man, there wasn't anything she could do about it. In all honesty, Chance would appeal to any woman. And it wasn't that she was a prude, or at least she didn't think of herself as one. Many a night she'd wondered how it would feel like to have a man make love to her.

Amanda was about to pass the saloon when she changed her mind. This was one place she'd stayed away from, but her inquisitiveness continued to eat at her. Women—decent women—never entered such establishments. But what difference did it make now? No one would know.

Feeling deliciously wicked, Amanda entered. In the silence, the clicking heels of her boots sounded loud and sharp. She stopped and glanced around. There were only tables and chairs, spittoons, and stairs leading to the upper floor. Was that where the prostitutes' rooms were that the boys had teased her about when she was young? What she assumed was the bar ran the length of the far wall.

Behind that was a large mirror over a counter lined with bottles and glasses, all entwined with cobwebs. The saloon had the same musty odor the stores had.

Amanda was disappointed. Well, she asked herself, what did you expect? Men drinking and women wearing scarlet dresses as they mingled with customers? How long had it been since men had raised glasses of whiskey in here and harlots had prowled? One thing she had discovered, the people who had lived here had been hardworking. Most of the clothes she found were sturdy, well-made working garments—the exception being the few lovely gowns she'd discovered, one of which Polly had destroyed in her determination to attract Chance.

Amanda was about to leave when she noticed a brass rod near the floor, running the length of the bar. Curious as to what it was used for, she moved forward. As she stood in front of the bar, she came to the conclusion that it was for men to place a foot on. She rested her elbows on the smooth mahogany, her eyes taking in the different kinds of whiskey bottles. Then she saw the picture on the wall at the far end of the bar, and felt herself blush from head to toe. It was a painting of a woman seated on a bench, holding a snake. But the woman had nary a stitch of clothing on! Horrified, she turned to leave, only to bump into a hard chest. Looking up, she saw Chance Doyer standing in front of her. "What are you doing here?" she blurted out.

"I saw you come in and thought I'd join you for a drink."

"Drink? I don't drink." His closeness was making her nervous.

"If you don't drink, why did you come in?"

"Well, I...I... It's none of your business!" He moved closer, and Amanda had to press her back against the bar to keep him from touching her. Not knowing what to say, she blurted out, "Why aren't you with Polly?"

"Why should I be with Polly?"

His voice was low and husky, and Amanda could feel his breath on her face. "Because she was looking for you. I think you should—"

"Polly can wait." Chance's gazed traveled from her thick black hair to her eyes, eyes that showed a strange combination of fear and wonder. "I wanted to talk to you. I'm sure you're aware of how desirable you are."

"Yes ... I mean, no ... We've already talked."

He looked at her lips. Full, tempting lips. How would she react if he kissed her? "I want to hear more about your father."

Amanda tried to move aside, but he placed his hands on the bar, trapping her in between them. How am I going to get out of this mess, she wondered desperately. I should never have come in here. I didn't even bring a gun! "My...my father is a small man" was all she could think to say.

It amused Chance to see how fidgety the normally calm Miss Amanda had become. "I wonder what it would feel like to loosen your hair from that bun and run my fingers through it."

"I demand you move your hands." The words didn't come out nearly as strong as Amanda had wanted.

"And what are you going to do if I don't?"

"Surely you wouldn't..."

"Wouldn't what? Kiss you? Caress your desirable body, savoring the feel of you until I can't wait a moment longer to make love to you?"

Amanda gasped at the blatant words. "I'm a lady," she whispered. "Gentlemen don't say such things to a lady."

"Gentleman? I assure you, my dear, I'm no gentleman."

When Amanda saw Chance lower his head, she instinctively knew he was about to claim a kiss. She squeezed her eyes shut and grabbed the sides of her skirts, refusing to shudder when his loathsome lips touched hers. But he placed soft kisses on her eyes and the corners of her mouth. Then his tongue trailed the outline of her lips while he muttered, "Damn, you taste good." His mouth touched hers, causing her head to spin. She opened her own to protest, only to feel his tongue slide inside, causing goose bumps on her arms. When he drew back, she knew she should give him hell, but she wasn't even sure she could speak. Never had a man kissed her in such a manner. His lips had removed all thoughts of refusal.

Seeing her eyes still closed and the dreamlike look on her face, Chance was tempted to take it further, but he had more important things to take care of. "Now, unless you want me to carry this further, *Miss Amanda,* I suggest you tell me exactly where you've hidden my horse. And while you're at it, maybe you'd like to tell me why you and Polly have remained in Springtown."

"What?" Amanda asked in disbelief.

"You heard me."

Quickly regaining her composure, Amanda stared him straight in the eye. The bastard had kissed her for information! "You didn't have to go to all this trouble to get an answer, *Mr. Doyer,*" she said angrily. "All you had to do was ask. If you want your horse, you're going to have to go looking for him. We told you the horses got away, and that was the truth." Why wouldn't he move away? She could still feel his body heat. "But when those men left, they didn't have the buckskin with them. So I can only guess he's running loose somewhere. As for why we haven't left Springtown, we have no means of getting out of here. *That's* why we stole the horses."

"All right, I'll accept that . . . for now. But believe me, kissing you was certainly no trouble." He removed his hands from the bar and stepped back. "Now, how about that drink?"

"Like I said, I don't drink. And even if I did, it wouldn't be with the likes of you." Amanda headed toward the door.

"Whoa, now." Chance grabbed her arm and spun her around. "Just what have you got against me? I've kept my word about not harming you as long as you don't try putting something over on me."

"That statement is just one example of why I don't trust you. You keep saying you'll leave us alone, but then you turn right around and try to intimidate us in order to get answers. Well, how about giving me a few answers?"

Chance leaned against the bar. "Ask away."

"Why are *you* here?"

"I told you, I was chasing that gang."

"Then why are you staying here instead of going after them?"

"Like you, I have no horse. But I'm in no rush. They travel slow." His gaze slowly traveled the length of her. "I have to admit, I'm beginning to like this place."

"Then give us your horse and *we'll* leave."

"Even if I catch my horse, I don't think I'd be willing to turn him over to you."

"I see." Amanda turned to go, tilting her chin upward. "I hope you have a miserable day."

"In case you're interested, I'll be going to the lake to bathe in about an hour." He grinned wickedly when she paused. "Care to join me again?"

"You are the most miserable excuse for a man I've ever known."

"Don't jump to conclusions until you have something good to compare," he called. As she went out the door, he added, "You needn't rush off." And then he broke out laughing.

"I wonder where Chance went after I saw him in the saloon," Amanda said as she climbed into bed next to Polly.

"I don't know, and at this moment, I don't care. Amanda, I'm scared to death about this ghost thing." Polly adjusted her nightcap. "Maybe it wasn't such a smart idea for me to be with you after all."

"Nothing's going to happen to you, Polly. I just want to be sure I haven't been dreaming. Now blow out the candle and go to sleep. I'll wake you if he appears."

"I know I'm not going to be able to sleep a wink."

A few minutes later, Amanda heard Polly snoring, but she had every intention of remaining awake. Tonight she was going to find out if she'd seen a ghost or not.

Amanda thought about the conversation she and Polly had had at supper. Polly had been pouting because she hadn't seen Chance since morning. Finding out that Amanda had been the one to tell him about his horse had only added to her sulking.

Trying to understand Polly was practically impossible, Amanda decided. A few minutes later, Polly had laughed, saying she wished there were more available men. When Amanda told her about Chance taking advantage of her, Polly had proceeded to preach about how lucky Amanda was to be so cold-natured.

Amanda rolled over, turning toward Polly. According to her mother, fornicating was something only whores and men enjoyed. It was a painful and distasteful burden that a good married woman was forced to put up with. Since Amanda had turned fifteen, miners had forever been trying to steal kisses from her, and some had even succeeded. But those kisses had been nothing compared to the one Chance had bestowed on her. It had made her insides feel...strange. It had been a wonderful kiss, and she hadn't wanted it to stop. It made her want to find out who was telling the truth—Polly or her mother.

She flopped onto her back and allowed pictures of Chance's naked body to fill her mind. His handsome face, his lean hips, his long powerful legs and... Would it hurt? He was so big! It didn't seem to bother Polly. *I shouldn't even be thinking about such things!*

She turned onto her side again and tried to concentrate on the gold. But her thoughts kept drifting back to a pair of blue-green eyes, eyes full of daring, and a man who had certainly mastered the ability to charm, even if he was a no-account.

Amanda climbed out of bed and went to the window. It was pitch-black outside. How many years did she plan to wait until she discovered the mysteries shared between a man and a woman? She was twenty years old and should be married and have children by now. Was Chance interested in sharing his bed with her? After all, he was the one that had stirred up these flaming desires that she'd thought she had smothered. And he was the perfect man to initiate her into the facts of life. Once he left Springtown, she'd never see him again. No one would ever have to know.

On the other hand, though he'd kissed her, he couldn't have been too interested, or he wouldn't have pulled away. And was she willing to sacrifice her virginity, which her mother had said was so important to take to the marriage bed? What if she became pregnant? What if she never found a man she wanted to marry?

Aggravated at herself, Amanda returned to the bed. Polly stirred, but didn't wake. Amanda elected to never let any man take her down the unpleasurable path of bedding! Yet, if she didn't want to experience it, why was she so curious? She closed her eyes, trying to fight off a need she didn't even understand, and soon drifted into a restless sleep.

When she awoke, she glanced toward the window, surprised to see the faint hues of dawn. So, she thought bitterly, the ghost was nothing but a dream. She should have known better than to think there was such a thing. It wasn't going to be easy telling Polly that all their dreams for a wealthy future had fallen down a bottomless pit. They were back where they'd started from, and it looked like Chance was their only hope of getting out of town.

Chapter Six

The early-morning air had had a nip to it when Chance had left town to find his horse. But that had been three hours ago, and after all the walking and climbing over mountainous terrain, he was now hot and sweaty. The temperature had to be nearing a hundred degrees, and he'd still seen no sign of the beast. Amanda might have been lying about Gus not taking Cactus, but on the slim chance she had told the truth, he continued looking.

Standing on top of a large boulder, Chance pulled off his hat and wiped his forehead while scanning the lush vale below. The floor was covered with tall... He jammed his hat back on to block the glare of the sun. An animal was grazing peacefully on the tall grass at the far end, but he couldn't be sure it was Cactus. Placing his fingers between his lips, he released a shrill whistle that broke the quiet and echoed around the surrounding cliffs. The animal raised its head, and Chance could clearly see the black mane and swishing tail. He whistled again. Hearing a familiar whinny, he started working his way down the boulder.

When the buckskin came galloping toward him, Chance felt a strong sense of relief. Aside from the hollow sound of hooves striking the ground, which told him that Cactus's shoes were loose, the big stallion appeared to be in excellent condition.

The stallion came to a sliding halt, then stretched his thick neck forward and lovingly nudged Chance's chest. Chance caressed his velvety nose. The two of them had been through a lot together, and the horse had even saved his life once.

"Well, big boy," Chance crooned, "it's been a while, hasn't it?"

Cactus nickered and tossed his head, appearing to understand Chance's words.

"Guess the first thing we need to do is take care of those shoes before they start causing you trouble." Chance took the rope he'd brought and looped it around the powerful neck. Holding the ends, he grabbed a handful of mane, then swung himself onto the horse's back. Knowing he'd have to ride to the town of Murphys to get Cactus shod, Chance neck-reined the stallion toward the south. After the short spell of freedom he'd enjoyed, Cactus was frisky, but Chance had no problem holding him to a trot.

As they passed less than half a mile from Springtown, Chance realized for the first time just how well the town was hidden. Not only did scattered trees block a man's view, but Springtown was also situated in a small mountain valley and up against a big cliff. And it was away from any of the well-traveled roads. No one would know it was there, unless, like Gus, he was deliberately staying off the beaten path and happened to stumble upon it.

Now that I have my pistol and my horse, maybe I should just keep going, Chance thought as he guided Cactus down a rocky incline. But there was the matter of the gold he'd left hidden in Springtown. A goodly sum to just up and leave behind.

Chance chortled, remembering how he'd told Polly he had no idea where Sacramento was. He'd lied because she was so determined not to tell him how she and Amanda had landed in Springtown. He'd even told her it was a three-month trip from Springtown to Angels Camp, just to see what her reaction would be. Hell, Angels Camp wasn't much more than seven miles away, and Murphys not over five. But she'd appeared to buy his story, and she hadn't asked any more questions.

The two women were a mystery. And what was all that foolishness Amanda had fed him about needing horses to get away from there? Unless they'd come down from the north, it would have been practically impossible to miss all the mining towns scattered about. And Polly kept muttering something about Columbia that didn't make any sense at all. Still, whatever their reason for remaining in Springtown, it really wasn't any of his business.

When Chance rode into Murphys, he headed straight for the blacksmith. He wanted Cactus taken care of as quickly as possible, so that he could ride back to Springtown, grab the gold and be on his way.

"Howdy," the blacksmith said as Chance slid off Cactus's back. "What can I do for you?"

"My horse needs to be shod," Chance replied congenially.

"You're in luck, mister. Right now I ain't busy, so I can get right to it." The blacksmith lifted Cactus's foot and took a look. "Yep, I'd say it's time. This shoe is as thin as hell and 'bout to come off. How come you ain't got no saddle and bridle for him?"

Chance smiled at the bull of a man. "I didn't steal him, if that's what you're thinking. I'm the only person I know that can stay on his back. Tried crossing the Stanislaus

River at the wrong spot. Thought sure I was a dead man. I don't know how the saddle came off, but at least me and my horse made it to safety." Chance shoved his hat back on his head and looked down the road.

"How come you didn't take Parrott's ferry across?"

"I was too far north. Where's a good place to buy gear?"

"'Bout two blocks down."

"How about a saloon?"

"You'll pass one on your way. Mighty fine-looking animal," the blacksmith commented as he ran his hand over Cactus's withers. "Would you be interested in sellin' him?"

"Nope, it'd be hell finding another one like him." He handed the blacksmith the rope still circling Cactus's neck.

"Where you goin' from here?" The blacksmith tied Cactus to a post.

"Springtown."

The blacksmith laughed, exposing yellowed teeth. "That's the biggest joke I've heard all day," he finally said, a big grin still spread across his face.

"Why do you say that?"

"'Cause there ain't no such town."

What does he mean by that? Chance wondered. Hell, I just came from there!

"Mister, if someone told you about Springtown, they was feedin' you a big line of bull. Ain't nobody but greenhorns believe that story."

"What story?"

"That there's actually a town named Springtown, *and* a ghost, *and* a heap of hidden gold." The blacksmith laughed again. "Hell, stories like that ain't nothin' but miners' tales. Miners will tell you some cock-and-bull story, then turn around and swear to God that it's the truth. I sure haven't met nobody who ever came from Springtown. I think that tale was made up so people like yourself would take off lookin' for the place, leaving more gold for others to find. If I was you, I'd give up ever tryin' to find Springtown. You know, that reminds me of a story about—''

''Thanks for the information,'' Chance cut in. ''I'll be back later to pick up my horse.''

As Chance headed down the street, his blood was already throbbing through his veins. He hadn't felt this way since he and his brother had found their first vein of gold. One thing for sure, he *knew* there was a Springtown, and hadn't Polly mentioned something about a ghost and gold? He entered the first bar he came to. Even if it took all day, he was going to find out if there were others who knew about the mysterious town.

After sharing a bottle of whiskey with an old-timer and the bartender, Chance left the saloon. Purchasing tack had already been forgotten. The two men at the saloon had told him just about the same story the blacksmith had. Though Chance didn't believe some ghost haunted Springtown, he was sure as hell giving a lot of thought to the possibility of hidden gold. Now he knew why the ''ladies'' had stayed. Either they knew where the gold was, or they were searching for it. Well, they were in for a big disappointment if they planned on keeping it for themselves. He had every intention of sharing their wealth.

Chance returned to the blacksmith's shop.

The flat-faced man greeted Chance. ''He's all ready to go. Thought you was goin' to pick up tack.''

Chance gave him a sheepish grin. ''Never got any farther than the saloon. How much do I owe you?''

After paying the man, Chance swung up on the stallion's back. "Where's the livery stable? Thought I might stay a couple of days."

"Go down the street and take the first left. Have you given any more thought to sellin' your horse?"

"Nope." He reined Cactus around and headed him down the street.

By the time Chance left town, he was quite pleased with himself. He'd paid the two-month fee to board Cactus and left the stallion there. Then he'd rented the roan gelding he was now riding. The hawk-nosed stable man hadn't batted an eye when Chance asked if the horse would return to the livery stable if he turned him loose. Chance had told him that he had a little mine and he didn't want anyone knowing where it was. He just needed the horse to get him there.

A mile from Springtown, Chance dismounted, then gave the gelding a hard slap on the rump. The horse took off kicking, but then settled down and made a beeline for Murphys. Chance continued on foot.

Polly and Amanda sat in Polly's kitchen, drinking coffee and counting money. The entire morning had been spent darting from one store to the next, collecting what Amanda had put back, and anything else they could find.

"I think he's gone," Amanda said despondently when the counting was completed.

Polly clicked her tongue. "I told you we should have asked him to take us out of here."

"I say we're lucky to be rid of him."

"Who knows how long it's gonna be 'fore someone else rides through? Chance was the only one we've seen that could have gotten us out of here," Polly insisted.

Amanda tossed her hair back over her shoulder. In their rush, she hadn't taken the time to brush and twist it into the usual bun on top of her head. "Well, there's no use bemoaning it now. You said you saw him leave town, and he certainly hasn't returned."

"What are we gonna do now?"

Amanda rested her elbows on the table, her ring glittering as it met the sunlight filtering in from the window. "Polly, aren't you just itching to go through all the houses to see what's in them? I am. Now I can take my time looking at the beautiful furniture, the clothes . . ."

"And the jewelry?"

"And the jewelry. It's like going on a treasure hunt. Think of the china and silver. . . ."

"Amanda, I miss havin' men around." Polly looked at her friend seated across from her. "You don't even know what I'm talking about." She tipped her china cup up and finished off the coffee. "I miss the excitement when a man is yelling that he's hit the big payload. I miss the music, the poker games, the men who look at me like I'm somethin' they can't live without. Damn it, I miss feelin' alive. There's nothin' happening here. At first it was all right, then Chance came, and now that he's gone, I'm already bored. At least Chance made things more interesting." She banged her cup down on the table. "I have to get away from this place, or I'll go mad."

Amanda tried to understand what Polly was feeling, but while Polly wanted to leave, Amanda was quite content. She liked the serenity of the town. But how would she feel after months of not seeing another soul, or when winter arrived and the ground became crusted with ice and snow? "I guess you're right. We can't stay here forever. Give it a couple of more weeks. In the meantime, we'll try catching that burro. We need him to carry the supplies we'll have to take."

Polly nodded as she swatted at a fly that kept buzzing around her head.

"It's such a hot day," Amanda commented, "I thought I'd go to the lake and wash off. Why don't you come with me?"

"I don't know how to swim, and water scares me. With my luck, I'd drown. No, I think I'll go to the saloon and get drunk."

Amanda thought about trying to dissuade her from drinking, but Polly was old enough to take care of herself. Amanda was surprised to be experiencing sadness because Chance wouldn't be returning. Was it possible that she'd miss him, too? Or maybe the feeling stemmed from the knowledge that all the doubts and questions she'd hashed over the night before were to no avail. Or was it the disappointment that her one chance for possible fulfillment had been lost? What difference did it make? He was gone now. "I'll see you later," she said as Polly left the kitchen.

Amanda felt downcast as she left the house. Polly was right. She had refused to think of Chance as a means of escape. But she'd also thought there was hidden gold. Surely that counted for something. She looked at the shops as she passed by. The town did indeed seem dead. The only thing that moved was dirt being kicked up from the road by a hot breeze. Polly's life had sounded so exciting, even though Amanda knew she would never be happy living like that. But what had she done in her lifetime? Nothing. Here she was, soon to be twenty-one years old, and she couldn't think of even one single exciting moment.

* * *

By the time Chance returned to town, it was midafternoon, and he was convinced it was hot enough to fry an egg on a rock. In the last few weeks he'd walked more than he had during most of his life.

He stopped at the well in the center of town, reeled up the bucket, then took several long drinks of cool water. When his thirst was finally quenched, he glanced up and down the street, wondering where the women were. A small whirlwind worked its way down the road, kicking up dirt and causing broken shutters to bang, but apart from that, everything remained quiet. He decided to grab a bottle of whiskey from the saloon, then head down to the lake for a refreshing swim. Tomorrow morning he'd start searching for mines.

As he entered the saloon, it took a moment for his eyes to adjust to the dim light. He had just strolled behind the bar to grab a bottle when Polly came swaggering down the stairs, laughing. She was regally adorned with a short, bright purple dress that clashed with the disheveled red hair she had piled on her head. In one hand, she held a large ostrich-feather fan that she waved back and forth. The other hand gripped the neck of a whiskey bottle. "Well, just look who we have here," he said with a broad smile as he stepped from behind the bar.

"Chance!" Polly slurred, trying to sound enticing. She tripped and almost fell, but managed to straighten up again and descend the stairs with her hips swaying. "I thought you'd left." She held up the bottle. "How about having a drink with me?"

"It would be my pleasure, pretty lady." He was enjoying the spectacle of Polly so obviously in her cups. After joining her at the bottom of the stairs, he took her hand, then led her to a table and pulled the chair out so that she could be seated.

"Oh, I do like your gentlemanly ways. Where have you been, Chance Doyer? I've missed you." Polly tried batting her eyelashes, but they didn't seem to want to move simultaneously. "Do you know what's upstairs?"

"I can take a guess."

Polly took a drink from the bottle, then handed it to Chance. "Rooms with beds. How 'bout you and me goin' up there together?"

"I can't think of anything that would please me more, but I'm not sure you can make it back up."

"Of course I can."

"Why don't we just sit here a minute and talk? I'm tuckered out from looking for my horse. If we go upstairs, I certainly wouldn't want to be a disappointment."

"Oh, I'm sure you wouldn't be. All right, then we'll talk...at least for now. How come you kissed Amanda?"

Chance grinned. "So she told you. She was being snippety, and I decided to get even."

"Amanda hasn't had much experience when it comes to men, so I suggest you leave her alone. Now, *I* know how to please a man."

"I'll just bet you do. And I have to admit, you're all woman. You know, while I was out looking for my horse this morning..."

"Did you find him?"

"I'm afraid not. Anyway, I got to wondering why Amanda is so unfriendly." He took a long drink and returned the bottle.

Polly tried fanning herself, but she changed her mind when the feathers tickled her nose. "Don't pay her any mind. But at the same time, leave her alone." Polly became as serious as her inebriated state would allow. "That's a warnin'. Amanda's the best friend I ever had . . . the only friend I've ever had . . . and I'd kill anyone that tried to harm her. She's been good to me."

"Come on, Polly, you know I don't want to harm either of you." He reached out and patted her hand. "It's just not in my nature. But I still can't figure out what she's got against me."

Polly's eyelids were getting heavier by the minute, and she was having an increasingly difficult time talking. "She thought you was like them others that rode through talkin' about robbin' the Wells Fargo in Columbia."

Chance found that piece of information quite interesting. Maybe this time Gus had bitten off more than he could chew.

Polly released a tired sigh. "Then, when the ghost talked to her about the gold," she continued, "Amanda didn't want you gettin' any of it. I wasn't suppose to tell you that, but it don't matter now." She leaned over and rested her head on the table.

"Here, Polly, have another drink."

Polly straightened up again.

"Why doesn't it matter now?"

"There ain't no gold. It was all a dream." Polly's eyes closed.

Chance had to give Polly credit. Even drunk, she was still trying to convince him it was all a bunch of hogwash.

"Where's Amanda now?"

"Some lake."

Polly slowly leaned forward, and Chance caught her before her head hit the table.

After carrying Polly upstairs and laying her on one of the beds, Chance left the saloon. Since Polly had been

surprised at his arrival, he could safely assume she and
Amanda had concluded he'd left for good. On the off
chance that Polly had told the truth about Amanda going to the lake, he took off in that direction.

Chance moved through the shrubbery with the silence
of a cat. He wanted nothing to warn her of his arrival until he found out what she was up to. He didn't, however,
expect to find her bathing.

Not bothering to remain hidden, Chance stepped out
onto the sandy bank, openly gazing at the wet chemise
and pantalettes that clung to Amanda's ripe body. She was
only knee-deep in the water, and her taut nipples and long
legs were clearly visible. Pangs of desire clutched at him,
the likes of which he hadn't known in years. He could see
fear in her large, whiskey-colored eyes as she backed into
deeper water, and he knew he should get the hell out of
there, but instead he moved closer to the water's edge.

Chance had never taken a woman by force, and he
didn't intend to do so now. But his need was strong. Too
damn strong. He cursed himself for even momentarily
allowing *any* woman to have that much of an effect on
him, and he was about to turn and leave when Amanda
slipped backward and fell. She disappeared beneath the
water, then came back up, thrashing and coughing. She
had drifted out over her head.

When she came up sputtering a second time, Chance
realized she didn't know how to swim. He yanked off his
boots and ran into the lake. Before he was even waist-
deep, he was using long, powerful strokes to take him to
where he had last seen Amanda. Immediately he dived
beneath the surface, going deeper and deeper, but she was
nowhere in sight. He came back up for air, then dived
again, worry starting to clutch at him. He was about to go
to the top the second time when he felt a hard kick in the

middle of his back. It was followed by another that knocked out what little breath he had left. With a strong thrust of his legs, he managed to break water, only to receive another blow, to the side of his head. Again he was submerged, but this time it wasn't his doing.

When Chance came back up, he was furious. Treading water, he had to turn practically full circle before spotting his attacker. Swimming with the agility of a fish, Amanda was practically to the bank, and he took out after her. By the time he'd reached the shallow water and could stand, Amanda was already on the dry bank with a thick branch clutched in one hand. Even though she was rushing to pick up her clothes, she was watching him. Chance kept moving forward, never slowing his pace, never taking his eyes off her. She was barefoot, and she sure as hell couldn't run through all the thick brush.

Knowing she didn't have enough time to pull her shoes on, Amanda dropped her dress and grabbed the branch with both hands. Her only defense was to hit him while he was still in the water. She hurried forward, stopping when she was only ankle-deep, and waited. He looked huge and mean, but anything was better than being raped. She'd seen the hungry look on his face when he was watching her in the water.

The moment he was close enough, she clenched her teeth, swung the heavy branch back, then brought it forward with all her might. But he raised his arm to block the blow. The wood splintered as it broke across his forearm. She was defenseless. Terrified, she threw the end still clutched in her hand, turned and ran. She hadn't taken more than five steps when a hand grabbed her ankle. She let out a whoosh of air when she hit the ground. Rolling to her side, she kicked at his hand in an effort to free herself, but he grabbed hold of her other foot. Then he was dragging her toward him. She screamed and dug her fingers into the soft dirt, but she couldn't get a good hold. He kept pulling until he was able to roll on top of her. She spit in his face and tossed her head back and forth. Her chest heaving, eyes wide, she stared up at him, hating him for his ability to overpower her.

Chance pulled his head back, satisfied that he'd finally stopped her damn screaming. "What the hell were you trying do out there?" he growled. "You deliberately tricked me into thinking you were drowning! If you were a man, I'd break your neck!"

Amanda clamped her mouth shut and continued to glare at him. She refused to show the stark fear that was taking hold of her. She could hardly get her breath after all her struggling, and his wet body was crushing her into the ground. The muscles in his jaw were taut, his eyes were blue-green ice, and she bit the insides of her cheeks to keep from panicking. To fight was useless. Now she could only wait and hope that he would position himself in such a way that she could plant a knee or foot right in his groin.

"Damn it, I want an answer!"

"You were going to rape me," Amanda whispered.

"Rape you? Is that what all this is about?"

"Damn it...I can't...breathe!" To her relief, Chance rolled off her, but a strong arm remained wrapped around her waist, preventing her from going anywhere.

"I may have wanted to try coaxing you into doing something, but believe me, raping you wasn't what was on my mind."

"Then let me go."

"And let you get away with what you tried to pull? Besides, I'm in no hurry, and I know for a fact that there's nothing pressing waiting for you in town."

Amanda's heart pounded in her chest. His low, quiet voice was more threatening than if he'd yelled at her. She was agonizingly aware of his closeness, even more so than when he'd been on top of her. Even though they were both dripping wet, she could feel the heat of his body pressed alongside hers. She was also aware of how little clothing she had on. "Polly will be worried. She'll come looking for me."

Chance knew Polly wasn't going to bother anyone for a good many hours. "I guess we'll just have to deal with that when it happens," he replied softly, even though he was still angry as hell. He raised up on one elbow so that he could see her better, then slowly moved his hand to her flat stomach, her ribs, and stopped just below her full breast. "Have you ever had a man, Amanda?"

She glared at him, refusing to dignify the question with an answer.

"Have you ever wondered what it would be like to have a man make love to you?"

Amanda ground her teeth together. She struggled, but he held her in place with little effort.

"I don't know why you're so nervous," Chance said smoothly. "If I'd wanted to rape you, I would have already done it. And other than keeping you on the ground, you have to admit I've done nothing...yet."

"You're touching me, you're talking about things decent women don't discuss, and damn it, we're practically naked!"

He grinned. "You've got a point, but 'practically' isn't the same as 'actually.'"

Chance's words slowly penetrated Amanda's anger. He was right! If he had wanted to rape her, he could have already done so. Suddenly she felt more in control of the situation, and she was convinced she could talk her way out of it. "All right, I apologize. But you have to understand that I thought I was protecting myself. If the situation were reversed, you'd have done the same. Since we're going to be living within hollering distance of each other, I think it's time we start acting more like friends. I'm willing, and you can start by letting me up."

"Oh, I would very much like to be your friend. But, like I said, I'm in no rush." His thumb caressed the underside of her breast. "How come you've never let a man make love to you?"

Amanda didn't dare move. It might cause his hand to shift. "That's a man's pleasure, not a decent woman's. Now if you'd—"

Chance lowered his head and nibbled on her small earlobe. "So I take it decent women are immune to physical desires."

"Leave my ear alone," she demanded. She tried jerking her head away, but without much success. She didn't like the pleasurable feeling that his teeth were creating.

Until now, Chance had just been determined to get even. But her ridiculous statements prodded him on. "So you're saying that since you're a lady, you couldn't possibly feel desire?" By moving her head, she'd exposed the creamy hollow of her neck. Chance trailed his tongue down it and sucked gently, smiling against her skin when her breathing became erratic.

"I've had enough of this!" Amanda rolled onto her side and tried shoving him away. She only succeeded in landing in his arms, her face only inches from his. Realizing her mistake, she tried to pull away, but he held her tight. His hand slid to her buttocks. To her outrage, he molded her against him as tight as the skin on an onion. "Stop this right now. You said you weren't going to rape me."

"And I'm not. Does being close to a man bother you?"

"It's not proper, and you know it."

"You haven't answered my question."

"What question?" she asked breathily. His teal-blue eyes were magnetic, and she had to force herself to look away. Her gaze landed on his stubbled chin, and on full lips that reminded her of their last, heated kiss. She gulped for air, inhaling the scent of his skin, an oddly pleasurable mixture of lake water and sunshine.

"I asked if since you are a lady, does that mean you don't feel desire. . . ."

Amanda gasped when his hand covered her breast, searing her flesh. His thumb stroked the sensitive bud, and she could feel it all the way down to the pit of her stomach. "What are you doing? Get your hand off me!" She tugged at his hand, trying to remove it.

"What difference does it make, my sweet? As you said, ladies are devoid of passion. Remember, that's only for men. You are a lady, aren't you?"

"Yes," she whispered, even though she could no longer deny the strange, wonderful sensations he was creating with each stroke of his thumb. One part of her demanded that she not let this have any effect on her. Another part wanted the sensations to continue.

"Then we have nothing to worry about."

To Amanda's shock, he turned her loose. She watched in disbelief as he reached for his boots and pulled them on.

Chance stood and looked down at the beauty still lying on the ground. He cocked an eyebrow and grinned. "Amanda, whoever told you ladies don't have needs was a damn liar."

Her mouth hanging open, Amanda watched him disappear into the tall bushes. She sat up, not sure what her reaction was. Last night she'd wanted him to make love to her. But when she'd seen him on the bank she'd been convinced he intended to have his way with her, and she'd panicked. Rape was a lot different than making love. And what right did he have to touch her body? No man had ever been allowed to do that!

Grabbing her dress, she expelled a deep groan. She could still feel his hands on her, and his soft, teasing lips. Damn! She stood and pulled her dress over her head. She'd had the perfect opportunity to find out once and for all what mating was like, and she'd fouled everything up! She looked out over the lake and smiled. She knew exactly what she wanted to do now. Chance had lit a smoldering fire inside her, and if she had her way, he was going to be the one to put it out.

Chapter Seven

Chance was still angry when he entered the house. However, he wasn't sure who his anger was aimed at—Amanda or himself.

Yanking off his boots he proceeded to the bedroom to change his wet clothes. He was angry at himself for being attracted to another conniving woman. And he was angry at Amanda *because* she was conniving. Maybe he should write a book on conniving women. He'd had enough experience with them to do that even before he'd met Amanda.

He picked up a bottle of brandy he'd taken from the saloon and poured a healthy amount into a snifter. It wasn't the best brandy he'd ever had, but it would do. As he took a sip, he thought back to when he'd met Patricia Turner, the first woman to take him for a fool. He had bumped into her as she came out of the bank in Auburn, but now he knew it had been a setup right from the start. He'd heard of too many other men she and her brother had cheated out of money.

He'd thought she was a lady, and her brother Logan a gentleman of considerable wealth. She'd been shy, and that had appealed to his male pride. When they made love several months later, she had explained her lack of virginity by saying she'd been raped at a young age. And, because of that terrifying experience, she had never let another man touch her, until Chance had come into her life. She even pleaded with him to be gentle.

Chance leaned against the fireplace mantel and took another drink. How big a sap could a man be? He'd believed everything she told him. Then, one day, Logan had cornered him, irate at having learned of Chance's affair with his sister. To save her reputation, Logan had demanded Chance do the right thing and marry Patricia. Chance had thought of Patricia as a delicate flower, someone who needed protection. So he'd proposed, thinking it was time to settle down and raise a family. Especially now that he and his brother Ned had struck it rich with their mine. They had immediately made arrangements for a large house to be built.

Chance felt his gut twist at the memory. It had been a fine house, the fanciest one in Auburn, and he and Ned had been looked upon as gentlemen and pillars of the community. They had even accompanied Logan and Patricia to church. But Patricia had never had any intention of saying her wedding vows. Chance knew he'd never forget what had happened after that. His brother had related the story with his dying breaths.

Chance had left for Sacramento to see about buying another mine, and while he was gone, Patricia and Logan had arrived at the house. Patricia's excuse being that she wanted to surprise Chance by decorating his new office. Ned had left her alone while he and Logan entered the sitting room to enjoy a drink and discuss the forthcoming wedding. Instead, he and Logan had proceeded to get drunk.

While they were drinking, Patricia had apparently gone through the open safe and took out the deeds to the mine,

as well as the house. An hour or so later, she had present-
ed them to Ned, explaining that they were merely legal
papers to place her holdings in Chance's name and that
she needed Ned's signature as a witness. By that time, Ned
had been well into his cups, and quite happy to oblige. He
hadn't bothered to read what he was signing.

When Ned visited the mine two days later, he'd found
a group of strangers working it. He'd protested, but a man
had shown him papers proving *he* was the legal owner and
stated that Logan Turner had handled the sale. Then Ned
had remembered the papers Patricia had had him sign. A
quick trip to the county office had confirmed that he had
signed away not only the mine, but the house, as well.
Chance's signature had appeared on the deeds, too, and
Ned had known Logan must have forged it. Proving it was
an entirely different matter. Ned had gone looking for
Logan and Patricia, but they'd already left town.

Chance poured himself another drink, then went over
and sprawled out on the divan. If he hadn't taken the trip
to Sacramento so that he could add to his already considerable wealth, or if he hadn't fallen into a trap set by a
woman with innocent blue eyes, Ned would be alive today. He clenched his fist at the memory of how he'd felt
when he'd returned and found other people living in his
house, the mine sold, and Ned nowhere to be found. The
marshal had told him Ned had gone in pursuit of the
crooked pair.

Chance had followed, but too late. He'd found Ned in
a doctor's office in Grass Valley, dying from two bullet
wounds in the back. Ned had found the crafty pair and
confronted them, but he'd made the mistake of turning
away to go fetch the marshal. That was when Logan had
shot him in the back. Ned had blamed himself for everything, and his last words had begged for Chance's for-

giveness. Chance had told his brother he was not to blame for anything, but the words had fallen on deaf ears. Ned was already dead.

Chance threw the crystal goblet across the room, watching it shatter and the unfinished brandy drip down the wall. He sat up and placed his head in his hands. He and Ned were quite a pair. Both blaming themselves for what had happened, when in truth, neither was at fault. Now he needed to learn acceptance of what had happened and get on with his life. Something that was easier said than done. For a year he'd traveled from one mining town to another with only one thing on his mind. To find and kill Patricia and Logan Turner.

The pair had had a sixth sense, and had always left town just before he arrived. And it had been another man who was smart enough to catch up with them and put an end to their miserable lives. Maybe he should be grateful to him, but Chance knew the year he'd spent hunting the pair had taken its toll. There was a cold bitterness left in him that he might never rid himself of. And it was that same cold determination he'd felt while tracking Patricia and Logan that was now directed toward finding the Springtown gold. He'd go somewhere and start his life again. No matter how much she schemed, Amanda wasn't going to keep him from accomplishing his goal.

Having changed into her night clothes, Amanda sat on the edge of the bed and glanced around the small hotel room. What she needed to do was to think about how she should approach Chance about taking her and Polly away from Springtown. She also needed to figure out how a woman encouraged a man to make love to her. She'd thought about just coming out and asking him, but she knew she'd never be able to work up the nerve. She tried running her fingers through her matted hair, but the effort proved futile. The thick mane was like a beehive of sand and dirt. Just visualizing what it was going to take to brush it out made her wince. If only she could talk to Polly about her dilemma. But Polly would get all puffy-jawed, because she, too, had an eye for the fetching man.

After leaving the lake, she'd searched everywhere for Polly. Finally, she'd thought to check the upstairs portion of the saloon. She hadn't been the least bit happy about finding her friend on a bed, snoring and wearing the most gaudy, brazen dress she had ever laid eyes on. She had tried waking Polly, but had gotten no response, so she'd covered her with a thin blanket and left. Knowing how long it took her father to sleep off a binge, she was sure Polly wouldn't be up until morning.

"You haven't gotten rid of the drifter. He and Polly deserve each other."

Amanda's back stiffened. This was no dream. She was wide-awake. Slowly she turned her head, scrutinizing the room from wall to wall. "Are...are you there?" she whispered. Then, not more than four feet in front of her, she saw a figure starting to appear. This time there was no fog. Amanda held her breath as the image grew stronger and stronger, until he looked as real as any *live* man would, had one been standing there. Amanda was so frightened she felt sure she was going to fall into a dead faint.

"I wish you'd stop being so scared every time I come to visit you," the ghost said casually as he moved over and sat on a chair. "I'm simply trying to be your friend."

Amanda gaped in disbelief. He looked to be about her age, and not much taller. A black top hat was perched on the top of his head. His straight black hair, black, penetrating eyes and perfectly shaped nose, and a fine mustache that tilted down at the sides, all combined to create an extremely handsome man. Despite the scar above his left eyebrow, he was every bit the gentleman in his long black tailcoat, white high-necked shirt and black trousers. And he had no gun belt, which wasn't uncommon.

Amanda suddenly realized that her mouth was still hanging open. "Why are you here?" she finally managed to ask.

"This is my town. Besides, I'm drawn to you."

Though his voice was not deep, like Chance's, Amanda liked the sound of it. There was something dangerous about him, yet even that was appealing. She cupped her shaking hands and rested them in her lap. "Why would you be drawn to me?" She watched his eyes twinkle with mischief as he laughed.

"I'm attracted to all beautiful women. But believe me, *señorita,* you outshine any woman I've ever known."

"Oh? Do you really think so?" Though she kept telling herself this whole conversation was ridiculous, Amanda still felt a definite quiver of pleasure from the compliment.

"And your body..." He rolled his eyes.

"My body? What do you mean, 'my body'?"

"There I go worrying you again. Please, sweet Amanda, there's no need for you to get upset. After all, I'm merely a ghost. However, even a ghost should be able to have some pleasures."

Amanda was stunned. "Are you telling me you watched me undress?"

"A good many times."

Amanda thought of Chance. The way things were going, she might as well run around naked all the time! "I demand you promise to stop... peeking!"

"Very well, but how will you know I'm keeping my word?"

"I won't. I'll just have to rely on your honor."

"My dear, how can you deprive me of one of the few earthly pleasures left to me?"

His smile was as intimate as a kiss, yet the glow of it caused Amanda to relax and grin. "I must insist."

"You have my word as a gentleman."

"Are you Spanish?" Amanda asked as she went to the washstand to pour a glass of water. Her mouth was as dry as Polly's mush.

"No, but I've spent a great deal of time in Mexico, and old habits die hard. Have you been thinking about the hidden gold?"

Wanting to hide her excitement, she slowly turned to face her visitor. "Yes, I..." He was no longer sitting on the chair. She glanced around the room, but he had disappeared. "Wait!" She had no idea why she was whispering. "What's your name?" Her shoulders slumped when there was no reply. But the next moment she was filled with a giddiness. There really was gold—it hadn't all been a dream, and her ghost was not only a fine-looking man, but quite charming, as well.

Her thoughts running in all directions, Amanda set the glass down, the water untouched. As if in a trance, she walked over and picked her brush up off the bedside table. Gold. Pulling the thick mane over her shoulder, she began working at the knots. Gold! Was there a lot? If so, she could go anywhere she wanted and live like a queen. She'd be rich! "Ouch!" she yelled when a tangle refused to give. She could even hire someone to dress her hair! Her hand paused in midair. But...how would she get the gold out of town? And where would she go? Most importantly, how would she keep Chance from finding out about it? "Damn! If it's not one complication, it's another!"

Amanda woke and jerked straight up in bed. Disoriented, she looked anxiously around the darkened room, listening for any sounds. There was only dead silence. The dream had seemed so real! She was still shaking with fear after watching all those terrified men and women frantically running in every direction. Screams had filled the air as one shot after another was fired and bodies dropped to the ground. Even though Amanda now knew it had been nothing more than a vivid dream, she still had to force herself to lie down again. Feeling the need for some kind of protection, she buried herself beneath the covers and tried closing her eyes. But she couldn't rid herself of the horror she'd experienced at seeing a small child shot down in cold blood. Not until the sky started turning light was she finally able to relax and sleep.

A little past noon, Amanda stood in the bedroom of Polly's house, watching the redhead change into a blue cotton dress. "I can't believe you don't remember something as important as whether or not you told Chance about the ghost and the gold," she scolded.

"I was drunk! And don't talk so loud, my head's splittin'." Polly slid the last button into the buttonhole, then leaned over and smoothed out her long skirt. "And what difference does it make if I did tell him? It was all a dream."

"Do you remember anything about being with Chance?"

"I doubt if I'd forget something like that, Amanda, no matter how drunk I was."

"Well?"

"No, damn it. Nothing happened."

Amanda smiled inwardly. As they left the bedroom, she said, "Polly, I saw the ghost again last night."

Polly stopped so fast, Amanda almost ran into her.

"And did this ghost awake you from a sound sleep?" Polly asked with a considerable amount of disbelief.

"No. I was wide-awake."

"Amanda, I'm never quite sure whether to believe you or not. Answer me one thing. If there is a ghost, how come he didn't show his face when I was with you?"

"I don't know, I didn't get a chance to ask. And there's no reason for you to be frightened." Amanda smiled. "He talked about the gold again. It's hidden. That's why it's so important for you to try and remember if you said anything to Chance. If he so much as suspects there's gold, he'll never leave!"

"Do you really think there's hidden gold?"

"Yes."

"Then we gotta start searchin'."

"But if we do that, Chance will get suspicious."

Polly rubbed her throbbing temples. "I can't think. Maybe I'll do better after I've had a cup of coffee."

"I already made some. Just try to remember what you said to Chance."

As soon as they entered the kitchen, Amanda poured Polly's coffee. "I have a plan," she said as she handed her the cup.

"I'm almost afraid to ask what it is." Polly took an appreciative sip of the steaming brew.

"While I was waiting for you to wake up, I had time to do some thinking. Why did Chance picked a house and move in instead of just sleeping upstairs in the saloon?"

"Because he wants to be comfortable?"

"Because he's planning on staying here! Now why would he want to do that?"

"Amanda, he's only been here a few days. In a week or so he could up and leave."

"I don't think so. At first I thought it was because you were being so welcoming, but I changed my mind when I realized there had to be a stronger reason. Since he doesn't know about the gold, I've decided he's a wanted man and he's using this as a place to hide out."

With each sip of coffee, Polly was feeling a degree closer to normal. "Maybe he's staying because, like us, he has no horse to leave on. It could be a hundred miles to the next town."

"I thought about that, too, and I came to realize something I should have thought of before. There are mines around here, so we're probably in gold rush country. That means there have to be other towns closer than any hundred miles. It also means Chance had to pass through, or close to, other towns to get here. I think he knows exactly where the closest town is."

"I think you're letting your imagination run away with you again."

"We're going to be nice to him."

"Then he may never want to go."

"After a few days, we're going to start begging him to guide us away from here."

"But if he's a wanted man, he won't want to leave."

"We'll convince him we're helpless, destitute, and appeal to him as a man to get us out of this mess. We can even have him help us catch that burro. Then, when we reach a town, we'll turn him over to the law, and he'll be out of our hair once and for all! After he's taken care of, all we have to do is purchase a couple of horses to pull our wagon and return to Springtown."

"Amanda, so far none of your schemes have worked out. Why can't we just ask him flat out to take us away?"

"I got us the horses, didn't I? It wasn't my fault they escaped. And we have to make him think we're desperate to leave. Otherwise he might get suspicious."

Polly wasn't sure why she let Amanda talk her into things, but Amanda did have a convincing way about her that she couldn't argue with.

Chance pushed on one of the heavy timbers supporting the mine entrance. It appeared to be sturdy and in good condition. But, like the other three mines he'd located, it had green shrubs cluttering its entrance. There were no footprints or broken twigs to indicate that any of the mines had been entered recently. He turned and studied the surrounding cliffs. There were some orangish-yellow mine tailings scattered about, but that didn't mean those were the only places where mines could be located. The mother lode was deep, and when it came to hard-rock mining, the tailings were often shoved back into the mines to keep them from collapsing, which happened often. Up above, he'd located air shafts, which proved that gold had likely been brought out. But that only gave birth to more confusion. Because of the depth of these mines, and the hard labor involved in working them, two women couldn't possibly do it, and certainly not by themselves. That left the possibility of placer mining. He decided to start following the creek and see if he could find a slough or anything else that might show where Amanda and Polly had been panning.

It was dusk when Chance returned to his house. He flopped down on the bed, hungry and worn out from his day's efforts. He still had no idea where—or if—the women were collecting gold from some presently un-known source. However, he was convinced that the tale of hidden gold had some validity. But was the gold already mined, or was it just a rich vein that hadn't been worked?

Something else had occurred to him while he was searching. Assuming there was gold, what if the women didn't know where it was, either? That would certainly explain why they'd stuck around. They could very well have heard the same story he had—and, like him, figured that since there really was a Springtown, there had to be ore. Hearing someone enter the house, he swung his legs over the side of the bed and sat up.

"Chance?"

Smiling, Chance rose to his feet and walked out of the bedroom. "Well, Polly, I see you've survived yesterday's binge."

Polly stepped forward and ran a finger down his chest. "I would have survived better if you'd have joined me. If you intend to stay awhile, you're gonna be needing a woman."

So, Chance thought, Amanda hasn't told Polly about what happened at the lake. "I absolutely agree. Unfortunately at the moment I'm worn out."

Polly frowned. His words sounded familiar. "Did you tell me the same thing yesterday?"

"I don't think so."

"Well, we can talk about it later. Amanda saw you returning and thought you might be hungry. Since we're the only three living in this town, she said there was no reason for us not to eat together."

"Oh? I was under the impression she wanted nothing to do with me."

"She realized her suspicions were unfounded. Anyways, supper will be ready in thirty minutes." She glanced into the parlor. The furnishings here were much nicer than in her house. She wondered if she should select another place to live. "So, will you be eating with us? Amanda's even made bread."

"I thought you did all the cooking. I didn't know she knew how."

"I do all the cooking because... I never thought about it. When we came here, I just started doing it. Believe me, she's a much better cook than I am."

"Then I'll be looking forward to our meal."

"Good. See you later."

Chance watched Polly's fanny swing seductively from side to side as she left. So what kind of scheme was Amanda cooking up? As he returned to the bedroom to change clothes, he wondered why he continued to resist Polly's advances. It certainly would be an easy way of alleviating his need, and Polly was an attractive woman.

He pulled out a clean shirt form the chest of drawers and tossed it on the bed. Maybe Polly's lack of appeal had something to do with his age. At twenty-nine, he was no longer interested in seeing how many women he could bed. He liked Polly, but she didn't appeal to him. He released a sigh. But the moment Amanda had walked into the bedroom where they were holding him captive, he'd known he wanted her. The challenge had made him even more determined to have her. At least he'd finally come to his senses and backed off. He didn't trust her. His brother had died because of a woman.

He picked up a towel, but stood staring into space. It still seemed like only yesterday when Ned had discovered... Chance shook his head. He'd gone over the whole thing in his mind at least a million times, so why did he continue to torture himself? Besides, he had to hurry if he was going to arrive at Polly's house on time.

* * *

Chance was surprised when Amanda answered his knock on the door. As he stepped inside the small foyer, his gaze traveled the length of her. Damned if she wasn't the most beautiful woman he'd ever laid eyes on. Even a lavender dress with a high neckline, long sleeves and pinafore failed to hide her luscious body. Just looking at her full, ripe breasts caused his groin to tighten.

"I'm so glad you accepted our invitation, Chance," Amanda purred. "As I told Polly, this squabbling is uncalled-for, especially since we're the only ones living in Springtown. I want us to be friends."

Chance gave her a lopsided grin. "I absolutely agree."

"I wanted this moment alone with you to say I'm sorry about what happened at the lake. I understand why you were angry, and hope you can understand why I acted the way I did." She smiled shyly. "And yes, you were right. Ladies do have feelings."

Chance was completely taken aback by her words. What game was she playing now?

"What's takin' you two so long?" Polly called from the kitchen doorway. "I've got the table all set."

"My apologies, lovely lady," Chance replied with a grin. "I was just telling Amanda how much I'm anticipating a well-cooked meal."

"Well," Polly said sweetly, "come along before supper gets cold."

When Chance entered the dining room, he was more than a little impressed. A damask tablecloth had been spread over the table. Linen napkins, polished silverware, fine china and sparkling crystal adorned each place setting. But what really drew his attention were the bowls of food. There were sweet potatoes glazed with syrup, thick slices of cured ham resting on a platter, two loaves of perfectly baked bread, snap beans, redeye gravy, and canned peaches floating in their own syrup. It seemed like years since he'd sat down to such a feast. "Ladies, you've truly outdone yourselves," he said sincerely. Remembering his manners, he started to move around the table to seat the ladies, but they were already seating themselves.

"We thought it only proper that you sit at the end of the table," Amanda commented cheerfully. She'd seen the pleased look on Chance's face as he'd scanned the table. Not until this moment had polishing silver seemed worthwhile.

By the time Chance had taken his place, his stomach was already growling with anticipation.

"Don't be shy," Amanda said encouragingly as she handed him the bowl of sweet potatoes. "There's plenty, so eat your fill."

After the food had been passed around, Polly said, "I'm sure glad we're going to be eatin' together from now on. It's like bein' a family."

"I agree," Amanda told her. "Chance, do you like the heel of the bread, or the next slice?"

"The heel will be fine," he replied between bites of ham. He couldn't help but wonder why they were being so nice. They wanted something, and he had no doubt in his mind that he'd find out what that something was before long.

Amanda sliced the bread, making sure the heel was a healthy size, then passed the plate. "Polly told me you've been searching for your horse. I must admit, I'm sorry you haven't located him. At least you could have left Springtown and sent back others to help Polly and me get out of here."

"I'm sure he's long gone and enjoying his freedom."

"Is that what you were doing again today?" Polly asked.

"Uh-huh. I still haven't given up hope." Chance took a bite of the bread. "Amanda, this is excellent."

"Thank you." Amanda found herself studying the handsome man. She suddenly realized he'd trimmed his thick, sandy-blond hair. It hung just past the collar of red shirt. But it was his hands and his long, tapered fingers that drew her attention. Lord, his hands... Her stomach clenched, and a shiver raced up her spine. The man had the most incredibly beautiful hands.

"Am I correct in assuming you ladies are anxious to leave Springtown?"

Amanda said nothing. She was still trying to remember how to breathe.

"The sooner the better," Polly answered.

Chance stabbed a piece of ham with his fork, then held it in midair. "Personally, I like the area. I'm in no hurry to go anyplace."

Amanda drew a deep, steadying breath, brushing his words aside. Her plan could still work. It had to! All she had to do was keep a rein on the desire he seemed to stir in her with nary a hint of effort. She just needed to keep her mind on the important things. "What about those men you were chasing?"

"They'll probably get killed when they try robbing Wells Fargo."

"But why would you want to stay here?" Polly asked. "This town is as dead as a graveyard!"

"Don't get me wrong. I don't plan on staying for the rest of my life. I've been thinking about checking some of the mines around the area." He watched Amanda's whiskey-colored eyes become the size of round saucers.

Just looking at Chance's handsome, sun-bronzed face and broad shoulders, just listening to his deep, caressing voice, was truly having an effect on her. "Would you care for some peaches?" she asked.

Chance chuckled. "I want something far sweeter."

"Since we have nothing more to offer, you'll have to settle for peaches," Amanda replied. She started dishing some into a saucer, but her hands were shaking so badly the peaches almost slid onto the tablecloth. "Polly and I were hoping you could help us catch that burro that strolls into town."

"Thank you," Chance said as Amanda handed him the saucer.

"What did you mean by 'sweeter'?" Polly asked.

Amanda groaned. "What about the burro?"

Polly leaned forward, thoroughly enamored with this handsome man who was now giving her his full attention. "You mean candy, that sort of thing?"

"A lovely woman is also sweet, kisses are sweet...."

"I absolutely agree," Polly gushed out.

Amanda was having more and more difficulty concentrating on her objective. The image of Chance's naked body flashing through her mind didn't help matters. "Are you going to help us catch the burro or not?"

Chance wiped his mouth with his napkin, then returned it to his lap. "Why is catching that burro so important to you?"

"Polly and I want to get out of Springtown. Hopefully we can pack enough provisions on the burro to last until we can reach a town, a house, anything." Amanda had already decided he would show her the pleasure of being a woman before he left. But it wasn't worth going through all this discomfort. The room even seemed to have heated up.

"And leave me here alone?" Chance feigned shock, but the next moment he broke out laughing.

"What's so funny?" Amanda demanded.

"I was wondering if I have been invited into this house just to catch a burro, or if you ladies have something else on your minds? Perhaps you want me to take you to the nearest town?"

"Well, now that you mention it," Amanda said sweetly, "that's exactly what we were hoping. Just two women and a burro traveling across the foothills could be dangerous. What if we came across the type of men you were chasing?"

Chance grinned. "Yes, I can see where that could be a problem."

"Amanda? Are you feelin' all right?"

Amanda looked across at Polly. "Of course. Why do you ask?"

"Your face is so flushed, and you've hardly eaten a bit of food."

"I'm sure it's just the heat. Baking the bread warmed the house up considerably. I'm fine." Amanda took a bite of beans to prove her point. What she really wanted was to get this meal over with. No, that wasn't true. What she really wanted was for Chance to make mad, passionate love to her, taking her to the wild, glorious heights of sensation that Polly was so good at describing. She was consumed with desire, and the man hadn't even so much as touched her!

Polly rose from her seat. "Amanda, I'm really worried about you. Your face is almost scarlet! Lean back in your chair. I'm goin' to get a wet cloth for your face." She hurried toward the kitchen.

Amanda darted a glance at Chance, then immediately looked away. He, too, had stood. She hoped he'd have the decency to leave. But she knew she wasn't going to be that lucky when he came to a halt beside her chair. Though she didn't look around, she could feel his nearness.

"Polly's right. Perhaps I should escort you to the bedroom."

The possibility of that happening made Amanda's blood surge through her veins. But this wasn't exactly the time or the place. "Honestly, I'm fine. I just became a little overheated."

"Then maybe you need some fresh air."

He placed a hand on her shoulder, and Amanda was certain his touch had seared her skin. She reached up and shoved it away. How was it possible to suddenly feel such a strong need for a man? "Would you leave me alone? I said I'm fine!"

"You sure are a stubborn woman."

Chance pulled her chair back, and before Amanda could protest, he'd scooped her up in his arms and was headed for the hall. "No!" she gasped. Her breasts were pressed against his hard chest, and feeling his body heat blending with hers, she was sure she was going through a living hell. She placed a hand on his chest to shove at him, then immediately jerked away when she came into contact with the curly mat of hair just above the top button of his shirt.

"Where are you going?" Polly called when she returned with the wet cloth and saw Chance carrying Amanda out of the room.

"I'm taking her outside for some fresh air," Chance replied over his shoulder.

Polly hurried after them.

"You know, sweetheart," Chance whispered to her as he carried Amanda out the door, "you shouldn't let your imagination run away with you."

Amanda was embarrassed all the way down to the bottom of her feet. Did he know what she'd been thinking? "You can let me down now."

Holding Amanda in his arms was all it took for Chance to change his mind about claiming what he already desired. There was little doubt that she was enamored with him. He'd seen it tonight in both her eyes and her actions. "If you should have any more flashes of desire, you know which house is mine."

Amanda was immediately on the defensive. "Are you accusing me of—"

"Here's the cloth," Polly said as she caught up with them.

Chance stopped and lowered Amanda to the ground. "I don't think Amanda will need it now, Polly. If she just stands out here in the cool night air for a minute, I'm sure she'll be just fine. Now, if you ladies will excuse me, I'm going to get a good night's sleep. Thank you for the meal. It was delicious."

"What about taking us away from here?" Polly asked.

"I'll think about it."

"You'll be eating with us tomorrow, won't you?" Polly inquired anxiously.

"I wouldn't think of missing it." He walked away.

As Chance strolled toward his house, he was smiling. He'd been looking at everything entirely wrong. Liking women had never been one of his problems. Trusting them was an entirely different matter. But, since he knew Amanda was up to something, there was no reason why he couldn't enjoy her pleasures. They wanted him to take them away from Springtown, but why? There was something he was missing, but there was no doubt in his mind that he'd eventually come up with the answer. In the meantime, he'd play their little game, which could turn out to be quite enjoyable. But if he didn't come up with some answers about the gold soon, he was going to have to find a way to drive a wedge between Amanda and Polly. Divide and conquer.

Chance had just turned out the oil lamp and climbed into bed when he heard the front door creak open. Reaching under the pillow, he grabbed his pistol and curled his finger around the trigger. But his hand relaxed when he heard the tread of a woman's soft-soled shoes. He smiled and waited for Amanda to enter the bedroom. The full moon shining through the window allowed him to see Polly enter the doorway and just stand there. Her heavy perfume drifted across the room. This wasn't quite what he'd been expecting.

"Chance?" she called out softly.

He knew that if he didn't do something fast, he was going to have a big problem on his hands. He needed Polly as an ally, not an enemy, and he could ill afford to insult her. Besides, he'd grown fond of the minx. From across the room, he watched her begin to unbutton the front of her blouse. The easiest solution would be to just go ahead and bed her. But, for some ungodly reason, she just didn't appeal to him. So how the hell was he going to get out of this? There was no time to think.

As Polly slid her blouse off her shoulders, Chance knew he had no recourse but to take the coward's way out. With the bed being across the room and in the night shadows, he doubted Polly could see him. She had already removed her blouse, and was now unbuttoning her skirt. Keeping an eye on her, he began carefully working his way toward the edge of the bed. Silently he slid off the bed and scooted under it. Moments later, he heard Polly crossing the room, barefoot.

"Chance, are you asleep? Damn! He hasn't even gone to bed yet. Oh, my big lover," she said joyfully, "are you in for a surprise when you return...."

Polly climbed into bed, and then, to Chance's aggravation, she began bouncing on it, causing the bottom part to come dangerously close to his face. He groaned inwardly. Was she ever going to settle down?

For the next hour, Polly was on and off the bed. She paced the floor, talked to herself, sang songs, bounced on the bed some more. To Chance's relief, she finally settled down, and a few minutes later he heard her snoring. He waited another five minutes before sliding out from under the bed. Silently he left the room. Tonight would be spent at one of the other houses. At least he'd finally get some much-needed sleep.

Chapter Eight

It was her name being called that awoke Amanda from a sound sleep the next morning. At first she thought it was the ghost. However, the second high-pitched call was easily recognizable. Polly's voice sounded far away, so she had to be downstairs. Amanda stretched languidly, then tossed the covers aside as Polly's calling turned into yelling.

"Are you going to answer me, Amanda? Where the hell are you?"

Amanda climbed off the bed. What could Polly be angry about this time? She stretched again before heading for the closed door. Polly's voice was closer now, so Amanda knew the redhead had made it up the stairs.

"You answer me right now, Amanda! What room are you in?"

Amanda opened the door. "I'm right here, Polly," she answered.

Polly marched forward, her green eyes flashing. The minute she entered the room, she went to the armoire and opened it. Then she got down on her knees and looked under the bed.

"What are you searching for?" Amanda asked.

"Chance! Did you two have a good time last night?"

"I have no idea what you're talking about."

Using the bed for support, Polly struggled to her feet. "Don't try acting innocent with me. You and Chance spent the night together!"

"Did he tell you that?"

"How could he tell me if he was with you?"

"This is ridiculous." Amanda turned away and went to the night table to retrieve her brush. "I was asleep until you woke me. I don't know where you come up with these ideas. I haven't seen Chance since supper last night."

"If you were sleepin', how come you already got your dress on?"

Amanda blushed. "Because my ghost said he liked to watch me undress."

"A likely story. You might as well 'fess up. I was in Chance's bed all night, and he never came home. Where else could he of been except with you?"

Amanda spun around. "You did what?" She gripped the brush in her hand to keep from throwing it. Was Chance planning on starting a harem? What upset her the most was her jealousy that it hadn't been her! At least nothing had apparently happened, or Polly wouldn't be in such a bad mood. "Just what were you doing in his bed?"

"I went there seekin' pleasures of the flesh," Polly said brazenly. "That's somethin' I'd of thought you knew nothing about, until last night!"

"What do you mean by that?"

"I mean I thought you'd turn red-faced from such a frank statement, until I found out you'd spent the night with Chance!"

"I didn't spend the night with Chance!" Amanda snatched a dress from the armoire. "However, Chance isn't your sole property, Polly. He's a grown man and can certainly choose who he wants to be with. If it was me, that's none of your business!''

''Well, he sure ain't your property! Remember? You're the one that didn't want anything to do with him when he first came here!''

Amanda tossed the dress on the bed. ''I'm not going to argue about this. You're just upset because you didn't get what you wanted.'' She was feeling a considerable amount of satisfaction at the knowledge that Polly had failed. ''This is absurd. I can't believe we're having words over the man. If he wasn't with either of us, what do you suppose he was doing all last night?''

''You mean he really wasn't here?''

''That's what I've been trying to tell you.''

Polly went to the mirror and turned from side to side to check her appearance. ''I should've known better than to think he was here,'' she said smugly. ''You're not his type.''

''Not his type?'' Amanda exclaimed. ''If that's true, why did you think he'd spent the night with me? Not his type, indeed. Let me tell you...'' Suddenly she had second thoughts about saying what had been on the tip of her tongue. She wanted Chance to bed *her,* not Polly. She would be wise to follow her own advice. She went to the open window to get control on her temper. ''Chance is up to something. I can feel it. Polly, we can't keep getting into fights, and we can't drift apart over some worthless man.''

Polly's shoulders slumped. ''You're right. I shouldn't have let it upset me. It's just that I was lookin' forward to havin' Chance knock me,'' she said with a pout.

''Knock you?'' Amanda sounded shocked. ''Knock you?''

''That's what we called it at the saloon.''

"Stop thinking between your legs, Polly. When we finally leave here, there will always be other men."

Polly nodded.

Amanda sat on the flat boulder above Springtown, enjoying the serenity. Though the climb had been arduous, it had been worth it just to get away from Polly. For the past three days, the woman had dogged her heels, wanting to know when they would ask Chance to take them away or why the ghost hadn't reappeared. And as if Polly weren't enough, she also had Chance to contend with. After two more nights of waiting for him to decide about taking them to another town, he still had not given his answer.

Although she kept telling herself she was not going to leave while still a virgin, she couldn't conjure up the guts to surrender herself. It wasn't so bad during the day, when she had things to do, but at night her thoughts and desires returned. She seemed to be obsessed with thinking about it. Even the gold didn't distract her one-track mind. Polly had even told her that it hurt like the devil the first time a man entered a woman. If that was the case, why was she so determined to go through with it? She had to be a glutton for punishment. But if she didn't let Chance make love to her, she'd always wonder what it was like. Besides, when would she ever have such a perfect opportunity again? If she could just get up her nerve, all this wondering and anticipation would be over with.

Amanda looked up at the few puffy clouds decorating the pale blue sky. Three buzzards were circling in the distance, and that seemed rather appropriate. Chance, Polly, and herself. All avaricious. What an unlikely trio they were. Three misfits. None of them worth a penny, and thrown together in a place called Springtown. No, she was wrong. They did have something in common. Lust.

Amanda frowned. Things couldn't keep on the way they were going. She had to get Chance out of Springtown. Not only because of the gold, but for her own peace of mind, as well. Maybe then she'd stop thinking about him when she was alone in bed. Surely any other man could handle her problem just as adequately. They all had the same trappings. But there were no other men. Amanda released a heavy sigh.

Amanda raised her knees and wrapped her arms around them, making sure the faded blue cotton skirt wasn't hiked up. There was another problem. She hadn't seen the ghost again. At the rate things were going, she'd still be here five years from now. She'd even given up the idea of wearing her clothes to bed. Why should she make herself uncomfortable? If the ghost was going to watch, there wasn't anything she could do about it.

As her gaze traveled across the trees surrounding the town, something caught her attention. She cupped a hand over her eyes to shade them. It looked like a mine. As she scanned the hills, she could see other signs of mines.

"You must be deep in thought not to have heard my approach."

Chance's voice sent a flutter of excitement charging through Amanda's body. She clenched her teeth to try and keep from thinking about what might happen now that they were alone.

"Mind if I join you?"

"Not at all."

He sat beside her. "It's not working, is it?"

Amanda straightened out her legs. "What's not working?" she asked, keeping her eyes directed at the town below.

"Just being friends."

"I don't know what you're talking about."

"Oh, yes, you do. Every time I'm around, you're as skittish as a doe. Did you honestly think either of us could ignore what happened at the lake and just be friends?"

"Polly is more than willing to satisfy you." Amanda wanted to bite off her tongue.

"But it's not Polly I want."

His words, and that deep, husky voice, sent her head spinning. Why didn't he just take her in his arms? It would certainly make things a lot easier if she didn't have to ask him to do it. "How did you find me?"

"I followed you." He picked up a rock and tossed it over the cliff. "Amanda, my dear, why do you keep fighting me?"

It suddenly occurred to Amanda that she had a golden opportunity right in the palm of her hand. She just had to keep her wits about her and not allow her foolish desire to take precedence. "Are you saying you desire me?"

"What do you think? Unlike you, I haven't bothered to hide it."

"I'll make you a bargain."

"Oh?" He chuckled. "This should prove to be interesting."

"I'll come to you willingly—after you've taken Polly and me to another town." There, Amanda thought proudly. That wasn't so difficult.

"I'm agreeable to that, with one exception. You come willingly *before* I take you."

Amanda wanted to laugh with joy. She'd known he wouldn't accept her proposal, but she had to keep him thinking he was getting his way. "After. I don't trust you."

"And I don't trust you. So it would appear we have a stalemate."

Amanda started to stand and act resigned to his proposition, only to be jerked back down. "What do you think you're doing?" she demanded as she yanked her arm free.

"I'm tired of these cat-and-mouse games, and I want some answers."

"I don't know what you're talking about."

He reached out and started pulling out her hairpins, watching her hair tumble down her back. Amanda tried scooting away, but to her delight, he pulled her to his side. "You have such beautiful hair." He ran his fingers through the thick mane, relishing the feel of it against his hand.

Amanda's stomach was churning with anticipation. At last it was going to happen. No, that wasn't right. She had to get him to agree to take them to another town first.

"Why are you in such a hurry to leave Springtown?"

"Why not? There's nothing here but three people and a burro."

Chance placed his arm around her shoulders and felt her quiver. He knew she wanted him every bit as much as he wanted her, but she was a stubborn minx. "You and I could stay here indefinitely." He nibbled her ear.

Surely he could hear her heart pounding. "I offered you a bargain, and you chose not to accept. So... stop kissing my neck!"

"But you taste so good, and you always smell like orange blossoms."

She gasped with pleasure when his hand covered her breast. "I will not succumb to your advances until..." She felt weak all over. His hands were already making her body scream for more.

"You already are. However, if you really want to put a halt to this, tell me where the gold is hidden."

His words snatched Amanda back to cold reality. "G-gold? What gold?"

"Don't try to act as if you don't know what I'm talking about." Chance turned her loose, then leaned back on his elbows. "When Polly was drunk, she began rambling about some ghost and hidden gold. That's why you've remained here, isn't it?"

Damn Polly! Amanda thought. She knew she could hardly deny anything now. Her mind raced to try and come up with a plausible story. "All right...we heard a...a tale. But we've searched every inch of this place and haven't found anything. So we've finally given up. The problem being, we don't know how far it is to the nearest town, and the horses we had to pull our wagon somehow got out of the barn. I guess we didn't tie them up any better than we did you. Then the old man and his sons arrived, so we tried stealing their mounts. But a hard wind came up, and they got away, too.

"Polly wasn't supposed to tell you about the tale, because I knew if you had any inkling of gold you'd never help us get out of here. Now, you've heard the whole truth." Amanda leaned forward and brushed the dirt off her skirt. "Getting us out of here can be to your advantage, too. When we find a town, we'd be willing to buy you a horse so you can continue after those men you wanted to get even with. So, will you help us?" She was quite proud of the story she'd concocted.

Chance silently mulled over what Amanda had said. It made more sense than anything else he'd heard. He was about to say he'd help—after he'd felt her naked body against his—when he suddenly remembered something. If the house he was staying in had been searched, they would have found the pouches of gold. And hadn't Polly told him they'd only been here a short time before he'd arrived? So Amanda was still lying. Why? He suddenly knew the answer. Once the ladies were rid of him, all they'd have to do was circle back, and they'd again have the town to themselves.

"Well?"

Chance shifted his gaze to Amanda. She was not only one of the most beautiful women he'd ever met, she was also devious. He gave her an ingratiating smile. "If you'd told me this to begin with, you and Polly would have been long gone from here. As a man, I feel it's my duty to help two lovely ladies out of their predicament."

"Oh, thank you, Chance," Amanda said with an overabundance of sweetness. It was all she could do to keep from giggling. "But first, we have to catch the burro so he can carry provisions. How long do you think it will take before we can reach another town?"

Chance could clearly see her excitement. Her whiskey-colored eyes had become as bright as a candlelit Christmas tree. Maybe they didn't know how near they were to Murphys, but he wouldn't have taken any bets on it. "You seem quite pleased with my decision."

"I am. More than you'll ever know." Amanda got to her feet. She'd already started to walk away when she realized Chance hadn't moved. "Aren't you coming? We have to get things ready."

"No, I'm in no rush."

"What do you mean? Look below. That confounded burro is standing in front of the saloon. If we hurry, you can catch him."

"Well, Amanda, you know the old saying—you scratch my back and I'll scratch yours."

"What are you talking about?"

"I'm saying that, though I'm willing to help, you're going to have to make it worth my time."

"I...I don't have much money, and after I buy you a horse..."

"I'm not talking about money."

Knowing she now had everything under control, Amanda smiled sweetly. "Like I said, once we reach town—"

"And like *I* said, I want payment in advance."

"But it will be an incentive. The sooner you get us to our destination, the sooner you'll receive your reward," she said enticingly. "Don't you believe I'll keep my word?"

"Nope."

"But—"

"Let's cut the bull. Either deliver, or I won't help you."

"You haven't left me much choice. I'll have to think about it."

Chance rose to his feet and studied the petite woman standing in front of him. "I'll give you until tomorrow noon." He tipped his hat and was about to leave, but then, suddenly, thought of something. "While you were doing all that searching, did you happen to find out why Springtown is deserted?"

"I believe it was yellow fever."

"I guess you're right. Oh, I killed and cleaned a deer. At least we can have fresh meat. See you at supper, and don't forget—noon tomorrow." He strolled off.

"Damn, damn, damn!" she muttered. "He knows about the gold!" Yet she'd been fairly sure she'd convinced him there was no gold, and he'd said he was willing to help them leave—if she obliged him. Amanda broke out laughing. The wily ways she'd learned from her father had certainly come in handy. Her father had told her many times that if you offer something freely, the other person is going to become suspicious. So always offer the opposite of what you really want. Chance thought he had the upper hand, but in reality, everything had gone exactly the way she'd planned it. Except for the gold. If only Polly had just kept her mouth shut.

As Amanda made her way back down the cliff, she was surprised to find that Chance was nowhere in sight. How had he gotten down so fast? He must have found an easier way down. So she was going to be the sacrificial lamb? She laughed again. Once her sacrifice had been given and she had him out of town, he would be out of her life forever. Now if only the ghost would reappear. Knowing where the gold was hidden would make her feel a lot more secure. She was banking an awful lot on someone who wasn't even human.

When she returned to town, Amanda took off in search of Polly. She wanted the redhead to know she'd rattled her mouth once too often.

Feeling restless, Chance walked into the parlor and collapsed onto the wine-velvet chair. He hated idleness. He also wasn't particularly pleased about the bargain to get Amanda in his bed. He much preferred a woman to come to him of her own free will. But she'd started it. He'd followed her to the boulder hoping that she'd be more talkative away from Polly. Well, she'd been talkative, all right, but she'd given him all the wrong answers.

He'd known she had no intention of keeping her promise to come to him willingly. So he didn't feel any qualms about not taking the two of them to another town. But if she did come to him, he sure as hell wasn't going to refuse to bed her. Then, when the gold was found, he'd leave with it and send someone from Murphys to take them out of here. He knew Amanda would do exactly the same thing to him if she found the gold, with the exception of sending someone back to fetch him.

He glanced around the room, taking in each finely shaped piece of furniture, the lace curtains, the velvet drapes that were properly hemmed so as not to touch the hardwood floor. Who had brought all this to Springtown? The place was nicer than what he'd had as a child, but nothing compared to the place he and his brother had built in Auburn. Just thinking about other people living in his house made his blood boil. Ned was probably turning over in his grave. Ned. It didn't seem like a little over a year since he'd been killed. God, how he'd loved his younger brother. Before he knew it, Chance's thoughts were drifting to the past.

Ned had been leaning against the parlor wall of their small Texas home, tears running down his cheeks. Chance, who at the time was ten and considered himself a man, had stood beside their mother. She'd just received a note from their gambling father stating that he was tired of family life and was leaving them.

"Don't cry, Mother," Chance had pleaded. "It doesn't matter that Father's left. I'm big and I can work."

Chance's throat tightened at the memory of the look of hurt and defeat on Cynthia Doyer's small face.

She had stroked his head and said, "You and Ned will continue going to school and get learnin'. I never had that opportunity, and I'm not goin' to take it away from you boys. Mrs. Parkinson has agreed to let me be her housekeeper. We'll do just fine."

And for the next seven years, they were fine. Then everything started going wrong. Mrs. Parkinson up and died, and his mother couldn't find employment. Though only seventeen, Chance was already working at the mercantile store, and he managed to keep food on the table.

Since the day she'd received the news that her husband had deserted her, Cynthia had had continual health problems. Six months after Mrs. Parkinson's death, his beloved mother passed away from pneumonia. She'd made Chance promise he'd always watch over his brother.

Embittered at what his father had done, and hurt over his mother's death, Chance delivered Ned to their aunt. Knowing his brother would be taken care of, Chance took off to parts unknown. Not caring what happened to him, he joined a gang that had a particular liking for strongboxes loaded on stagecoaches. They also found it profitable to steal cattle and sheep and deliver them to Mexico. For four years he rode with outlaws, but once a month he returned to check on Ned and deliver the money needed to feed an extra mouth.

Chance steepled his fingers and stared into space as he thought about his last visit to his aunt's house. A smile tickled the corners of his mouth. He'd spent a week with his brother before leaving again. About five miles away from the house, he realized he was being followed. He rode his horse behind a large boulder, then climbed on top. When his pursuer passed beneath him, he jumped down, knocking the rider to the ground. Chance chuckled, remembering how he'd raised a fist, but hadn't delivered the blow. The rider was Ned. After a lengthy argument, Chance finally gave in and allowed Ned to go with him.

Those were the good days. They rode with different gangs, spent money as fast as they got it, slept with women, and raised hell. The Doyer brothers became feared and wanted.

It was Ned who heard about gold being discovered in California. Because their faces had become too well-known, they agreed that it was time to leave Texas and make their fortune at a place called Sutter's Mill. And they did make their fortune. But it was at Auburn, not Sutter's Mill. They worked hard, and he and Ned became rich.

Chance stood. Knowing what he knew now, it would probably have been better if they'd stayed in Texas. On the other hand, they could have had it all if he hadn't allowed Patricia and her brother to bring everything crashing down on their heads.

Chance glanced around the room again. Instead of reliving the past, he should be thinking about the present. Suddenly he remembered seeing a diary when he'd searched the place. Why hadn't he thought about the diary sooner? Perhaps it would reveal what had really happened in Springtown. Better yet, it might disclose where the gold was hidden.

"Now where did I see that diary?" he muttered as he left the parlor. He didn't relish the idea of having to search the whole house again. He stopped in the hallway, trying to decide which room to tackle first.

Chance had already searched one of the bedrooms before he finally remembered he'd seen the diary in the cellar. Damn! He was going to have to go down there again! Trying to convince himself that this time it was going to be a piece of cake, he grabbed the lantern off the chest of drawers, lit it and left the house.

As Chance descended the creaking stairs, the musty odor of earth and stale air caused him to wrinkle his nose. As soon as he reached the bottom, he raised the lantern, determined to keep his mind on why he was down there.

He recognized the few jars of canned vegetables and jams,
but where had he seen the diary? Slowly he moved the
lantern to the left, then to the right. Perspiration was already starting to trickle down his temples. Think, damn
it! He'd found it on the floor behind that old milk pail....
He'd picked it up, and he'd been holding it when he
checked the shelves behind the empty canning jars. He
went over and shoved the jars aside, not caring that some
fell and broke on the hard-packed earth. He silently
cursed the spiders that had already spun new webs around
them. Then, to his relief, he saw the diary.

Grabbing the book, Chance hurried back up the stairs
and slammed the cellar door shut. His body was covered
with perspiration, and his shirt clung to his back. Even so,
he welcomed the sun's warmth as he drew fresh air into his
lungs. The diary had better be worth the effort, he
thought, because that was absolutely my final trip into
that hellhole! He opened the book to the last page.

Susan was married today. It was such a beautiful
wedding. Everyone in town attended. Willard looked
quite handsome and proud. I caught the wedding
bouquet. Perhaps I will wed next.

Angered because the passage revealed no answers, he
started to toss it on the ground, but then he changed his
mind. Since he had nothing else to do for the rest of the
day, he might as well read it.

Amanda entered the hotel lobby and was about to go up
the stairs when something on the floor caught her attention. It was in the dark corner of the registration desk and
the wall. Because of its size, her first thought was that it
could be a tarantula. She'd seen the large furry spiders on

walls or going down the street on more than one occasion. The thought of this one possibly going up the stairs held no appeal. It wasn't moving, so she decided to see if it was dead.

As Amanda drew closer, she realized that the object actually looked nothing like a spider. It was a rock, but this rock was yellow! She reached down and picked it up, unable to believe her eyes. It was a gold nugget, every bit as big as a large egg.

Amanda hurried up the stairs and into her room. As soon as she'd closed the door behind her, she again stared at the nugget. "Fool's gold?" she whispered, still unable to believe her good fortune. It even felt warm in her hand.

"No, it's real."

Amanda looked up and saw her ghost standing in front of her.

"I've been waiting for you to return." He smiled warmly. "I've missed you."

"It's—it's real?" she sputtered. "It must be worth a fortune."

"It's my proof to you that there really is gold here."

"Here? In the hotel?"

"No, my dear."

"Then where?"

"That's a question I'm not ready to answer yet."

"Why?"

"Because when you collect the gold, you'll want to leave."

He was standing so close, but when Amanda reached her hand out, it went right through him. "Why can't I touch you? You look so real. How did you get the nugget here?"

"So many questions. In time you'll have your answers. But first I want you to get to know me."

It occurred to Amanda that she wasn't the least bit frightened. "Do you have a name?"

"That I do, most beautiful lady." He made a deep, dramatic bow. "Jack Quigley, at your service, ma'am."

Amanda laughed at his antics. "You appear to be quite the ladies' man."

"I've been known to have a way with the fairer sex."

"Before you go disappearing again, I think you should know I'm going to take over one of the houses. I'm tired of staying in this hotel. But if you'd tell me when you'll be appearing, I can—"

"I have just the house for you. Tomorrow, go to the end of the street and take a left. Pass the stand of trees, and you'll see it."

"Will you be able to visit me there?"

"Of course."

"You can do that?"

"I can move about quite freely." He gave her a broad smile. "I can even lift things." He went to the commode, then raised the pitcher to prove his point.

Amanda was properly impressed.

She suddenly broke out in peals of laughter.

"You should laugh more often, sweet one. It's most becoming."

He reached his hand out, and Amanda could have sworn she felt it caress her cheek. "Why do you use such endearing words?" she asked as she sat on the bed. "You really have no right to say such things to me."

"I think I have every right! I am falling in love with you. I'm a man, not a *caracol!*"

"That's impossible. How can a ghost love a mortal?"

"With all his heart," Jack replied softly.

Amanda was shocked at his sincerity. "What's a *caracol?*"

"A snail, in Spanish."

"Well, nevertheless, I don't want you to think I can return your affection, even if I am flattered."

Jack stopped in front of Amanda. "Oh, but you can. I can tell you're already starting to feel something for me. You just have to accept that you can love a ghost."

Amanda started to protest, but stopped when she saw him fading from view. Instead, she cleared her throat. She stared down at her opened hand, expecting the nugget to vanish, too. She laughed with joy when nothing happened. Yes, sirree! She was going to be rich!

Amanda took another bite of the delicious venison steak, but remained silent. Chance sat at the end of the table, obviously enjoying his meal. Polly, who was seated across from her, was still pouting over the verbal flaying she'd received for having told Chance about the ghost and money. Being upset certainly wasn't hindering her appetite, however. Amanda had chosen not to tell Polly about the nugget or the ghost's return. The redhead couldn't be trusted not to tell Chance.

Amanda surreptitiously glanced at Chance. Why couldn't he have a flabby body, instead of one that rippled with muscles?

All afternoon Amanda had thought of nothing but the gold and Chance. The time for vacillating had come to an end. Tomorrow she would no longer be able to think of herself as pure. There was one little problem. Though she had every intention of going through with it, she was starting to get cold feet. Thank heaven it would all be over tomorrow at noon. Then they could leave for some other town.

Chance watched the different expressions playing on Amanda's face. Apparently she was trying to come to a decision about tomorrow. If she agreed to his proposal, it would be proof of her desperation to get him out of town. Still, there was that niggling doubt in the back of his mind. He'd changed his mind about not taking them to Angels Camp. He'd take them, and then he'd come back to Springtown and wait. If they showed up, as well, he'd know that everything Amanda had told him was a lie, and that she was returning for the gold.

Chapter Nine

Amanda was up early the next morning. She'd had another dream about innocent people being slaughtered last night. Though she was still badly shaken, by the time she completed her toilette the sounds of screams and pleading voices were finally beginning to fade from her mind. Needing to shut off any thoughts of her dream—as well as her noon meeting with Chance—Amanda left the hotel and went in search of the house Jack Quigley had told her about.

As Amanda walked around trees and through tangled vines, her anticipation was building. Why was the house so far away from the others? But the question slipped from her mind when she saw it looming in the distance. It was a magnificent two-story structure. Her feet moved faster. Then she was standing in front of it, thrilled with her discovery. *This* would be her house. She went up the three steps, across the wide porch, then placed her hand on the doorknob and turned it. The door creaked opened, and she stepped inside.

The foyer alone was larger than the shack in Columbia. Soon she was excitedly rushing from room to room, delighted at her good fortune. Though dusty, the furniture was like nothing she'd ever seen before. There were marble-topped tables, and even a piano. Upstairs were five bedrooms, and off the biggest one was a separate bathing room, tub and all. The armoires were full of clothes of every description. There were racks of women's hats and shoes. There were large closets filled with linens.

Finally Amanda stopped and caught her breath. She leaned on the upstairs banister and stared down the wide circular staircase. It was beautiful! "I don't know if you can hear me, Jack," she whispered, "but if you can, thank you."

Amanda wanted to start cleaning immediately, but she knew she would just have to do it all again when she returned to Springtown. If she had her way, she, Polly and Chance would be leaving soon. Then she would claim her house. Since it wasn't anywhere near noon yet, she decided to pass the time by taking a room at a time and inspecting it thoroughly.

As Amanda neared Chance's house, her steps slowed. No matter how many times she told herself this was what she wanted, it didn't make the doing any easier. She had no experience in such matters. Why couldn't Jack Quigley be mortal? He was a perfect representation of what a man should be like. Gentle, kind, thoughtful and charming. No, she thought again, it wouldn't have been easy with him, either.

Amanda reached the door and raised her hand to knock, but couldn't. What was she supposed to say? I'm here, do what you want with me? She took a deep breath. She couldn't back down now. After all, there was the gold to think about. Surely all she'd have to do was nod her head and he'd do the rest. There was no reason she couldn't handle this in a ladylike manner. The door suddenly swung open, and she was almost knocked over as Polly bounded out of the house. "What are you doing?" Amanda demanded.

"Damn sure not what I wanted to do!" Polly's pink checked dress flew up in the back as she scurried down the walk. "Wash my face, indeed!"

Again riddled with doubt, Amanda forced herself to enter the house. "Chance?" she called. A moment later he stepped out into the hallway. He looked so intimidating, and her knees were already shaking.

After Polly's visit, Chance was not in the best of moods. "Right on time. Have you made your decision?" he asked Amanda without any indication of interest.

There was a coldness about him that Amanda had never seen before, and it increased her nervousness. "What did Polly want?"

"The same thing Polly always wants."

"And...and you turned her down? Is that why she was so angry?"

"That's right."

"But why?" she asked, suddenly suspicious. "She's so beautiful. You've never struck me as a man who would refuse an offer from any woman."

"But then you don't really know me, do you? You know nothing about me. You don't know if I'm mean, good, kind or cruel. I'm just someone who has stepped uninvited into your life. Now what is your decision?"

"You don't have to take your anger at Polly out on me!" Amanda stated in a huff. "Sounds like she turned you down, instead of the other way around."

"Polly has nothing to do with us. Now I asked what your decision is."

Unthinkingly, Amanda started wringing her hands. "You promise that if I agree with your terms, you'll take Polly and me to a town?"

"That's what I said."

"You're not making this easy for me."

"Why should I?"

"Well, a gentleman would—"

"I told you once before, I'm no gentleman. Well?" He raised a meaningful eyebrow.

Amanda bravely tilted her chin upward. "Very well, I agree." Nothing happened. Instead of him taking over from here, he just stood staring at her, his face as cold as granite. Angry at his lack of sensitivity—and at herself for going through with this—she began tearing at the buttons on her dress, wanting to get it over with.

"Stop right there."

Amanda's hands paused, but she couldn't look at him. Her embarrassment was too deep.

Chance raked his fingers through his sandy hair, then placed his hands on his hips. This wasn't the way he'd planned on bedding her. And why was he angry? "You don't have to go through with it." He couldn't believe he'd said that. "Get out of here. I'll take you to Angels Camp anyway." He turned and went back into the parlor.

At first Amanda was actually relieved that he'd turned her down. Relief quickly faded, however, and shock yielded to fury. Was he saying that, like Polly, she wasn't good enough for him? The nerve of the man! She marched into the parlor. "Just what makes you think that you're so irresistible you can pick and choose any woman you want?" she spat out contemptuously. "I have news for you, Mr. Doyer. Contrary to what you may think about yourself, you are far from being a man women dream about! You are nothing but a worthless drifter, and I'll be glad when I've seen the last of you!''

"If I were you, I wouldn't go around casting stones." His quiet voice held an undertone of cold contempt. "You're getting what you want, so don't do anything you might regret."

When he turned his back on her, Amanda's temper snapped. She walked to an end table, picked up a vase and hurled it at him. Her mouth dropped open when the delicate glass crashed against his back and the shards fell to the floor. As he slowly turned, she stepped back. His stoic face was even more frightening because it gave no hint as to what he was thinking. Then she saw the muscles in his jaw flex, and she knew he was angry.

"You're absolutely right. Indeed, who am I to be so picky? We've made a deal, and I'm obliged to stand by it."

Amanda's eyes widened. This was not at all the way she envisioned this. He was supposed to be kind and gentle and— And what? All her fantasizing had been exactly that. Images made up in an overimaginative mind. She'd made him into a prince who had come to take her away from a humdrum life. She'd made a mistake. A big mistake. "That won't be necessary," she assured him as she took two more steps back. "I was in the wrong. I should never have said those things." She knew she was babbling, but she couldn't seem to stop. "Did I hurt you? Sometimes my temper is my own worst enemy." Again she stepped back. "I'll just be on my way."

"I wouldn't hear of it. After all, we still have business to take care of."

"But... but you said I didn't have to go through with it."

"I've changed my mind."

"I should have known. All right," she said bravely. "Where's the bedroom? I want to prove *I'm* not a person who goes back on her word!" To her shock, her excitement was starting to build.

Chance sauntered forward until he stood directly in front of her. He crooked a finger beneath her chin, forcing her to look at him. He gazed into her fathomless eyes, then leaned down and kissed her tempting lips. "Not here."

His lips teased hers as he spoke. Amanda was sure she was going to swoon, and she had to lean against him for support. "Why?"

"We wouldn't want Polly to come barging in on us. We'll meet after supper, at that boulder you were on yesterday." His tongue traced the outline of her lips. He crushed her to him, then kissed her deeply, letting her know exactly what she could expect later.

It wasn't until he released her and stepped away that Amanda saw his cold grin.

"You know, Amanda, you always make me wonder who you're really fighting. Me, or yourself?"

The slap across his cheek resounded through the room. Amanda spun about and left.

Chance released a bitter chuckle directed at both of them. Instead of kissing her, he'd wanted to throw her over his knee and spank her. When she'd accepted his bargain, it had made him furious, which didn't make a whole lot of sense. After all, he was getting what he wanted.

He went to the window and watched Amanda walk down the stone path, her thick, glossy hair shining in the sunlight. Even her green work dress couldn't hide the rigidity of her body. He rubbed his cheek.

He turned away when she disappeared from view. He was still infuriated that she would prostitute herself to get her way. He had been right all along. Women were all alike, and Amanda wasn't any different.

He glanced at the open diary resting on the armchair where he'd left it, then went over and picked it up.

Amanda sat at the dinner table, picking at her food. Knowing she was to meet Chance on the boulder after supper was making her as jittery as a long-tailed cat in a room full of rockers. When Chance looked at her, his eyes seemed to reach into her very soul. The tension that stretched between them grew. She was alternately thrilled and frightened. Polly's quietness didn't help matters. Amanda felt that if someone didn't break the silence, she would scream! Yet, for the life of her, *she* couldn't think of a thing to say.

"Polly—" Chance leaned back comfortably in his chair "—did Amanda tell you I've agreed to take the two of you to another town?"

Polly's face came alive. "Really? When?"

"How about the day after tomorrow? I caught that burro this afternoon and staked him out by the stream. Of course, I'm assuming Amanda is in agreement."

Amanda didn't miss his sly grin.

"Finally!" Polly exclaimed excitedly. "Amanda, we can start packing tonight!"

"But Amanda hasn't given us her answer."

"Of course she wants to leave," Polly said.

"Amanda?" Chance raised an eyebrow, waiting for her reply.

Amanda cleared her throat. "Yes...that would be fine."

"Good. I just wanted to be sure we have an understanding."

"Oh, we have an understanding, all right," she snapped at him. "I understand that you'll stop at nothing in order to get what you want."

"Then that means we're very much alike, doesn't it?"

"Amanda!" Polly gasped. "How can you talk like that? Chance has agreed to take us away from here! Don't go spoilin' it!"

Amanda was nervous. This mating had taken on entirely different connotations. She had thought she was trapping him, but in reality, she was the one being trapped. The sooner it was over with, the sooner she'd be able to dismiss Chance from her mind. She looked him straight in the eye. "Don't worry, Polly. If Chance is a man of his word, we'll leave Tuesday morning."

"Whew!" Polly laughed joyfully. "I was beginnin' to think we was gonna die here!"

Amanda stood and started collecting the dirty dishes. "I have something to take care of later, and the sooner I get it over with the better. Come on, Polly, let's get the dishes washed." She curled her lip when she heard Chance chuckle.

The steep climb up the hill was even more difficult in the dark, and Amanda silently cursed Chance for having picked such a meeting place. At least the moon allowed her enough light to see by. She wasn't even sure Chance would be waiting. She'd had a devil of a time getting away from an overly excited Polly, who was already planning what they should take on their trip.

By the time Amanda reached the top of the flat boulder, her breathing was labored. She glanced around, but Chance was nowhere in sight. She'd done her part, and as far as she was concerned, if he wasn't here, that didn't nullify their agreement. But she wasn't surprised at the feeling of disappointment that washed over her. She tried assuring herself it was for the better. But her body was already aching for his touch, and there was that desperate need to have him teach her all the wonders that so far had been denied her.

Somewhere in the distance, an elk released its eerie call. Amanda was reminded that she was alone in the dead of night and she hadn't brought anything to protect herself.

Chance stood in the shadows of the trees that edged the boulder, watching Amanda nervously move back and forth. The way she kept looking down the incline, he knew she was thinking about returning to town. He had half a notion to let her go. But if he did that, she'd be getting her way.

The moment Chance stepped into the moonlight, Amanda saw him. He was tall, rugged and beautiful, and she could see the muscles of his arms bulging against his shirtsleeves. "All right, let's get this over with," she said with a heavy dose of sarcasm, trying to hide the excitement, the anticipation, she was feeling. "I can't believe I'm letting the likes of you have your way with me."

Her cutting words put an end to Chance's vacillating. "Very well. Take your clothes off."

Amanda was dumbfounded. "But . . . shouldn't we do something first? Like kiss?"

"Why?" He started unbuttoning his shirt.

"Well . . . that's what we did before."

"You said you wanted to get this over with." He dropped his shirt, then reached down and pulled off his boots.

"I didn't mean . . ." She held her breath as he began unbuttoning his pants. With the moonlight so bright, she could see him clearly, even though he was still several feet away.

"You didn't mean what?"

"You don't have to act so damn cold!"

Chance saw the moonlight glistening on the two tears that trickled down Amanda's cheeks before she turned her back to him. He placed his hands on his hips and looked up at the stars. He was being an insensitive bastard. He was sure Amanda was a virgin. And at no time had he taken into consideration how difficult this must be for her, whether or not she was doing it to get her way.

He walked over and placed his arms around her waist. "Amanda, you don't have to go through with this," he said softly.

"But I..." She couldn't hold back the flood of tears. "I wanted..." She tried brushing the tears away. "I'd hoped... I mean I thought..."

"Are you trying to say you want me to make love to you?"

Amanda could only nod her head.

Chance gently turned her around. He wrapped her in his arms and kissed the top of her head, inhaling the fresh fragrance of her hair. "Amanda, I..."

Amanda pulled back and looked up at him. "Please, Chance, don't make me b—" His lips joined hers, and she leaned into him, savoring his kiss. His tongue caressed her lips, and when he placed her arms around his neck, it all seemed so right. Not sure what she should do, she tentatively returned his kiss and heard his groan of pleasure. His hands caressed her back, then slid down to her hips, drawing her to him. She gloried in the feel of his body pressed against hers. She drew her strength from his passion, feeling more sure of herself with each passing moment. He kissed her neck as he released the pins from her hair.

Chance knew that if he kept this up, there would be no turning back. He raised his head and looked into her eyes, eyes that were already clouded with passion. "Are you sure?" he asked.

"Oh, yes," Amanda whispered. "I would die if you stopped now."

Slowly he unbuttoned her dress, not wanting to rush anything. As he slid it off her shoulders, the moonlight bathed her pale skin. He leaned down and gently suckled each nipple hidden behind her chemise. His need almost overpowered him when she gasped with pleasure and arched her back. As he removed each piece of her clothing, she became bolder. She stood on her tiptoes and kissed his neck, all the while running her hand across his chest.

Lifting her in his arms, Chance carried her to the other side of the boulder and laid her on a thick patch of grass. As he removed his trousers, he was surprised at her lack of embarrassment at being naked, and at the bold gaze that swept across his body. He lay beside her, his hands and mouth feeling, kissing and caressing until he knew every curve, and knew what gave her the most pleasure.

Not until she was writhing with passion did he enter her. Her body stiffened, but then, as he slowly moved, kissing and caressing away the pain, she began to move with him. She became wild and untamed in her desire, seeking, but not knowing what it was she was seeking. He encouraged her every move as she reached her climax and he took her dancing among the stars.

The sky was already turning light when Chance silently pulled on his pants and boots. He stood, looking down at the beauty sleeping peacefully at his feet. Her thick, dark hair was spread out like a halo, and her face had the sweet look of innocence. There was nothing he didn't know about her body. He knew what places to touch to turn her into a wanton tiger. Yet he knew nothing about what went on in her head, except that she was determined to get her hands on the gold. But then, he really didn't know that, either. Yet if she returned to Springtown, he'd know once and for all if this had been a ploy to get rid of him.

He walked to the edge of the boulder and looked down on Springtown, watching as the sun bathed it with light. Amanda had given him every bit as much pleasure as he'd given her. He scratched the back of his head. Too bad they hadn't met before Springtown.

Hearing Amanda move, he turned back around. She was sitting up, her dress clutched to her breasts. Her lips quivered in an uncertain smile. Leave it be, he told himself. You were bitten once. Don't let it happen again. "We'll leave tomorrow morning at dawn," he said softly.

Amanda nodded. "Thank you," she whispered.

"You're not sorry?"

She smiled. "How could I be? I've never experienced anything so wonderful."

Chance chuckled. "You'd better get dressed."

Amanda began putting her clothes on. Had their mating had the same effect on Chance as it had on her? She loved him, or at least she thought she loved him. Just having him near made her feel all warm inside. She wanted to be with him, to feel his strong arms around her and recapture the blissful—

"Are you ready?"

"Yes."

Her delight soared when he took her hand and led her away from the boulder. His hand was so large that it practically swallowed hers. "Isn't it a beautiful morning? Oh, wait!'' She reached down and picked a wild sweet pea. ''Such a pretty pink,'' she commented as she took hold of his hand and they continued on. When they came to a narrow path, she laughed. ''I wondered how you got down so fast.''

''And I wondered why you came up the hard way.'' Amanda looked up at him, and he grinned. Her face glowed, and she was all but dancing down the hill.

She probably thinks she's in love, Chance thought. He'd felt the same way so many, many years ago, when he'd had a woman for the first time. He'd even wanted to marry Betty Lou, but fortunately, at thirteen, it wasn't possible. A month later she'd moved. He broke out laughing. It wasn't more than a month later that he'd found out he wasn't the only boy Betty Lou had shared her favors with. And he couldn't have been too much in love, because when he'd found out, it hadn't bothered him in the least.

''What are you laughing at?'' Amanda asked cheerfully.

''I was just thinking about what it took to catch that burro. I'd like to leave before dawn tomorrow.''

Amanda felt the marvelous feeling slipping away at his second mention of their leaving. She was tempted to tell him about the ghost and the gold, but she kept her silence. There had been no promises between them, just a wonderful moment in time shared by two people. Now they both had to get on with their lives. However, what happened once they reached the next town might be an entirely different story. It would be sheer madness to try the fruit only once. And who was to say what might happen the second time? She could hardly wait to find out.

Amanda entered the lobby of the hotel and her humming stopped. The sudden cold, prickling sensation told her Jack Quigley was near. He was seated on one of the benches. He looked so real! "Have you been waiting long?" was the only thing she could think to say.

Jack stood and smiled. "Any time I wait to see you is like an eternity, my love."

Amanda returned his smile. "Really, Jack, you shouldn't be saying such things."

"But, my dearest, surely it can't be wrong to pour my heart out to you. You mean everything to me."

Amanda longed to hear Chance say such things, but was quite uncomfortable having it come from a ghost.

"What were you doing last night? I searched for you, but you were nowhere about."

An unforeseen sense of guilt swept over Amanda. What with Jack expressing affection for her, she felt as though she'd been unfaithful. Did he know she'd been with Chance?

"I can see you're upset about something. Did you find the house I told you about?"

"Yes." It suddenly occurred to Amanda that he couldn't read her thoughts. Polly had said that ghosts knew everything about a person. Either Polly didn't know what she was talking about or Jack didn't fit all the ghostly requirements.

"And did you like the place?"

"It's like a dream castle," Amanda said excitedly as she thought about the house. It would be the perfect place for Chance and her to live. "Is that where the gold's hidden?" He laughed with delight, and she could see the twinkling orneriness in his black eyes. "You're playing games with me!" she accused. She went over and settled down on the bench he'd been sitting on. "There isn't any gold, is there?"

"Don't be saddened," he said, still grinning. "I would never lie to you. You are my heart and soul."

Amanda watched him go behind the registration desk and start pulling out drawers. As each one fell to the floor with a bang, she jumped.

"Do you know what I miss the most, other than feeling a lovely woman's arms around me?"

"No."

"A good drink of whiskey."

Amanda dredged up the courage to ask a question that had been on her mind for some time. "Jack," she said softly, "I've been wondering . . . How did you die?"

"I don't like to talk about that, but maybe I'll tell you in a week or so."

"Then perhaps you'll tell me why the people left Springtown."

"I don't think so. It will be a little mystery for you to figure out. After all, it's not as if—"

"Every time I ask a question, I get the same reply." Amanda's patience was starting to wear thin. "Do you ever plan on telling me where the gold is?"

"Absolutely. But we wouldn't want Chance to find it, would we?"

"Then there really is gold?"

"More than you could carry. Didn't I prove that by leaving you the nugget?"

To Amanda's amazement, he walked right through the registration desk and came to a halt in front of her. The air seemed to move when he moved.

"You mentioned games. I've always liked games. Each time I see you, I'll give you a clue. My first clue is that the light shines on it at certain times each day."

"That could be anywhere."

"Exactly." He grew serious. "But at the same time, it will keep you here with me, and your love will grow stronger each time we meet. Oh, my sweet Amanda, if only I could share my body with yours, and show you the depths of my love. You must never leave me." He reached out as if to caress her, but his hand went right through her arm.

"Jack, we're..." Before Amanda could finish, he had disappeared.

That night, Amanda had another terrifying dream, but this time, she saw a man being hanged. And although she couldn't see his face, she could hear the crowd cheering.

Chapter Ten

Amanda pulled her floppy hat down to shade her eyes. They had been walking since dawn, and Polly's constant complaining had started almost immediately. If she wasn't expressing how unaccustomed she was to walking so far, she was whining about the growing blisters on her feet, the insects, or how burnt her face was from spending so much time in the sun. Chance always had an encouraging word, but he continued to push on with the determination of a bull. He held on to the rope that was attached to the burro's harness, and the burro gave him no trouble.

Amanda watched Polly stumble over a small clump of grass, and saw Chance, who had been bringing up the rear, give her a helping arm. Polly looked up at him with adoring eyes. "Thank you, Chance. It's plain to see we couldn't of ever made this trip without you." Amanda gritted her teeth. She'd stumbled several times, and Chance certainly hadn't bothered to help her. She was hot, sweaty, and every bit as exhausted as Polly. But, unlike Polly, she refused to ask Chance for any favors. He hadn't said more than five words to her since they'd left Springtown. It was as if she weren't even there. It hurt. And as time passed, she became angry. Angry that their night together had apparently been nothing more than a bargain kept.

Amanda looked ahead and saw nothing but more rolling hills, occasional live oaks, thorny purple thistle and grass that reached up to her waist. It was like trying to wade though mud. Just how long was this trip going to take? It was a question she should have asked before they'd taken off on their trek. Luckily, the insects didn't bother her as much as they did Polly, and because her skin was darker, her face wasn't the least bit burnt. She had enjoyed seeing deer occasionally, and hearing various types of birds calling to one another.

When Chance finally brought them to a halt beside a small stream, Polly immediately collapsed beneath a cottonwood. Amanda fell to her knees and splashed her face with the cold mountain water, not caring that it was running down her bodice. Feeling better, she joined Polly under the trees, convinced she'd never be able to rise again. She watched Chance remove the packs from the burro and hobble him. Amanda had to admire Chance's stamina. Never once had he shown any signs of fatigue. Though her body ached, Amanda rose to her feet. If Chance could keep going, so could she! She picked up the sleeping rolls and laid them out. Then she proceeded to gather kindling for a fire. Polly didn't move an inch.

To his credit, Chance cooked their meal, which consisted of flat cakes, venison and gravy. Amanda found it to be surprisingly tasty, but she was too exhausted to eat much. Polly devoured the rest of her share, as well as her own.

As soon as she was finished eating, Amanda cleaned her tin plate and spoon. When they were put away, she climbed on her bedroll, ready to call it a night. A surge of jealousy shot through her when Polly—who had constantly complained about how tired she was—chose to join Chance by the campfire rather than lie down. The two spoke quietly, and though Amanda strained her ears, she couldn't hear a thing they said.

By the time Chance returned from washing off in the stream, both women were asleep. After checking to be sure the campfire was completely out, he settled down on his bedroll, tucked his arms beneath his head and stared at the stars. Though he was tired, he knew that sleep wasn't going to come easily. All day he had watched Amanda trudge along with nary a complaint. At times she'd even helped Polly, even though he knew she had to be worn out herself.

His admiration for her continued to grow. Though she tried to maintain a tough demeanor, there was a vulnerability about her that appealed to him. He not only desired her, he was beginning to like her, and he felt guilty about taking a day and a half to only go seven miles. There was something between them that he couldn't have put into words. It was like a limb swaying in the wind—it could go in either direction. If she returned to Springtown, the limb would break and fall. If she didn't, then there was a possibility that the limb would remain sturdy and flourish. That was what he had to find out, and that was what would take him back to Angels Camp.

They hadn't gone more than half a mile the next day when Polly plopped down on the ground and was swallowed up by the grass.

"Here—" Amanda offered her a hand "—let me help you up."

"Just leave me be. I'm not gonna move another foot."

As far as Amanda was concerned, Polly's attitude reminded her of a child throwing a temper tantrum. Polly's chin jutted out in defiance, and her gray skirt was hiked up to her calves, allowing a good show of her white stockings and buttoned-up shoes. Her hair stuck out in every possible direction, and to emphasize her stubbornness, she had crossed her arms over her ample bosom. Amanda knew that to give in to Polly would be a bad mistake. "Then just stay there! I hope you're well hidden when a wolf comes by looking for a feast."

"What's the matter?" Chance asked as he joined them.

"Polly says she's not going to move another foot," Amanda replied as she walked away.

"Why can't I ride the burro?" Polly whined.

Amanda quickly returned to Polly's side. "Because we need the provisions!" To Amanda's amazement, Chance began removing the packs from the burro. "You can't do that!" she demanded. "What about our clothes and provisions?"

"Polly's right," Chance drawled as he released the last pack. Only the water canteens were left. "She's at the end of her rope."

"No! I won't let you do this!" Amanda persisted. "She can walk just like the rest of us."

"She'll never make it." Chance lifted Polly up and sat her on the burro. "There you go," he said with a smile. Holding the lead rope, he continued on.

Amanda was furious. Both her dress and Polly's were soiled beyond repair, and he was leaving their only other dresses behind! What were they expected to wear? "What about food?" she yelled at Chance, who had already moved a good distance away. Knowing that catching up would be more difficult the longer she tarried, she gave one of the packs a hard kick and hurried forward.

* * *

After getting directions to the assayer's office and the dry goods store, Amanda left the Angels Hotel. It wasn't a large hotel, but their rooms were quite comfortable.

Considering how many dresses she had in Springtown, Amanda had held off purchasing another one. But her soiled clothing was a constant embarrassment. Seeing no other recourse, she'd decided to purchase a dress before going to the assayer's office. She didn't want him to think she'd stolen the gold nugget. None of it would have been necessary if Chance hadn't allowed Polly to have her way.

Amanda scurried down the street, hoping against hope that she might see Chance. At least for a little while, she was rid of Polly. It had only taken a day and a half to reach Angels Camp from Springtown. Yet for the past three days Polly had been in bed *recuperating*. Amanda did feel sorry for her, but her patience was running thin. She had even gone to the Scribner Drugstore to get Polly a cure-all tonic. But the redhead continued to groan— unless she was sleeping. Admittedly, the shoes Polly had insisted on wearing had been too tight, and the long walk had caused multiple blisters. And yes, they would have been worse if she hadn't ridden the burro.

Amanda thought about how Polly had sat on that burro looking like some queen going to her coronation. Had Chance bothered to explain that they had less than a half day's travel left, Amanda would have looked at the situation differently. But he'd just let her rattle on, never saying a word. For a man who said he wasn't interested in Polly, Chance certainly gave the woman a great deal of attention!

By now, even Polly would be forced to believe that Chance cared nothing about either of them. He'd taken them to the hotel, and they hadn't seen him since. He hadn't even asked for the horse she'd promised to buy him! Her dreams of them making love once more had diminished the moment they'd left Springtown. In two days, she'd loved and lost. Surely that had to be some kind of a record.

Amanda watched a woman miner moving down the street, leading a burro loaded with mining equipment. It was the men's clothing she was wearing that drew Amanda's attention. The sight wasn't that uncommon in mining towns, but for the first time, Amanda could see the advantages of doing so. It would make the trip back to Springtown a heck of a lot easier.

Amanda shoved her new hat on her head and walked out of the dry goods store. Feeling self-conscious, she quickly glanced up and down the street to see if anyone was gawking at her. Since no one appeared to be paying her any attention, she slung the saddlebag she'd also purchased over her shoulder and took off down the street. The shirt and vest she had on were quite comfortable, even though she felt indecent wearing men's jeans in public. But as she continued on toward the assayer's office, she began to enjoy the freedom that the pants allowed. Her stride became longer, and soon she was walking at a jaunty pace.

In many ways, Angels Camp reminded Amanda of Columbia. There were doctors, butchers, a post office, and many other businesses. On her way back, she planned on stopping at the Nunenger Bakery to purchase some of their delectables. And there were people. Old people, young people, and children. Until their arrival, she hadn't realized how much she'd missed seeing people. She felt more alive than she had in a long time, and she had a ready smile for a passersby. It was plain to see that though she'd thought she would like living alone in Springtown, it simply wasn't true. She found herself dreading the return.

Seeing the assayer's office, Amanda walked through the open doorway. By the time she left, she was feeling extremely apprehensive. The nugget Jack had given her was top-grade ore. But the assayer had asked pointed questions about where she'd discovered it. Afraid that word would get out of a find—and that she'd be followed and robbed—she hurried back to the hotel.

"Polly," Amanda said as she bounded into the redhead's room, "we have to get out of this town immediately." It came as a relief to see Polly finally off the bed and standing in the middle of the room. "Good, you're finally up."

"I'm not going anywhere! And what in heaven's name are you doing dressed like that?"

"You should try it. It makes getting around a heck of a lot easier. Polly, we have to return to Springtown—now."

"Why? I haven't even had a good look at Angels Camp. And where is Chance?"

A knot formed in Amanda's throat, but she refused to let Polly see how his desertion was affecting her. "I have no idea." She walked though the open doorway to her room and began stuffing her toilet items into the saddlebag. "When will you realize he doesn't care what happens to us?"

"I don't believe that. You saw how much attention he paid me on the way here. I think he's just shy."

Amanda's laugh had a sharp edge to it. "I don't think even you could believe that. Stop deluding yourself. Is there anything in the room that you need to take?"

Polly rested her hands on her ample hips. "I said I'm not going anywhere. At least not for a week or two."

"Fine. Then you can find your way back to Springtown alone."

"I wouldn't know which way to go!" Polly complained.

Amanda shrugged her shoulders.

"Can't you at least tell me what the big hurry is?"

Amanda stared at Polly, wondering why she even wanted her company. Because she couldn't stand the loneliness, she admitted to herself. She started to tell her about the nugget, but changed her mind. No telling what Polly might blab to the locals. And, if the redhead should discover that her companion really didn't want to return to Springtown alone, Polly would make her wait weeks before they went back. Amanda knew she was going to have to bluff. "Suit yourself. I'm not going to wait. I've been talking to Jack, and he assures me he'll tell me the location of the gold as soon as we get back. If you're not there, don't expect me to come looking for you."

"Who's Jack?"

"Since you chose to remain in a constant huff the last few weeks, I didn't tell you the ghost's name is Jack Quigley. We've talked a great deal. I'm using some of Lester's money to purchase horses and food, and I'm riding out of here." She placed the saddlebag over her arm. "Whether or not you come with me is up to you. I would think you'd want your share of the gold."

"Of course I do!"

"Then the sooner we get back and find it, the sooner we can leave Springtown behind us."

Chance relaxed on the boulder overlooking Springtown. It had been five days since he'd left Amanda and

Polly in Angels Camp, and they still hadn't returned. With all the problems Polly had had, he'd felt guilty about taking them the long way so that he could beat them back. Still, they'd had plenty of time to return. Assuming they were going to.

He pulled a Cuban cigar from his vest pocket and lit the end. He'd found a box of cigars in one of the houses as he searched for clues to where the gold was hidden. Other than the cigars and some good whiskey, he'd found nothing of interest, or value. But it did help while away the hours. It was also frustrating. He'd found nothing to indicate there was any hidden gold, or why the town had been deserted.

At night, he read Emily Howard's diary. He was already past the part where she and her family had moved to Springtown. Her father had not only owned the dry goods store, he had also had a mine somewhere in the hills. She'd written about the people in town, and Chance was beginning to feel as if he knew them. Emily had been quite happy living here. She had even mentioned a miner named Billy whom her father had had over for supper. She seemed quite taken with the man.

But reading Emily's diary increased Chance's loneliness. In fact, he could never remember having felt so completely alone. Even the town itself seemed to possess a deadly quiteness. It was as if it were waiting for something to happen.

He studied the cigar resting between his thumb and forefinger. Had he been wrong about Amanda wanting to get rid of him so that she'd have the town to herself? He'd already decided that if the women didn't return within the next week, he was heading back to Angels Camp. Having had plenty of time to think, he'd come to accept how much he really cared for Amanda. If she were agreeable, he was actually thinking about marriage and settling down. If he found the gold, it would help matters, but he had no doubt that they'd manage.

Wondering what their children would look like, he raised the cigar to his lips, took a long pull, and looked out over the land. He was letting the smoke trail slowly out again when he saw something move in the distance. The sun was starting to dip behind the mountains and he squinted to get a better look. The corner of his mouth twitched, and his eyes became hard as stones. There was no doubt about it. Two mounted horses were coming from the west, and he had a good hunch as to who the riders were. He stood, dropped the cigar, crushed it out, then started down the hill.

As they neared town, Amanda's heart was pounding against her breast. Her gaze was riveted on the tall, broad-shouldered man resting his hip against the stone wall of the well. His hat was tipped low on his forehead, the sleeves of his light blue shirt were rolled up, and his jeans were tight over narrow hips and long, muscled legs. If she had questioned her love before, there was no doubt now. She had been such a fool. Because of her scheming and greed, she'd almost lost the one person she cared the most about.

"It's Chance!" Polly said excitedly.

Amanda nudged her horse to a quicker pace. She couldn't wait to declare her love, whether he loved her or not. But as they drew closer, she could see his taut jaw and set lips. She brought her horse to a halt in front of him, and when he tipped his hat back, she stopped breathing. Never had anyone looked at her with such cold, unforgiving eyes.

"Welcome to Springtown," Chance said, without enthusiasm.

"Did you miss me, Chance?" Polly cooed.

"No. I knew you'd be back."

A hard, painful knot twisted in Amanda's gut. "You bastard," she whispered. "You used me. You knew all along what we were up to."

"Yep. And now that we know exactly why we're here, there won't be any more need for pretending."

Amanda was furious. The man really didn't give a damn about her. Trying to keep tears from forming, she swung down from the saddle and began untying her saddlebag.

"I see you've decided to change your style of clothes."

Having taken charge of her emotions, Amanda squared her shoulders. "Why all the talk? Like you said, there's no longer any need to beat around the bush. When we find the gold, don't expect us to split it with you."

"Chance, would you help me down?" Polly asked sweetly.

The bright pink dress Polly had insisted on buying before they left Angels Camp was covered with pink bows, and her skirt was hiked up to her knees.

Polly's sudden coyness was more than Amanda could handle. "You've had no trouble getting on and off that horse for two days," Amanda bit out.

Chance ignored Polly's plea. "I take it it's going to be every man for himself."

"More or less." Amanda stroked her horse's glossy neck. "But it's one man against two women."

"And how do you feel about that, Polly?"

Polly let out a heavy grunt as she climbed off her horse. "As much as I like you, Chance, I do have to look after myself."

"Oh, I can understand that, but why share the gold with Amanda?"

"It won't work, Chance," Amanda said as she gathered up the reins. "Polly knows I'll share with her, but she'd be a fool to think you'd offer the same deal. Like I said, it's two against one."

Polly spoke up. "And Amanda's ghost is going to tell her where it is."

Amanda wanted to throttle her.

Chance stared at Polly, then broke out laughing.

"What's so funny?" Polly demanded.

"A ghost? And you actually believe that?"

Polly glanced at Amanda. "Well, yes..."

"Come on, Polly," Amanda said, butting in. "Let's get these horses put away. Chance is just trying to cause trouble." She turned to leave.

Chance's smile vanished as he pushed away from the well. "You didn't answer my question, Polly."

"I... Amanda told me about him." Polly didn't like the way he was intimidating her.

"And do you believe everything Amanda tells you?"

His soft, deep voice and blue-green eyes sent shivers of delight spiraling through Polly's body. He looked so magnificent. "I guess—"

"Of course she does, because she knows I don't lie to her! Tell him, Polly, so we can get these questions over with once and for all."

Polly hadn't realized Amanda had rejoined them and was now standing by her side. She released a heavy sigh. "She's right, Chance. We've been through a lot together, and I'm not going to side with you against her."

"There! I hope you're finally satisfied."

"I don't think Amanda has told you everything, Polly."

Amanda jerked her hat off and slapped it against her leg. "Don't do it, Chance," she told him threateningly.

"What do you mean she hasn't told me everything?"

"Don't listen to him, Polly. He's trying to cause trouble."

"She didn't tell you that she let me make love to her."

"She did what?" Polly screeched. Polly spun around so fast that a bow fell off her dress. "How could you do that?" she demanded. "You knew I wanted him. But no! You kept telling me to keep away from him. Now I know why!"

"Polly, let me explain." But Amanda's plea went unheard as Polly marched toward her house. Amanda dropped the reins and turned to Chance, her fury overcoming her common sense. "You no-account bastard!" She doubled her fist and socked him in the stomach with every ounce of strength she could muster. She had caught him off guard, and when he leaned over, she delivered another blow to his chin for good measure. She was about to grab her horse's reins when a big hand clamped around her wrist. Chance jerked her to him, his face a mask of rage. "What are you going to do? Hit me?" she challenged.

It was all Chance could do to keep his temper. "Don't tempt me. But we're even now. From here on, it's every man for himself. Excuse me. Every person." He released her wrist, tipped his hat and walked away.

Not wanting him to have the last word, Amanda picked up a good-sized rock and hurled it. She let forth a laugh when it struck him in the back, then stuck her tongue out at him when he kept walking. "I hate you, Chance Doyer!" she yelled.

Amanda turned and was about to reach for the horse's reins again when she saw a huge dust devil coming down the road, picking up momentum. The horses were already backing away. Amanda yelled, "No!" She couldn't bear the thought of them losing their mounts again. Then the dust devil was upon her, and she was enveloped with dirt and debris that flayed her from every direction. She felt a sharp pain when something struck her on the forehead.

Hearing Amanda yell, Chance turned and saw the horses galloping directly toward him. He had to make a flying leap to one side to keep from getting trampled beneath their hooves. Then he scrambled to his feet and ran into the barber shop to avoid the twister, which was now coming at him. He slammed the door shut and leaned against it.

If Amanda hadn't yelled, he'd be dead right now, or at least badly mangled. Suddenly the silence he'd been experiencing since his return covered everything like a thick blanket. He'd shrugged it off before, but he realized now what it was. There were no birds. No breezes. Nothing. Just that deadly silence that could wear on a man's nerves. As he pushed away from the door, he suddenly remembered Amanda. He yanked the door open and ran back out into the road. She lay motionless on the ground, about a hundred yards away. He started running. "Is she all right?" he heard Polly yell from somewhere behind him.

As soon as he reached Amanda, Chance fell to his knees. Her pulse was strong, but her face was a bloody mess and she had a nasty gash on her forehead.

"Is she alive?" Polly asked anxiously as she slid to a halt.

"Yes, but she's unconscious and badly cut." Chance scooped the limp body up in his arms, and stood.

"Take her to my house. I've got needles and thread. That gash on her head needs to be closed."

"Can you do it?" Chance asked, a strong undertone of doubt in his voice.

"It won't be the first time. Now hurry. Maybe I can get it taken care of before she wakes."

By the time Chance had Amanda on the bed, Polly was already threading a hook needle. "Go get water and a cloth," she ordered. "Her face needs to be cleaned so I can see what I'm doing."

A moment later, Chance returned.

"Okay, Chance, it's bleedin' like hell, and you're goin' to have to keep the blood away as best you can while I sew. At least the blood's washin' the wound out." Polly took a deep, steadying breath, then stuck the needle in Amanda's flesh.

Amanda's head was pounding. She raised her hand to her forehead, but another hand stopped its progress. Her eyes flew open.

"You've been hurt, Amanda, and I had to sew a cut on your head," Polly said softly. When Amanda's arm relaxed, Polly removed her hand.

Amanda stared at Polly and Chance, who were standing by the bed, staring down at her. Chance's shirt was covered with blood, and Polly had blood smeared on her face, but neither of them appeared hurt. "What happened?" she asked weakly.

"You got caught in that twister," Chance replied. He was trying to keep his words soft, but he knew they sounded clipped. He was having a problem with his emotions. He hadn't liked the consuming pain he'd felt upon seeing Amanda laying motionless on the ground. Even now, her face was pale. "Try not to touch your face. Since you appear to be all right, I'll be going."

"So you can continue searching for the gold?" Amanda bit out. Her hands gripped the chenille bedspread as she watched him walk out of the room. She was empty inside. Was he so angry that he couldn't even feel a touch of compassion, or did he just downright hate her? Had he always felt this way, or was it just because she'd tried to get him out of town? "What happened to the horses, Polly?"

"They're gone, just like the others. Amanda, sometimes I'd like to swat you!" Polly stated angrily. "Chance is a good man, and it's beyond my understandin' why you treat him the way you do!"

Amanda refused to acknowledge the anguish she was suffering. "You're just smitten with him." She tried to raise up, but the pain in her head made her settle back on the pillow.

"You're a fine one to talk. You were knockin' around on the side and keepin' it to yourself. I was mad as hell when I found out."

"Polly..."

"You just listen to what I have to say." Her hands clasped behind her, Polly began pacing the floor. "When I saw you on the ground, I was worried sick, and so was Chance. He carried you here, and between the two of us, we got you pretty well cleaned up and your head stitched. But Chance is right. From this point on, it's every man for himself. That goes not only for the gold, but for Chance, as well."

"Polly, you don't know what he's like!"

"You let me finish." Polly stopped by the bed and looked down at Amanda. "You never liked Chance from the beginnin'. You couldn't even muster up a thank-you for what he just did. Well, I think I'm in love with him, and I don't appreciate all them cutting words you're always throwin' at him. And you can just wipe that shocked look off your face. Chance is my type of man, and I'm goin' to do everything I can to make him look my way. Now, you're welcome to stay in my house till you're feelin' better, but after that I think you should move out."

Polly left, leaving Amanda feeling both guilty and resentful. Another one of Polly's bows had fallen from her dress onto the floor. Her head pounding mercilessly, Amanda moved her legs over the side of the bed. A groan escaped her lips as she pushed herself into a sitting position. Seeing herself in the mirror straight ahead, she gasped. She looked as if someone had taken a pitchfork to her face. Tears trickled down her cheeks. Would she be scarred for the rest of her life? Slowly she stood, trying to fight the dizziness that assailed her. Her legs were wobbly, and she had to hold on to the nightstand for support. Gradually the dizziness subsided. Carefully placing one foot in front of the other, she left the bedroom.

"Amanda! What are you doing? You can't leave now!" Polly exclaimed.

"I'll not be beholden to anyone."

"Oh, Amanda, I'm sorry for what I said. You can stay as long as you like. Someone has to watch over you. It's just that—"

"I'm going to the hotel," Amanda replied, ending the conversation.

It was a slow, agonizing process, but Amanda managed to walk down the path and past the picket fence. Suddenly a pair of powerful arms were lifting her up.

"Damned if you're not the most stubborn woman I've ever met!" Chance growled.

"I don't want you carrying me!" Even talking hurt, but apparently, Chance had no intention of letting her go, and

Amanda was too weak to argue. "If you insist on doing this, take me to the hotel."

Chance turned and, seeing a worried Polly nod her head, he started down the road.

By the following week, Amanda's strength had returned to normal, and she was in the process of moving into her house. She had taken out the stitches in her forehead and was grateful that the scar was just above the hairline. Surprisingly, the rest of her face had cleared up quite nicely.

During her recuperation, Polly had brought her food and checked on her progress, but they had exchanged few words. Chance hadn't shown his face once, and she kept trying to tell herself she didn't care. But each day her resentment grew. She could just picture Polly and Chance frolicking together in bed. And as if that wasn't bad enough, the two had a head start at searching for the gold. What she couldn't understand was why Jack Quigley hadn't paid her a visit, and why her nightmares had returned.

After more than a week of searching for treasure, Amanda entered her house and collapsed onto the brocade chair. She was exhausted. And so far she hadn't found one single nugget.

She had just pulled the pins from her hair and allowed the thick mane to fall around the shoulders when she felt a chill and a prickling sensation she'd become accustomed to. Knowing she wasn't alone, she glanced around the large parlor. "How come you haven't paid me a visit sooner?" she asked angrily.

"I've been very upset with you."

Amanda turned toward the gaping fireplace and saw Jack standing there. "Angry with me? I'm the one who should be angry. I'm worn out from trying to find your gold. I'm beginning to understand what you meant about liking to play games." She placed the wooden pins she was holding on the small side table and stood.

"You deserve to be worn out. I've enjoyed watching you and Polly darting from one place to another. Chance is different, though. He's patiently waiting to see if either of you come up with anything, and I think in the meantime he's checking out the old mines."

He was walking toward her, so Amanda went over and sat on the piano bench. Now she was angry with Jack, as well as with Polly and Chance. She was beginning to feel like a shrew. "What do you mean, I deserve to be worn out?" Amanda suddenly realized that Jack's face was hard, almost frightening. He and Chance made a good pair. "Are you going to answer my question?" He stopped beside her, and this time she decided it wouldn't be wise to move again. Then his hand disappeared through the piano lid, and, though she couldn't see the ivory keys, she could hear them being struck at random. The eerie noise caused her to shiver.

"I have been upset with you, my love."

Amanda was relieved when he stopped banging the keys. "You've already said that. Why would you be upset with me?"

"You left me."

"I don't belong to you, Jack. I'm free to go and come as I please. However, you're the one who disappeared before I could tell you I had every intention of returning. I was trying to get rid of Chance."

"Don't leave again."

"Is that a threat?"

"Don't be angry with me, my beloved. I want you here with me where you belong. Haven't I been good to you?"

"I'm not sure." She stood and went to the window, surprised to see that it had already turned dark outside.

"I don't like you in men's clothes. Why don't you wear some of the fine dresses upstairs?"

"Because it's easier to move around, and I don't want to ruin them while searching for your gold."

"But the gold isn't in town."

"I'm beginning to believe there is no gold, Jack. I think it's all part of your little game."

"You'd do well to remember that I'm your only ally. The others have deserted you."

Amanda felt the tingling sensation leave her, and she knew she was alone again.

Having finished the diary, Chance snapped it shut. His thoughts were still on the last few passages of the book. Emily had gone into great detail describing the grand house her father was having built for them. The family had planned on moving into it the week after the last entry. Amanda's house fitted the description perfectly.

Chance laid the diary on the arm of the chair. When the family moved, it must have accidentally been left behind. He wanted Emily's next diary. It was the only sure way he knew of finding out what had happened in Springtown, and where the gold was.

But that would entail searching Amanda's house. Just thinking about the vixen brought forth memories of her breath, warm and moist against his face, as she'd strived to satisfy her need. His lips twisted into a smile. Amanda had used him to satisfy her curiosity. She hadn't just wanted to get him out of town. He'd be a damn liar if he said he didn't have feelings for her, but this time he wasn't going to end up on the wrong end of the stick. He thought about her socking him in the stomach and jaw and smiled. She also had a strong fist. He leaned back in the chair.

At least two good things had come out of all this mess. He cared for Amanda—though he wasn't crazy enough to be in love with her—and he'd gotten Polly off his back. On second thought, maybe he hadn't. Though she hadn't made any more direct advances, her friendliness and quick smiles gave him the distinct feeling he was being wooed. She had him over to her house every night for supper and tried to wait on him hand and foot. She'd even offered to wash his dirty clothes. He chuckled. How in hell had he ever ended up in Springtown with two crazy women?

Amanda tossed and turned in her large bed, then awoke screaming. Her body was covered with perspiration, and she had to gasp for breath. As before, the dream had been vivid, but this time, there was a bonfire in the middle of the road, and the light from it illuminated the face of a man who had been hanged. It was Jack Quigley. And it was all happening in Springtown.

She went to the commode and poured water from the pitcher into the bowl. After wetting the facecloth, she ran the cool material over her face and neck. She needed someone to talk to, someone who would understand. But there was no one, and they wouldn't understand unless they, too, had experienced the nightmares. Were the dreams true? Had such things happened in Springtown? That was ridiculous. People didn't dream of the past—at least not a past that didn't include them. On the other hand, she'd never believed in ghosts, either—not until she'd met Jack Quigley.

Chapter Eleven

Amanda wasn't able to go back to sleep. She was too fearful of having another nightmare. Still in her gown, she lit the lantern and carried it downstairs to the kitchen. A few minutes later, she took her toast and hot chocolate into the parlor so that she could relax. Dawn was already upon her, so she put out the lantern.

By the time she'd settled into the Queen Anne chair, the sky was already turning light. As she savored the sweet taste of the chocolate, she watched the day slowly light the whole room. Even the blue and gold of the thick wool carpet came alive. The crystal candle holders on the wall would have glimmered, but they needed cleaning. Where had the time gone? She'd cleaned a good deal of the house, but it was too much for her to keep up with while she searched for the lost gold.

She took another bite of toast and wondered what was happening to her. She had always been a cheerful person, at least when she hadn't had to put up with her father's shenanigans. Now her attitude was so bad that she didn't even like herself. In Angels Camp, there had been no nightmares, and she hadn't felt the gloom that now seemed to hang over her like a thick cloud. Why? Was she jealous of Chance and Polly? She'd never experienced jealousy before, and it was eating away at her. She had taken her anger out on Chance and Polly, when the problem was hers. She wanted Chance's attention and his love, but it wasn't something she could make happen.

And what about Jack? He was coercing her, and he, too, seemed to be suffering from jealousy. And was the gold something he'd made up? He had admitted he liked playing games. Other things came to mind. Jack had said the nugget was proof that there really was hidden gold. But why should he have placed it in a secluded corner where she might never have found it? Why not put it in some obvious place, like on top of her bed? And why hadn't he appeared to Polly or Chance? Was Jack using the tale of gold just to feed her greed and keep her here? I should leave Springtown, she told herself. A single tear trickled down her cheek. The thought of never seeing Chance again hurt deeply, even if he didn't love her. And what would she do if she left? She didn't want to live in Angels Camp. It reminded her too much of Columbia. But she could get a stage from there to Sacramento.

Amanda finished her hot chocolate and set the cup on the table beside her. When had she become such a weakling? How could she care for a man who considered her nothing more than someone to use? But, God help her, as hard as she tried to stay angry with him, she still wanted Chance to make love to her, to hear him saying sweet words and telling her how beautiful she was.

And Chance wasn't her only weakness. Jack had guessed right. She still hoped there really was gold hidden somewhere. The thought of never again having to wash someone else's clothes to keep food on the table and a roof over her head renewed her determination to find the lost gold.

She needed to make peace with Polly. She could no longer bear the loneliness. But, instead of going upstairs to get dressed, she curled her legs beneath her and leaned against the back of the chair. She was so tired. She didn't try fighting the peaceful sleep that settled over her.

By the time Amanda finally left the house, it was close to noon. She was anxious to have a talk with Polly, and, she hoped, dispel the feeling of mistrust that Chance had managed to wedge between them.

When Amanda was out of sight, Chance entered the house. Because of the clear descriptions in the diary, he knew exactly which bedroom had been Emily's. Taking the steps two at a time, he went up the wide staircase and turned left at the landing. The house was every bit as lavish as Emily had described. He followed the hall around to the last bedroom. Though there were cobwebs and dust, he could picture Emily sleeping here. The three windows made the room light, and everything was done in white and blue, her favorite colors. But he couldn't afford to dwell on the furnishings. Amanda might return at any time, and he didn't want to have to explain about the diary.

Chance glanced around the room, trying to decide where to start. He was just about to go to the armoire when something caught his eye. He watched, astonished, as a blanket slid off an old sea chest that sat between two of the windows. Curious, he walked over and raised the lid of the chest. Resting on top of a green satin dress was a diary. He opened the front cover and saw the name Emily Howard scrolled on the first page.

When there was no reply to her knock, Amanda wasn't sure what to do next. Polly should be up by now. But what if she wasn't alone? Should she just barge in? She looped her thumbs around her suspenders. Was Chance with her? It was one thing to suspect Chance was Polly's lover, but quite another to be faced with the actual fact. She took a deep breath. Maybe that was what she needed to finally rid herself of the hold he seemed to have on her.

She was about to barge in when the door suddenly swung open. Amanda's mouth dropped open. Polly's face and arms were covered with blotchy red spots.

"Amanda!" Polly said frantically. "I was fixin' to go find you. I think I've got that yellow fever!"

"What? Oh, merciful heaven! Where were you? I mean ... did it just suddenly break out?"

"The only thing I've done was go searching for berries by the stream yesterday!" She wasn't about to admit she'd been collecting the plants she needed to make an aphrodisiac. Her voice cracked when she asked, "Amanda, am I going to die?"

Amanda felt sure she knew exactly what Polly's disease was. "Let me take a look," she said as she stepped forward.

Polly backed away. "I can't let you catch it."

"I'm not worried. Just stand still." Seeing the watery blisters and swelling, Amanda had to swallow her laughter. "It looks to me like you've got poison oak."

"Poison oak? Are you sure?"

"Positive. I'll go to the drugstore and see if I can find some spirits of niter. In the meantime, don't scratch those blisters. They'll seep and cause it to spread."

"You mean this may never go away?"

Amanda smiled. "No, that's not what I mean. It's not so bad, Polly. I've seen worse." Amanda turned to leave.

"Are you still angry with me?"

Amanda looked over her shoulder and felt herself relax. "I don't think anyone could stay mad at you for long."

Amanda's smile broadened as she left the house. She couldn't blame Polly for being angry when she'd learned that she and Chance had made love. Only minutes ago she'd been having the same feelings at the thought of finding Chance in bed with Polly. But she'd been too hurt to see what had been staring her in the face all along. When Chance had made love to her, he'd been tender and caring, not the angry man she'd met the day she returned from Angels Camp. Could that anger have stemmed from knowing she had tried to get rid of him? She laughed aloud. One thing was certain. Polly's poison oak wasn't going to disappear overnight, which meant that, at least for a while, there wouldn't be any hanky-panky going on between Polly and Chance.

When Amanda returned with the spirits of niter, she found Polly sitting on the divan with her arms spread out, not moving a muscle.

"What are you doing?" Amanda asked out of curiosity.

"I don't want any scars."

"You won't have scars if we get to this right away."

"My ma was left with scars when she had the pox."

"You don't have the pox. What we have to do is bathe the red spots with the niter, then pop the blisters and bathe them again."

Polly glared at Amanda. "You can't be serious!"

"Oh, yes, I am."

For the next half hour, Amanda tended to the tedious chore, making sure none of the seepage got on her. She leaned against the back of the divan, relieved that the task was finished. If Polly hadn't continually fidgeted and complained, it wouldn't have taken so long. "There, it's done. If you see any new places, just do what I did. You should be healed in no time."

"It's terrible. I could never do it."

"Sure you can. It's better than having it all over your body. If you leave it alone, maybe in a few months it'll clear up."

"A few months?"

"I knew a woman once who had it so bad the doctor didn't even let her out of bed for six months."

"You're lyin'!"

"No, I'm not."

"Well…all right. Thank you, Amanda, for takin' care of me."

"You took care of me, so I think it only right that I return the favor."

Polly laughed. "I must admit, I felt terrible after all I said to you."

Amanda patted Polly's hand. "But you did keep coming to feed me and make sure I was all right."

"Have you seen the ghost?" Polly suddenly asked.

"Yes. I can't believe how mad he was because I'd left."

Polly looked wide-eyed at her friend, who was now relaxing on the divan. "Was he real mad?"

"I think so. He warned me not to do it again."

"Amanda, I just had a thought. Maybe he's the one that's been chasin' all the horses away. He could have even caused that dust devil that day you got hurt."

Amanda sat up straight and smiled. "Not likely. You may find this hard to understand, but he loves me. So it wouldn't make any sense for him to want to do me harm."

"I guess you're right," Polly commented thoughtfully.

"He's harmless." Amanda pulled her hat down on her head. "I think I'll go take a swim in the lake. I'll come back later and help you with those blisters. Maybe we can even eat supper together."

"Chance will be over, too."

Amanda felt the tentacles of jealousy clutch at her throat. "Oh. Well, maybe another time."

Polly should have been excited that Amanda didn't want to see Chance. But there was a sadness about Amanda that bothered her. "How come you came by to see me?"

"I wanted to make peace. I should have told you about what happened with Chance, but I knew you'd get angry. I have no excuses, and I can't even say it was all his fault. Polly, I've decided to search around for a few more weeks, then..." Amanda couldn't finish the sentence. What if Jack heard her say she was going to leave? Maybe Polly's fears were beginning to rub off on her. She saw Polly looking at her questioningly. "And then I think I'll start altering some clothes. Polly, you should come to the house. There are clothes of every description. From what I've seen so far, it looks like the woman of the house was about your size."

"Really?" Polly exclaimed excitedly. "As soon as I get rid of this stuff on my skin, I'll be over."

"Have you searched for the gold?"

Polly bowed her head. "To tell the truth, Chance and me agreed that I'll take care of the cookin' and he'll take care of the lookin'." It wasn't as if she were really lying, she just preferred to think that was their agreement.

"I see." Amanda wanted to tell Polly she shouldn't trust Chance, but she knew the advice would fall on deaf ears. Feeling lonely again, she stood. Chance really had used her to alleviate his male need. "I'll be looking forward to seeing you at the house."

Polly nodded. She felt like a damn traitor.

For the next week, Amanda thought constantly about leaving Springtown. There was nothing left here for her. She didn't even care about the gold anymore. But she wanted to talk to Chance first. The only problem was that she couldn't get up the nerve to pay him a visit. If he so much as kissed her, she'd fall into his arms. Then nothing would have been resolved, except that she'd feel used. How could she say she was sorry for the way she'd treated him, and thank him for helping Polly stitch her wound, without breaking into tears? Yet she knew she owed him that much.

When Polly arrived at her house, Amanda couldn't remember ever having been so happy to see someone. They spent the entire day together. They visited, laughed about their first meeting, looked in all the rooms and tried on clothes.

Even though Polly had promised to return the next day, Amanda felt even lonelier when she left. They were going to start making alterations to the dresses and underclothes they'd discovered. Amanda figured the sewing would take a week or two, and then she would leave Springtown. Staying was only making her increasingly miserable.

The following morning, Amanda awoke early. After a quick breakfast of oatmeal, she left for town. She wanted to collect needles and thread so that she'd have everything ready when Polly arrived.

As she strolled down the main street, Amanda paid scant attention to the stores she passed. Everything had become a familiar sight. She kept looking at the ground, hoping to find another ring like the one she now kept in her saddlebag. While in Angels Camp, she'd gone to a jeweler. The big piece of green glass had turned out to be an emerald.

Hearing an animal snort, Amanda looked up and sucked in her breath. Not ten feet in front of her were three men mounted on horses. She recognized them immediately.

"Son of a bitch, Pa, I told you I saw women that night the horses got away!"

"Well, Fred, I reckon you was right after all," Gus commented. His crystal-blue eyes raked the woman from head to toe. "And this one sure is mighty purty, even if she is dressed like a man. I'd say she's real ripe for the takin'."

"I get her first," Vern said as he swung to the ground.

"The hell you say!" Fred kicked the toe of his boots out of the stirrups, then leapt on top of Vern.

The two men scuffled on the ground, sending clouds of dust into the air. Amanda took the opportunity to run. She hadn't gone more than ten feet when a rope circled her waist and she was thrown to the ground. She tried scrambling to her feet, but every time she made a little headway she was yanked down again. She tasted dirt in her mouth and heard the men laugh. She had to warn Polly and Chance! She stopped struggling and began releasing one scream after another. She ceased her screaming when the old man rode up and delivered a kick to her chin, snapping her head back. She was sure he'd broken her jaw.

"That's more like it," Gus barked.

"Who gets her first, Pa?" Fred asked, already starting to unbutton his pants.

When Fred was close enough, Amanda raised her foot and kicked him hard in the groin. Fred doubled over and grabbed his crotch.

Gus looked down at the woman on the ground, already contemplating his own pleasure. "What's it gonna be, girl? You goin' to tell us where the gold is, or do me and my boys ride you all night until you finally decide to talk? Fred and Vern can be mighty hard on a woman."

Amanda stared at the old man's dirty face. "I don't know what you're talking about," she whispered. Her chin and mouth ached.

"Well, don't say I didn't give you a chance, little girl." Gus wiped his bulbous nose with the sleeve of his grimy shirt. "Neither of you boys is first. I am." As he leaned over to dismount, a shot rang out, nicking his ear. Gus leapt off his horse and shielded himself behind the animal.

Vern grabbed the pistol from his belt and held the end of the barrel to Amanda's head. "Pa, are you all right?"

"Hell, no. I got blood runnin' down my face. Whoever fired that shot," Gus yelled, "if you do it again, the woman's dead! Do you understand me?"

There was no reply.

"Ain't no cause to worry," Fred grunted. "I know who it is. It's that other woman I saw. I told you there was two of them."

"No cause to worry?" Gus blared. "She almost killed me! Button up your pants."

Fred began buttoning his pants, but kept his jaundiced eyes on Amanda. "You just wait 'til I get my hands on you, woman."

Amanda kept her head turned, refusing to let any of them see how frightened she was. She was positive Chance had fired the shot. But from where she lay on the ground, she couldn't see anyone. Where was he now? Had he decided just to let her die?

"Vern, keep your gun on the woman. Fred, you tie her hands and feet. I want that gold, and we're gonna get some answers real fast."

Vern backed away, and when Fred approached her, Amanda scrambled to her feet. She saw Vern's finger tighten on the trigger of his pistol. But another shot rang out, hitting him right between the eyes. As he fell to the ground, Amanda took off running. But Gus moved faster than she had expected. Grabbing her arm he swung her around and held her in front of him.

"Pa!" Fred yelled. "They've killed Vern!"

"Keep a horse in front of you and make for the hotel," he barked at Fred.

"But, Pa, we can't just leave Vern here."

"You damn idiot! Vern's dead, and if you don't get a move on, you're gonna be the next one lying there!" Using Amanda as a shield, Gus headed for the hotel.

Once they were inside, Gus gave Amanda a hard shove, and she tripped and fell to the floor.

"My brother's dead out there, woman, and you're gonna pay for it!" Fred raged.

Fred pointed his gun at Amanda, but Gus knocked his hand away before he could pull the trigger. "I don't want her dead. Not yet. Now, missy, I just lost a son, and I'm in no mood to quibble. Tell me where the gold is, and I guarantee your death will be quick. Don't tell me, and you'll die a thousand deaths before them pretty eyes is closed permanently. And don't try sayin' there ain't no gold. We done heard all about it while we was in Columbia."

Amanda stared up at the men towering over her. She was shaking so badly she wasn't even sure she could speak. "I—" A kick in her stomach doubled her over.

"That's for kickin' me!"

"Now, Fred," Gus said with mock concern, "we don't want the woman so bad off she can't tell us what we're wantin' to know." His beady eyes grew hard. "Now try again, missy. Where's the gold?"

"I . . . I don't know."

"Let me handle her, Pa. I'll make her talk."

"No, I'm gonna . . ." Gus rubbed his arms. "How the hell did it turn so cold all of a sudden?"

Suddenly, there was a loud banging noise. Both men turned to see what it was and stared in disbelief as they watched an iron poker drift through the air.

"What the hell—?" His hands trembling, Fred fired his gun. The poker suddenly came crashing down on his head.

Amanda scooted to the corner and huddled against the wall. Heavy footsteps thudded on the floor. She looked up in time to see the old man run out the door, trying to escape. A shot rang out.

"It's all right, my beloved. I will always take care of you."

Amanda opened her eyes and saw Jack Quigley standing in front of her. "You killed him," she said in a hushed voice.

"Of course I killed him. He hurt you." He glanced toward the doorway. "Remember, I hold your life in the palm of my hand."

Glancing at the dead man on the floor, Amanda could no longer hold back the bile rising in her throat. She was still retching when Chance and Polly ran into the lobby.

* * *

As the days passed, Amanda chose to remain in her house. After what had happened, she'd told Polly and Chance that she wanted to be by herself for a while. But her privacy was invaded by Jack Quigley's visits. And his visits were becoming increasingly frequent. He told her he was pleased that she'd chosen to have nothing to do with Chance and Polly, and he talked constantly about them always being together.

Amanda tried explaining her situation, tried to tell him that it was not her intention never to talk to the others again, but he didn't seem to want to listen. Nor had he said anything more about the hidden gold. For the first time, Amanda was afraid of Jack Quigley. What was to keep him from killing her if she tried to leave?

Amanda walked to a bush beside the house and plucked a perfect red rose. She held it to her nose and inhaled deeply, enjoying the sweet, heady odor. "I always wanted a rosebush," she murmured. She glanced around at the various trees surrounding the house and suddenly wondered why there were no chirping birds. She thought about going to see Polly, but if Polly and Chance were carrying on, she didn't want to know about it.

Tired of remaining around the house, but afraid to leave Springtown, Amanda decided to search for the gold once more, just in case Jack Quigley had been telling the truth. If she found it, she could give it to Chance and Polly, and they'd leave. She was also becoming concerned for their well-being.

Jack had said the gold wasn't in town, so she took off in the opposite direction. He'd also said that at certain times of the day the sun shone on it, which meant that it had to be partially hidden. Perhaps in a cave? Or maybe even just inside a mine?

It felt good to get away from the house. Amanda had had enough time for healing. Now she needed to get on with her life. She would search for a week. After that, she was going to find a way to escape from Springtown and from Jack Quigley. Though it was dangerous, she had to tell Polly and Chance about him.

Billy Hayes was killed in a cave-in at the mine. His body was brought out this morning. My grief is overwhelming. I loved him so, now we shall never be together again. Why has God done this to me? In two days we had planned to run off to Murphys and get married. I know I shall never love again. Mother says that is nonsense, but I know differently.

Feeling Emily's grief, Chance gently closed the diary. She had been a fine young woman, and it was too bad she'd lost her love. This was the end of her journal. Was there still another one, or had she been so grieved that she stopped writing? He hoped not.

Chance left the house. He was going to search Emily's room again. If there was another diary, she might have taken it with her when she left Springtown. But he had to be sure. He'd learned something of extreme importance from this last book. The other miners had been selling their gold to Emily's father, Robert Howard. According to Emily, Robert had been sure the people of the town were trustworthy, but he hadn't wanted to tempt anyone into trying to steal it. So he'd kept it concealed.

Which meant the tale of hidden gold was probably true. Knowing miners were prone to superstition, Robert could have made up the ghost, as well.

The pieces of the puzzle were beginning to fall into place. Now the question was, had the Howards taken the gold with them, or had it been left behind like the other things in town? And there was another question that was still unanswered. Why had the people of Springtown left?

Even though it would be a hindrance if Amanda was home, Chance was looking forward to seeing her. Though Polly kept assuring him that Amanda was probably fine, he wanted to see for himself. She'd been badly shaken by the episode with Gus and his boys. Though he hadn't said anything, he'd been every bit as concerned about Amanda as Polly had. Probably even more so, because at that moment he'd realized that he loved her.

When he'd watched Fred drag her into the hotel, he'd wanted to barge in after them. The only thing that had stopped him was the fear of Amanda being killed. After he'd taken care of Gus as he ran out of the hotel, he'd been sick with worry at the thought of what Fred might do to Amanda. He still couldn't figure out how she had managed to kill Fred with that poker. When he'd run into the hotel, pistol ready, his heart had ached at the sight of her huddled in a corner, trembling and wretching. Then, when he'd tried to console her, she'd wanted nothing to do with him.

At least Amanda's self-imposed solitude had allowed him time to get himself back in check. Though her attitude had made him furious, she'd actually done him a favor. He was better off staying away from Amanda. She was like poison in his blood. When it came to women, it seemed he was a glutton for punishment.

Chance crossed the wide porch and knocked on the door. When no one answered, he walked in. At first he thought something might be wrong with her. But once he'd decided she'd only left for a little while, he headed up the stairs.

As Chance entered Emily's room, he detected the same strange glow he'd experienced the last time. Yet it was nothing tangible, nothing he could put a finger on. It looked like any other room, and the only light was coming in through the windows. Disregarding the matter, he took a slow look around. If the diary he was looking for had been Emily's last, she would likely have kept it near her bed. But there was nothing but a lantern and a music box on the small bedside table.

He was about to search the room when he suddenly thought about the bed. Gripping the feather mattress, he pulled it forward, along with the covers. It was there—he'd found the diary. Retrieving it, Chance pushed back the mattress and smoothed out the covers.

It had been four days since he'd seen Amanda, and he decided to satisfy himself that she was all right. He searched the ground until he found the direction she had headed, and he followed her trail, wondering if she had come up with some answers regarding the gold.

Chance lost her tracks when he reached the rocks. Even more curious, he scanned the surrounding cliffs. Finally he caught sight of her, climbing around some small boulders above him. He held his breath when she slipped on the loose gravel, but she managed to recover and continue on, entering what looked like a cave. He squatted on his heels and waited.

A couple of minutes later, she came back out and stood at the mouth of the cave. She appeared to be studying the cliffs on the far side of the canyon. Obviously she was still looking for the gold. Suddenly he wasn't interested in what she was searching for. All he knew was that he couldn't take his eyes off her.

She'd left her black hair hanging loose down her back, and the mild breeze was blowing it around her face. Her breasts were pressed against her shirt, and her jeans showed off her rounded hips and long legs. There had been many women in his life, but never had he desired a woman as much as he desired this one. He wanted to take her back in the cave and make the rest of the world disappear. But it was out of the question. Amanda had done nothing but lie to him, and he had to protect his heart. He stood and walked back toward the trees.

Seeing movement, Amanda looked down at the floor of the canyon. Her lips curled into a sneer. So, Chance had followed her to see if she'd located the gold. Had he been keeping an eye on her all along? Did he also watch her house? she wondered angrily. Maybe he thought that, since he hadn't discovered anything, she'd just lead him to it. She'd already accepted the strong possibility that there was no gold. But he was going to be in for a big disappointment when he came to the same conclusion. It was almost worth hanging around to see. She knew she was being bitter, but that was better than all the crying she'd done in the past couple of weeks.

Chapter Twelve

After pulverizing the leaves, Polly set the pestle aside and picked up the mortar. Carefully she poured the juice she'd extracted into a glass vial and corked it. Now that she was rid of the poison oak and she had her precious concoction, the effort seemed worth it. At last she had the means to stir Chance's desire. She held her vial in the air and giggled.

"Being a harlot does have some advantages. A few drops of this, my sweet, and you won't be able to keep your hands off me." She straightened the skirt of her simple calico dress, then reached up and made sure her hair was properly smoothed back. Satisfied, she left the drugstore.

Polly hummed a lively tune as she hurried toward Chance's house. She was convinced that, once Chance discovered the joys she could give him, he'd never look at Amanda again.

When she stopped at Chance's door, she again checked her appearance. She had already decided to knock this time, instead of brazenly barging in. That way he'd think of her as more of a lady.

When Chance opened the door, his shirt was still hanging open. She had to keep her hands to her sides to prevent running them across his broad chest. He was so tall and handsome, and she knew she would never again meet a man like this one. "I came to have a talk," she said softly.

"What do you want to talk about?"

"I just want to visit. Aren't you going to invite me in? I promise to behave myself."

Chance looked at Polly's clean face. There wasn't even a smidgen of paint on it. She'd brushed her hair neatly back and secured it with a blue ribbon that matched her dress. Her complexion was flawless, and her pert nose and lovely green eyes were something to behold. Though not as pretty as Amanda, Polly could certainly hold her own when it came to looks. "Do come in." He smiled and backed away from the door.

As he followed Polly into the parlor, Chance thought that, even though they'd had their differences, he liked Polly. She never tried to pretend to be something other than what she was—a passionate, warmhearted woman. "What brought on this visit?"

"I just got to thinkin' that by each of us going our separate ways, we're not gonna get anywhere. So, I wanted you and me to join forces."

Still grinning, Chance nodded. "That's a pretty dress you have on."

Just knowing he'd noticed caused Polly's heart to flutter. "Does this mean I'm forgiven?"

"For what?"

"For helping Amanda get you out of town."

"To tell the truth, Polly, had the circumstances been different, I might have done the same thing," Chance said magnanimously.

"You don't know what a load you've taken off my mind. I know it's early, but can we drink to a new start?"

"I don't see why not."

"Good. Sit down and I'll pour the whiskey."

"You've got a deal." Chance sat in his favorite arm-chair, quickly shoving the diary under a cushion.

With her back to Chance, Polly slipped the small vial from her skirt pocket. She pulled the cork, then put two drops in one of the glasses. Thinking about how big Chance was, she put in another drop for good measure. It wasn't a strong aphrodisiac, but it would be enough to get the juices flowing. She corked the vial and stuck it behind a whiskey bottle, where she could retrieve it later. Already anticipating the results, she smiled as she poured Chance's drink.

"Do you really think Amanda has made up this whole thing about the ghost?" Polly asked as she placed the glass on the table in front of Chance. She made a point of sitting quite properly across from him on the divan.

"I have no reason to think otherwise."

"There *are* times when she lets her imagination get away with her." Polly kept staring at his glass, waiting for him to pick it up. "But what would it gain her?"

"I don't know. There are a lot of things about Amanda that are beyond my understanding."

"She always said she liked it here and didn't want to leave. Aren't you goin' to drink up?"

"Then maybe that's the answer. By making up the story, it could keep you here." He doubled a fist. "She tried getting rid of me, but it didn't work."

Polly's lips parted as what Chance was saying began to make sense.

Chance leaned forward. "I don't know about you, Polly, but personally, I don't take kindly to being duped. I once knew a woman that was a lot like Amanda. Believe me, they can be very tricky when it comes to getting what they want."

"Then why have you stayed?"

"There's something I want to finish first." He thought of the diary he'd been reading. "When I'm sure of the answers, I'll leave."

"Will you take me with you?"

Chance chuckled. "Why not?"

"Then let's drink to it." Polly lifted her glass in the air, waiting for him to pick his up.

Chance was just fixing to wrap his big hand around the glass when the front door banged open. He looked toward the noise. A moment later, Amanda walked into the room.

"When I couldn't find you, Polly, I figured you were here," Amanda stated. She knew she was making a fool of herself. But she was finding it increasingly difficult to keep her jealousy under control. At least they weren't sitting side by side. "I see you've been enjoying a few drinks." She noticed Chance's open shirt. "And other things, as well! Is this a conspiracy, or were you planning to invite me to the party?"

"We were just about to have a toast," Chance snapped back at her.

Polly suddenly realized this was a perfect opportunity. If Chance openly showed desire for her, Amanda would surely leave him alone. "I think havin' a toast to the future is a good idea." She rose from the divan. "I'll even fix you a drink."

"Don't bother. I'll have my drink, then leave you two lovebirds alone!"

To Polly's horror, Amanda picked up Chance's glass. "No!" Polly whispered, but it was too late. She was furious that Amanda had ruined all her plans, but there was nothing she could do about it now. Amanda's face turned a bright red from having downed the strong whiskey in one gulp, and Chance laughed. It was his look of total pleasure that made Polly head for the doorway. She already knew what the outcome would be, and she was damned if she was going to hang around and watch it happen. Polly had seen the light that had come into Chance's eyes the moment Amanda entered the room. Chance was in love with Amanda. She doubted that either of them had noticed her leaving.

Still laughing, Chance went to Amanda and began striking her between the shoulder blades to help her catch her breath.

Amanda jerked away. "Are...are you trying...to kill me?"

"Don't think I haven't considered it." Chance's sense of humor quickly deserted him. He led her to the sofa, then gave her a push on the shoulders. She landed on the seat, and her legs flew up in the air. "The time has come for us to have a talk, Miss Amanda. By the way, what's your last name?"

"Bradshaw." Her breathing having returned to normal, she tried to rise. He pushed her down again.

"Don't you bully me!" she snapped. "And keep your dirty hands to yourself!" Again she tried to stand, and again she was knocked back down, and none too gently!

"We could keep this up all day," Chance stated, without a hint of sympathy in his voice. "If you agree to just stay put, we can have our little discussion."

"I have nothing to discuss with you."

"I happen to think you have a lot to discuss with me. Are you going to stay put?"

"Fine!"

"Good!" He took the few steps to the armchair, checked to be sure she wasn't going to try and get up again, then sat down. "Now, assuming you're capable of telling the truth, just what did you hope to accomplish by making up some story about a ghost?"

"What do you mean, assuming I'm capable of telling the truth? If anyone's lying, it's you. There is a ghost! He killed that man in the hotel!" Amanda could see by the look on his face that he didn't believe her. That was something she hadn't even thought about. And she had no proof. There was no way of warning him.

Chance shook his head. "Let's try another question. Where did you find out about the gold?"

"You won't believe me."

"Try me."

"The ghost told me."

"I have to give you credit—you sure do try to stick to your story. But I'm not buying it."

"I didn't think you would." Amanda watched him run his fingers through his thick, sandy-colored hair. He did have wonderful hands. She wondered if he had gotten his blue-green eyes from his mother or his father.

"I know you were trying to get me out of town so you could keep the gold for yourself. But were there also personal motives?"

"No, I..." He has such a strong jaw line, and his lips... Oh, yes. His lips. Such soft lips. "Why was Polly here?"

"You answer my question first."

"What question?"

"Are you feeling all right?"

Amanda propped her elbow on the arm of the sofa and smiled. She was beginning to feel quite warm, but she'd be hanged if she'd tell him that. "Actually, I'm feeling pretty damn good. Maybe we should have another drink."

"Amanda! What does it take to get an answer out of you? I asked if there were more personal reasons for wanting me out of town."

"How many women have you slept with?"

"Why would you ask something like that?"

Amanda's gaze traveled slowly down the length of him as she began unbuttoning her shirt.

"Oh, no. You're not going to get out of this that way. It won't work."

Amanda shook her head. What was she doing? She felt so peculiar. "I don't know what you're talking about." She began putting the buttons back through the holes. After the second one, her fingers stopped moving. She was far too warm to close her blouse.

"You know damn well what I'm talking about. Now I want an answer, lady!"

"Chance, I..." There was a growing ache of desire in the pit of her stomach and a throbbing between her legs.

"You what?" Was that passion he saw in her eyes or was it just another trick to get what she wanted?

Amanda's need was growing so strong she couldn't even think straight. Her hand slid from the buttons and glided down her breast. "I can't remember what I was going to say."

Chance shifted uncomfortably. He wasn't going to let her evade his questions by trying to seduce him. Yet her hand moving over her bodice was stirring his blood. "We were talking about you wanting me out of town."

"Oh? I'd rather talk about...how I feel when you move your hands over my skin and—"

"Stop right there! We're going to..." Chance felt perspiration break out on his upper lip as she stood and walked toward him. Her gaze held his for a brief second before he stood and walked toward the window. After putting a safe distance between them, he turned and faced her again. "I want to know about the gold. If you think I'm going to leave without my share, you've got another thought coming. And you using your female wiles isn't going to change my mind."

Amanda was to the point of wanting to tear off her clothes and attack him. But another emotion was beginning to also take hold. As she stood in the middle of the room, it occurred to her that she was making Chance equally uncomfortable. She was elated at the effect she was having on him. She moved toward him, removing the pins from her hair and letting it fall down her back. "Are you trying to tell me you no longer find me attractive?" she asked in a husky, seductive tone of voice.

"I said I won't—"

"I don't care what you said."

Amanda stopped in front of him and reached out to touch his chest. Chance brushed her hand aside, his breathing already becoming heavy. "Damn it, ladies don't—"

"But you told me ladies do." She caressed his chest. "I want you Chance. I want you real bad."

Chance was fast losing every bit of his self-control. He told himself to push her away, but she was like a flame and he was the moth. She was so damn beautiful. Her half-closed eyes looked glazed with desire, and as she ran her tongue across her full lips, he wanted to lean down and claim them. It had to be an act. He'd given her no cause to become so suddenly passionate. She was only trying to get out of answering his questions. "I think you'd better leave."

"Damn it, Chance," Amanda demanded, "make love to me!"

"No! I—" She reached out for him and Chance knew he'd already lost his battle of denial. She was driving him mad, and he was no longer willing to deny his need for her. He lifted her in his arms. If she was putting on an act, she was going to have to accept the consequences. A guttural groan escaped his lips when she clung to him while at the same time nibbling and kissing his neck.

When Chance laid Amanda on the bed, he was shocked at her forwardness when she began unbuttoning his pants. By God, she wasn't acting!

By the time they lay naked beside each other, they were too sexually aroused for foreplay.

"Yes, yes, yes," Amanda uttered when he entered her. "Oh my sweet Chance, you make me feel so wonderful." She arched her back so that he could have access to her breasts, then ran her hands through this thick blond hair as he suckled a tempting pink bud. She had waited and prayed for the moment she would once again feel him in her arms, making love to her. She trailed her hand down his back, glorying in the feel of his flexed muscles and wanting to give back as much pleasure as she was receiving. But a crescendo was building, and all she could think of was her need to soar with the shooting stars. She moved her hips, encouraging him, wanting him, needing him, loving him. His hands trailed sublime fire over her body. She dug her fingers in his back, waiting, demanding. "I love you," she whispered. Her body stiffened, and she looked into his eyes as the towering sky exploded. She felt Chance shudder as he joined her in their eternal moment of bliss.

Feeling delightfully languid, and playful, as well, Amanda turned on her side so that she could look at Chance. He way lying on his back and his eyes were closed, but she knew he wasn't sleeping. "Can we do that again?"

Chance chuckled. "Not right away."

Amanda raised up on an elbow. "Why not?"

"Because, my love, it takes at least a few minutes for a man to recover. Especially with a woman like you."

"And just what kind of a woman am I?" she teased.

He opened his eyes and smiled. "A woman who has a special gift for taking what she wants and returning it twofold."

"Oh? Is that good?"

She snuggled down next to him and rested her head on his chest. When he wrapped his arm around her, she felt warm and protected. "So, how long do I have to wait?" She kissed his nipple.

He rolled her on top of him. "Not long. Not long at all."

"You mean..."

"I do indeed."

She moved her hips, and her smile broadened. "I see what you mean."

When their desire was sated, and Amanda was sure she wouldn't be able to move for a month, Chance kissed away the damp tendrils of hair clinging to her face. "You're beautiful," he uttered softly.

"So are you."

"Where are your parents, Amanda? Surely you have family somewhere."

"My mother went back to her family, and my father is probably still in Columbia."

"Do you plan on joining either one of them when you leave here?"

"Absolutely not."

Chance moved his thumb across her lips. "Why is that?"

Amanda told Chance about her life, and how she and Polly had ended up in Springtown. By nightfall, they were lost in a deep, satisfying sleep.

Polly ate little supper. She had been too busy feeling sorry for herself to think about food. But by the time she was cleaning the dishes, she'd come to accept the inevitable. She'd been in the business of pleasure too long not to look at things as they really were. Chance loved Amanda. She'd seen it in his eyes. And Amanda was of the same mind, or she wouldn't have been jealous at finding the two of them together. She sighed. If Amanda was the one he wanted, then she wasn't going to try to interfere again. Besides, though she and Amanda had fought on more than one occasion, she had a deep fondness for her friend.

A loud and unexpected clap of thunder overhead made Polly jump straight into the air. Not more than thirty minutes before, she'd been outside, and there hadn't been a cloud in sight, only a crescent moon and lots of stars.

A strong wind began whistling through the town. What's going on? she wondered as she looked up at the ceiling. The wind and thunder became so loud that she clasped her hands over her ears. She could even feel the floor shaking. Terrified, she climbed under the kitchen table. Convinced the house was going to collapse on top of her, she began weeping and mumbling long-forgotten prayers.

Amanda was also shaking, even though Chance continued to hold her tight in his arms. "What's happening?" she yelled over the loud noise.

"I don't know," Chance replied worriedly. Even his nerves were on edge. "I've never heard or seen anything like it. If we were in Texas, I'd swear it was a tornado!"

"Polly!" Amanda tried pulling away from Chance's arms. "I have to get to Polly! She must be terrified!"

"No, Amanda, it's too dangerous. We have to ride this out." Amanda screamed in terror when something banged against the side of the house. He clutched her to him. "It's going to be all right, Amanda," he said, trying to reassure her.

"Jack!" she shouted frantically. "Polly was right! Jack is doing this because he knows I'm with you! Let me go!" Losing all control, she began to hit, claw and bite. "Polly!" she kept saying, over and over.

Knowing that Amanda was determined to go out into the storm, Chance was left with little choice. He curled a fist and popped her on the jaw, knocking her out cold. He groaned. The blow had probably hurt him more than it had her. Then, as quickly as it had started, the storm stopped. Again there was that deadly silence.

After making sure that Amanda was all right, Chance scrambled off the bed and pulled his pants on. Without bothering to put on his boots, he ran out of the house, and he continued running until he reached Polly's place. The front door was hanging from one hinge. "Polly?" he called as he entered. Because of the dark, he had to rely on memory to find the bedroom. But he kept bumping into things, which told him everything inside had probably been toppled. "Polly!"

"Chance?"

Relief washed over him. She was alive, though the voice was faint. He didn't know where she was calling from. "Where are you, honey?" he asked, deliberately keeping his voice calm.

"Under the kitchen table."

He could hear the terror in her voice. "Are you all right?"

"I think so."

Chance began feeling his way. "I'll be there in a minute." When he reached the kitchen, he hit something with his shin and muttered a low curse. He shoved what felt like a chair aside, then felt a pair of arms clutch his leg. Reaching down, he pulled the soft body into his arms. Polly was shaking so badly that her teeth were chattering. She kept whimpering words he couldn't understand. "It's over, Polly. You're going to be all right. I'm taking you back to my house."

When they got to the house, the lanterns had already been lit. Chance placed Polly on her feet just as Amanda hurried out of the bedroom. The women ran into each other's arms, crying and talking at the same time. Chance noted that Amanda had calmed down and had taken the time to put her jeans and shirt on. He'd become used to seeing her in men's clothing, and he rather liked it. Convinced there was nothing wrong with either woman, he picked up a lantern and headed for the kitchen to make coffee. They could all use it. Whatever had happened, it didn't make sense. How could there be such loud claps of thunder and yet no lightning?

"Amanda," Polly whimpered, "Jack is doing this. He's angry. I know he's angry. He's gonna kill us all."

Amanda was thinking the same thing. She couldn't prevent a shudder. She wanted to tell Polly to leave and take Chance with her, but she didn't dare say the words out loud. And how was she going to convince Chance of the danger they all seemed to be facing? Damn him, he didn't even believe there was a ghost! There was only one way Amanda could think of to relieve Polly's fear. "Polly, you have to listen to me. There is no Jack Quigley."

"I don't believe you!"

"It's the truth. I made it all up. You have nothing to fear."

Polly pulled away from Amanda and stared at her in disbelief. "Why?"

Standing in the kitchen doorway, Chance also waited to hear Amanda's explanation.

Amanda turned her back to Polly. Her nerves were shattered, and it was hard to think. Then she remembered what Gus and his boys had said. She turned around again and leaned against the wall. "I'd heard about this place when I lived in Columbia. When I saw the name Springtown, I remembered the tale about a ghost and hidden gold. Just like you, I wanted that gold. But I was afraid you'd leave me all alone after Chance joined us, so I made up Jack Quigley." She rubbed her chin, wondering why it was so sore.

"What I did was wrong. Furthermore, I'm not sure there really is any gold. I think we all got caught up in something that wasn't real. We let our greed manipulate us. I wouldn't blame you if you and Chance left Springtown."

Polly jutted her chin out. "Are you trying to get rid of me?"

"I'm trying to make you understand. You were right all along. There's nothing here. You've wanted to leave this place from the first day. I'm simply saying I don't blame you."

"And if I go, will you leave, too?"

"No. As I've told you, I like it here."

"No, you want the gold all to yourself!"

"Damn it, Polly, why is it that every time I say one thing you say the other? If you want to stay, that's fine!" Amanda marched into the parlor and plopped down on the divan. She was scared, and worried. Someone could have been killed during the storm. If Jack Quigley had been behind it, there was even more reason for concern. But if Polly and Chance left—

"Here," Chance said. "I've heated up the coffee."

Amanda gladly accepted the cup he handed her.

"Polly, come in here and sit down," Chance ordered.

Polly dutifully entered and took her place on the armchair across from Amanda, refusing even to look at the other woman. Chance left the room, returning a moment later with two more cups. He handed Polly one of them.

"Ladies," Chance said as he set his cup on the fireplace mantel, "I think all of us have made a big mistake."

Both women looked up at him questioningly.

"The mistake we made was lack of trust." He crossed his arms over his naked chest. "Hear me out before either of you say anything. I can understand why you didn't trust me when I came here. But if I meant you any harm, I could have done something long before now. And, yes, to begin with, I wanted the gold all to myself. I no longer feel that way. If we find it, there's no reason why we can't split it three ways." He picked up his cup and took a drink of the strong brew. "I don't know if there's any gold, either. But I'd like to give it a few more weeks of looking. I do know one thing. Assuming there is gold, we're not going to find it unless we work together. Are you ladies willing to do that?"

"How many weeks?" Amanda asked.

"Three. After all the looking we've already done, if we don't come up with something by then, we're never going to find it."

"But if I go searching, I'll get poison oak again." Unthinkingly, Polly scratched the back of her hand.

"Not if you search the houses." Chance finished off his coffee. "Just make sure you don't come in contact with any more bushes."

"What about Amanda? After all the lying she's done, how do we know we can trust her? She might find the gold and not tell us."

Amanda rested her head against the back of the divan and closed her eyes. "I don't believe you, Polly. From the beginning, I was the one who talked about us sharing everything. We just had a terrifying night, yet you're sitting there making accusations. I didn't have to tell you about the gold. I think Chance has the right idea about working together. Maybe we can draw some sort of a map and point out where we've already looked. That way, we can start narrowing down the area. Besides, the gold isn't in town. It's somewhere the sun shines on it sometime during the day."

"How do you know that?" Chance asked.

Amanda's eyes snapped open. How could she have been so stupid? She glanced at Polly. "Well, I . . ."

Polly jumped out of her chair. "I knew it! You weren't lying about you seein' a ghost! What else has Jack Quigley told you?"

Chance spoke up. "Polly, you can't really believe that. We're all worn out. Look, it's starting to get light outside. I suggest we all get some sleep. Then we'll try discussing this later on in the day."

"I'm going to my house," Amanda said as she got to her feet.

Chance went to her and drew her into his arms. "You're dead tired. Why don't you just stay here?"

"No!" Amanda blurted out. "I can't do that." She jerked away from him. If Jack was behind this, she didn't dare remain with Chance.

"What the hell is going on?" Chance demanded. "A while ago you were more than content to lie in my arms, and now you're acting like you want nothing to do with me!"

"I'm only willing to help find the gold and share it." Amanda had to fight back tears. She wanted to stay with him forever. But she couldn't. Not until she talked to Jack. She took several deep breaths to calm herself. "You're right, Chance. I think we all need to get some sleep." She rushed out of the house. There was no telling what else Jack might do. No matter how tired she was, she had to find out if Jack had caused the storm.

Furious, Chance continued to stare at the doorway Amanda had passed through.

"Chance, I'd like to sleep here," Polly stated. "I'm still scared half out of my wits. Don't look at me like that. I don't mean sleep with you. You'll be pleased to know I've given up the battle." She walked over to the sideboard and removed the vial from behind the whiskey bottle and slipped it in her pocket.

"What's that?" he snapped at her.

"It was my gift to you."

"I don't understand."

Polly shrugged her shoulders. "It doesn't really matter. Chance, don't be angry with Amanda."

Chance grunted.

"What do you say we have a good stiff drink?"

Chance nodded.

Polly found two glasses up on the sideboard and un-corked a bottle of whiskey. "From the time I was a child, I was warned about ghosts. There's few things that scare the hell out of me, but ghosts is one of them."

"Don't start that again. It's just superstition, Polly."

"I think you should listen to what I have to say, for both our sakes." Polly walked over and handed him a glass of whiskey. "Maybe you're right about ghosts, and maybe you're not. I'm sure not all the tales I was told were true. I might not be as smart as Amanda, but I'm not dumb."

Chance furrowed his brow. "What are you getting at?"

Polly sat down in the velvet armchair.

"Did Amanda tell you how we ended up here?"

"Yes, but I still don't understand what all that has to do with ghosts."

Polly took a swig of liquor. "The night those men rode through town, I was wakened by Amanda's screams. She was scared out of her wits and wanted to get out of Springtown immediately. That's why we tried to steal them crooks' horses."

"That was before either of you knew I was around."

"Yes. But Amanda said she made up the story after you arrived. Now, I'm not gonna pretend to be brave, 'cause it would be an out-and-out lie. I can't even begin to tell you how scared I am."

Chance downed his drink. "Polly, I understand what you're saying, but even so, I just can't bring myself to believe there is a ghost haunting this place. And what would be the purpose of it?"

"Jack Quigley—that's the ghost—is in love with Amanda. Jealousy can be mighty potent."

"Hell! Do you expect me to believe that?"

"Well, how about this? We knew nothin' about the gold before comin' here. Jack told Amanda about it."
Polly suddenly shivered. "Do you feel a draft?"

"Yes. It's probably coming in through the window."
Chance stood and poured himself another drink. "If I heard the tale in Murphys, I see no reason why Amanda couldn't have heard the same thing in Columbia."

"I reckon I'm not goin' to convince you of anything! Would you just do me one favor?"

"What's that?"

"Either get us out of here, or—"

"I'm not going to be run off, Polly. You can leave if you want, but I'm staying until I get some answers or the three weeks are up, whichever comes first."

Amanda was appalled at the damage the storm had done. Many store windows were broken, doors were standing open, and some roofs were caved in. She hurried on, eager to find out if the lovely big house had been damaged. The sun was already coming up. Feeling the warmth and seeing the clear sky, it was hard to believe a storm could even have taken place. At least it hadn't rained and left the road all muddy. When she'd left Chance's house, she had been convinced that Jack was behind all the hell-raising. But in the light of day, it just didn't seem possible.

Not until the house came into view was Amanda able to relax. There appeared to be no damage to the outside. When she reached the front door, it was standing open. As she entered the house, she knew immediately that Jack wasn't in the foyer. She couldn't feel his presence. "Jack!" she hollered. "I want to talk to you!"

Amanda began going through all the rooms, but Jack was nowhere to be found. She stopped at the last room she entered. She'd never spent time in this room before. It was all the way back at the end of the hall, and out of the way. It was a lovely room, decorated in white and varying shades of blue. Even the wallpaper had tiny blue flowers on a white background. The decor and the perfume bottles and other toilette items on the dressing table made it clear the room had belonged to a woman. And, although she'd never noticed it before, the room felt both warm and safe. She looked at the bed. It was a high four-poster with carved corners. It looked so tempting. She climbed onto the soft feather mattress. She'd wait here for Jack. Moments later, she was asleep.

Chance lay on his bed, eyes wide open. He could hear Polly snoring in the other bedroom. Normally, that would have made him smile, but he was in no mood for humor. He almost wanted to believe there was some ghost drifting around. At least it would explain what the hell was going on. But he didn't believe in ghosts. In all his years, he'd never seen one, and he'd finally made Polly admit she hadn't, either. Then there was Amanda. Even now he missed having her beside him. And Polly's insistence that there really was a ghost named Jack Quigley bothered him. There was no doubt in his mind that Polly thought he was real, and so did Amanda. When the storm hit, Amanda had been scared out of her wits, and had accused Jack of being the cause.

Chance went to the parlor. After pouring a drink and lighting a cigar, he settled in his favorite chair. Now that he could no longer deny his love for Amanda, the situation was even more difficult. He felt a commitment to her. But was it a fool's commitment? If Amanda thought she was seeing some damn ghost, was it going to haunt her the rest of her life? And where did that leave him? Last night he'd thought a strong bond had developed between them. This morning she'd turned cold again.

His hand touched Emily's diary and he pulled it out. He hadn't mentioned the diaries to Amanda or Polly, because he hadn't wanted them getting excited over nothing. When he was through, he'd explain where the tale of hidden gold had come from.

Chance opened the diary to where he'd left off. As with the second book, he had turned to the last page and quickly perused it. There was nothing of importance there. Emily was telling about hiding in an armoire, the way she had as a child. However, Chance still wanted to read it. In the second book he'd learned about her father's hidden gold. Maybe this one would reveal something else of importance.

So far he'd learned that Susan, the girl who'd gotten married at the end of the last diary, was now pregnant. Emily thought Susan's secret love affair with Joseph was exciting. However, like the rest of the town, Emily's family was appalled when Susan's stomach began getting noticeably larger. Chance chuckled. Naughty Susan had only been married a week, and now the whole town knew of her promiscuous ways.

Chapter Thirteen

It was a little past noon when Amanda awoke, feeling more rested than she had in months. Just thinking about her wonderful dream brought forth a smile. She and Chance had been laughing as they ran across a field of wild orange poppies. Then he'd pulled her into his arms, and they'd made love. Such sweet, wonderful love that just thinking about it was kindling her desire. She wanted the dream to linger, but reality surfaced. Would they ever share the freedom and happiness that she'd felt in her dream? Chance had never said anything about love, but their time together last night had been magical and full of warmth, and she was sure he loved her.

She raised her arms and stretched, then glanced around the room until her gaze settled on the pine armoire. It was a large, ornately carved affair, and it probably held a lot of clothes. The thought of putting on a dress suddenly appealed to her. She hadn't even bothered to change out of her dirty jeans before falling asleep.

She slid off the bed and went to the armoire. It was locked, and the heavy door refused to give. Amanda stood staring at it for a moment. What difference did it make? There were clothes in the other bedroom, the one she'd been sleeping in.

Amanda descended the wide staircase, trailing her hand along the smooth mahogany banister. She took the last step, then turned toward the back of the house, where the kitchen was located. The moment she entered, she inhaled the smell of the herbs that she'd strung up to dry a week ago. She thought how wonderful it would have been to have this kitchen in Columbia. It was large, with plenty of room to move about. Pots and pans of every description rested on hooks, there was a fine coffee grinder, indeed everything a person could possibly need to prepare food. There was even a water pump! The stove looked as if it had never been used, and the big, round oak table and chairs allowed plenty of room to eat in the kitchen. But what really tickled her fancy was the series of bells hanging near the ceiling. It had taken some time for her to figure out what they were for. Each bell had a cord running to a certain room. Also, each had a different sound, so that when one was rung, the servants would know which room to go to. A truly wonderful innovation!

After a quick meal, Amanda gathered what was needed to clean the blue and white bedroom that she had decided to consider her own. The moment she walked in, her lips spread into a smile. Would it be possible to bring Chance up here?

As she cleaned, Amanda sang old miners' songs and contemplated what life with Chance would be like. Being in his arms was like being in heaven. But the feel of his hands as he brought her body to life... She paused in her dusting. Maybe that was something she *shouldn't* think about.

When the room was spic-and-span, Amanda stood by the bed and observed her handiwork, wondering why she had never explored this room more thoroughly. Tomorrow she'd take the feather mattress outside to air and go through the sea chest, the armoire... Her curiosity getting the better of her, she went over and tried once again to open the armoire. But the door held firm. Tomorrow she'd see if there was some way to pry it open. It was already late afternoon, and she needed to change out of her jeans and shirt and hurry over to Chance's house so that they could plan how to search for the gold.

Amanda was humming as she walked out the front door. She crossed the porch, and was about to go down the stairs when she suddenly jerked her foot back up. She clasped her hand over her mouth and stared at the dead dog lying on the step. There was a cord around its neck, and its body was thickly matted with drying blood. Amanda recognized the spotted animal immediately. It was the same one that had run toward them, barking, the day she and Polly arrived at Springtown. Because she hadn't seen him again, she'd assumed he was a wild cur. Tasting the bile rising in her throat, Amanda looked away.

Hiking her skirt up, she moved to the far side of the steps, then jumped. The moment her feet touched the ground, she took off running, as fast as her legs could carry her, and didn't stop until she entered the open door of Chance's house. Seeing no one, she ran into each room, only to find them empty. She stood in the hallway, catching her breath, telling herself she was overreacting. It didn't help. Chance had to remove the dog's carcass. She certainly couldn't do it! "Chance!" she yelled.

Amanda was about to go searching for him when she heard a woman's voice. Looking out the front door, she saw Polly and Chance coming toward the house. She rushed forward to meet them. "Do you have any idea what is on my porch step?" she asked as she stopped in front of them.

Chance shook his head. "Not the foggiest."

"A dead dog!" Seeing no reaction on either Polly's or Chance's face, she reiterated, "A dead dog! Didn't you hear what I said?"

"How could we help but hear?" Chance replied.

"Well, aren't you going to do something about it?"

Chance placed an arm around Polly's shoulders. When he saw Amanda's nostrils flare, he tightened his grip. Had he actually managed to make Amanda jealous? "What would you like me to do?"

In the throes of panic, Amanda hadn't noticed how cozy Chance and Polly were acting. But she was noticing it now. How dare he have his arm around Polly! And they were even smiling at each other! After her wonderful dream of love, and then finding a dead dog on her step, this was too much. "Bury it!"

"Very well," he drawled. "Let's go take a look." Chance was sure this was either another one of Amanda's made-up stories or a method of getting him away from Polly.

"Aren't you going to bring a shovel or something?"

"*If* there is a dead dog there, I'll get what's needed from your house."

Amanda marched forward. "What's wrong?" she said sarcastically when Chance caught up with her. "Isn't one woman enough for you?"

"I got the distinct impression this morning that you wanted nothing more to do with me."

"It certainly didn't take you long to latch on to someone else!"

"Well, come here and I'll give you a hug, too."

"That won't be necessary," Amanda snapped at him.

"I like your dress."

"I didn't think you noticed."

"Believe me, I noticed."

To Amanda's sadness and relief, the dog was exactly where she'd last seen him. Not about to go near it again, she watched Chance examine the carcass.

"Looks like someone tied the dog up and beat the hell out of him. Somehow he managed to get loose and make it to here." He pointed to the ground. "You can see where he dragged himself to the steps. I don't know how he—" Chance jerked his head around and looked down at the dog again. "That's Emily's dog!"

"Emily? Who is Emily? Are you going to tell me you knew the woman who lived here?" Amanda challenged.

Chance had to do some fast thinking. He didn't want to tell Amanda the whole truth about the diaries. "I went through this house while you were in Angels Camp and found some papers. They looked like part of a diary, written by a girl named Emily. She told about having a spotted dog about a year old. She adored him."

Amanda couldn't understand why Chance sounded so forlorn. He talked as if he had actually known the girl. "Will you bury it?" she asked quietly.

Chance looked toward the big oak tree. That was where Emily had played with the dog when he was a puppy. "I'll bury him. Right under that tree. Go see if you can find me a shovel while I carry the dog over there."

Amanda was stunned by how tenderly Chance lifted the dog in his arms. It made her love him all the more. She went around the house to fetch a shovel from the shed.

When the dog was buried, Chance dropped the shovel and walked away without saying a word. Realizing that the dog was Emily's had affected him deeply. In reading all of Emily's little secrets, sorrows and pains, he'd grown attached to her.

Chance could feel Amanda walking beside him, and was grateful for her silence. Emily's gentle spirit had reached out through time and touched him. Her gentleness had made him look at things honestly and put them in their proper perspective. There were the Emilys of this world, and there were the Patricias. Maybe that was why he was willing to let Amanda into his heart. Probably not a wise move, but certainly a necessary one. It was time to put the past behind him and get on with the future. "How would you like to go for a swim?"

The out-of-the-blue question took Amanda by surprise. "But Polly's waiting for us."

Chance took her small hand in his. "I think she'll understand."

Amanda knew she should refuse, but she wanted to be alone with him more than anything. "I'd like—" That sudden tingling feeling halted her words. Jack was nearby. She still didn't know if he was dangerous, but she couldn't afford to take any chances. She had to think of something that would not only pacify Jack, but Chance, as well. "I think we should join Polly. We've agreed on three weeks, and that doesn't give us much time to search for the gold."

Chance chuckled. "You're a determined minx, and you're probably right. However, it's getting too late to do anything today. I say we go for a swim."

"Let's go to the house and chart a plan so that, come morning, we can get to work."

"We can plan tonight."

"No."

"Yes."

Amanda jerked her hand form his and stopped. Though she no longer felt Jack's presence, she had an overpowering premonition of doom. "Chance, something terrible is going to happen," she whispered.

"Are you going to start that again?"

"Why won't you listen to me?"

Chance glanced around at the leafy cottonwood trees surrounding them. "I'll listen to you, but not until we have that swim."

"You have a one-track mind."

"Indeed I do." He grabbed her around the waist, then swung her up in his arms.

Amanda tried struggling, but her efforts were futile. "You put me down, Chance Doyer!"

"Be a good girl, Amanda," Chance teased as he headed down a narrow path.

"What will it take to make you listen to me? You're in danger, damn it!"

"And you're in danger if you don't stop struggling. Have you thought about taking off some weight?"

Amanda relaxed her body with a sigh. She was getting nowhere.

When Chance reached the sandy shore of the lake, his steps didn't falter. He walked straight into the water.

As Amanda felt the water rising up her legs, she started laughing, even though he was ruining her dress. "You're impossible," she stated, her good humor returning.

Chance let her down, but held on so that her face was even with his. "You've been so serious—" he kissed her soft, full lips "—that I was beginning to wonder if you had forgotten how to laugh."

"Did you really mean it when you said I should lose some weight?"

Chance threw his head back and let out a peal of laughter.

"What's so funny?"

"You," he replied, a wide grin spread across his face. "Now, how about that swim?"

"Swim? But I thought—"

"I know what you thought, but it's not going to happen."

"What do you mean, it's not going to happen?" she asked, her voice becoming husky with desire.

"I mean we're going to take a swim." Chance lowered her to her feet. The water came to her waist, and the skirt of the dress floated on top of the water. "I've ruined your dress," he said with a broad smile.

"And you've ruined your boots."

"Damn!" he exclaimed. "I didn't think about that. It's a good thing I have another pair." He reached down and pulled one off, then tossed it to the bank. A moment later, the other one went sailing through the air. His pants and shirt followed. "Turn around and I'll help you off with your dress. All that wet material will bog you down."

"If I had known you were going to dump me in the lake," Amanda teased as she struggled out of her dress, "I would have worn my jeans and shirt. They could use a good washing."

For the next hour, they laughed and frolicked in the water, splashing and dunking each other. By the time they returned to the shore, Amanda was exhausted, but it was a pleasant exhaustion. She couldn't remember ever having so much fun.

Chance sat on the ground and watched Amanda wring the water out of her long hair. Her wet pantalettes and chemise clung to her body, offering a most tempting sight. However, this time he wasn't going to submit to his desire. "Amanda, we need to get some things straightened out between us."

Amanda smiled. "Good. It's about time you told me something about yourself. You already know about my past." She began working her hair into a long braid. "Or is there some deep secret you don't want me to know? I was convinced you were an outlaw on the run. I was even going to turn you over to the law when we arrived at Angels Camp."

"Why didn't you?"

Amanda's fingers paused for a moment. "It didn't seem fair."

"Well, to set your mind at ease, I'm not a wanted man. I want you to tell me about your ghost."

Amanda swung the braid over her shoulder and stared out at the smooth, shimmering water. Soon it would be sunset.

"Why is it that the minute your ghost is mentioned you become solemn?"

"I told you, I made the whole thing up."

"You can say what you like, but you believe there's a ghost by the name of Jack Quigley."

"What's the use of talking about it? You don't believe me."

"How do I know what to believe? I've heard bits and pieces from Polly, and nothing from you. Polly told me he first appeared the night you stole Gus's horses."

Amanda wrapped her arms around her knees, then rested her chin on them. "No, the first time he only spoke to me. He didn't appear until later. He was such a gentleman. He spoke sweet words and offered compliments. I was flattered. Then, when we came back from Angels Camp, he changed. He was furious that I'd left. He's the one that killed that man in the hotel."

"How do you know?" Chance asked softly.

"I saw him do it. Chance, he scares me. He tells me I'm his love, and that he wants me to stay here forever with him. I'm afraid of what he'll do to keep me here. And then there're the nightmares. The terrible nightmares."

Chance wanted to pull Amanda into his arms and comfort her, but she was talking, and he didn't dare break the spell. "What are the dreams about?"

"At first they were about people screaming and running as they were being shot down in cold blood. Then they were about a hanging. The people were cheering, and there was a big bonfire. The man that had been hung was Jack Quigley, and I slowly came to realize it was all taking place here in Springtown."

Her chin was trembling, but Chance still held off taking her in his arms. "Amanda, is it possible that you've made this all up in your head? Neither Polly nor I have seen him. Maybe you needed to feel someone cared for you. Or it could be caused by the strangeness of the town. I've found it hard to believe that yellow fever made so many people up and leave without their possessions. Maybe you're having the same feelings."

"He wasn't around when I was in Angels Camp. I'm not losing my mind, if that's what you think. I knew you wouldn't believe me." Amanda reached for her dress.

"Very well, let's approach it from a different direction. Let's say you're right."

Amanda looked at him with distrust. "Yes, let's say that."

"We'll go a step further. Let's say it's just like your dream. He was hung in Springtown, and that's why he haunts the town. From what you've told me, he's also clever. If that's so, why can't he be using your fears to manipulate you? He must know you're frightened."

"I hadn't thought of that."

"You said he didn't appear when you were in Angels Camp. Why don't we just pack up and leave? Then you'll be rid of him once and for all."

"You'd be willing to give up the gold?" Amanda said in awe.

"Yep." He smiled at her. "There probably isn't any gold, anyway, so remaining wouldn't serve any purpose."

Amanda smoothed back her wet hair. "But if there is, we could all be wealthy." She turned and looked at him. "Chance, when those men had me in the hotel, they said they learned about the gold in Columbia. That's why they came back. There has to be some truth to the story."

"So what do you want to do?"

"I think we should remain for three weeks, as you suggested. And leave after that."

"What do you plan on doing after we leave?"

Her eyes became soft. "I guess I'll tag along with you, if you'll let me."

"And why would you want to do that?"

Amanda's heart sank. He didn't want her. "You're right. Maybe I'll go to San Francisco, or some place like that."

"If we don't find any gold, you know we won't have a cent to our names."

Amanda thought about the money she had stashed away, and the large nugget and the ring she kept in her saddlebag. "I think we could make do."

"Why did you want to get me away from Springtown, Amanda?"

Amanda bowed her head. "Because of the gold. But then we made love—"

"We left after we made love."

"Yes, but that was before I realized I was..." She couldn't say the words. Instead, she laughed. "Did you really only bring me here to swim and talk?"

He chuckled. "What other reason could I possibly have?"

"I had something else on my mind."

"Oh? Like what?"

"I'll show you." She scooted over to him and kissed him hungrily. She heard his guttural groan of pleasure, and then his arms wrapped around her and he was returning her kisses.

Polly was cooking supper when Amanda and Chance returned.

"I was beginnin' to think you two were never comin' back," she scolded lightly.

Amanda suddenly wondered if she and Polly had changed places. Polly looked lovely and proper in her high-necked, long-sleeved blue dress. Her red hair had been smoothed back into a chignon, and she appeared to be every bit the maiden. Amanda felt self-conscious. Her dress was wet, her hair a tangled mess, and she was the one who had been enjoying a man's pleasure. "I have to go change my clothes," she said as she headed toward the door. "I'll be back for supper."

Once she was outside and headed toward her own house, Amanda started laughing. She remembered how she'd looked down her nose at Polly when they'd first met. She had been so self-righteous that she had found it impossible to believe that Polly could have any redeeming qualities.

Not until she reached the trees did Amanda give some serious thought to what Chance had said. Was he right? Was Jack Quigley a figment of her imagination? Could she have made the whole thing up? Was it possible she had killed the man in the hotel herself?

As she left the trees, Amanda stood and stared ahead at the house. It looked cold and forbidding, and she was tempted to go back to Chance's place. Instead, she continued on. She had to deal with Jack Quigley, whether he was real or not.

When she opened the door, she felt the cool air and the familiar tingling sensation on her skin. She kept telling herself this wasn't real, that if she concentrated hard enough he'd be gone from her life. She headed toward the staircase and looked up. Jack was sitting on the landing, his once-handsome face twisted with anger. She closed her eyes, willing him to disappear. But when she opened them again, he was still there. Maybe she wasn't losing her mind. What Chance had said about Jack using her fear to manipulate her suddenly made sense. She was going to have to stop running scared and start using her head. As she waited for him to speak, she kept telling herself not to be frightened.

"Are you going to offer any excuses?"

"For what?"

Jack sneered. "I believe it's called unfaithfulness."

"Can you satisfy me?"

"I can give you my love!"

"When you were alive, didn't you have your women?"

"That's different. I was a man."

"And I'm a woman. I have every right to enjoy life and the pleasures it holds. Your life was cut short, and you want to do the same thing to me. Why don't you let me see your neck? Is it because you don't want me to see where you were hanged?"

Jack stood and began slowly descending the stair. "How did you know?"

"I saw it in my dreams. Jack," she said more tenderly, "if you were unjustly hanged, don't take you hatred out on others."

"I don't give a damn about others. Why are your clothes damp?"

"That's none of your business."

"You were with Chance again, weren't you? And you went swimming. With or without your clothes?"

Amanda backed away. Don't let him scare you! She stood her ground. "If I had been swimming naked, my clothes wouldn't be wet."

"You're trying to defy me, aren't you? Apparently you didn't learn your lesson."

"What lesson?" Amanda had to turn, because he walked right through her.

"That dust devil. I was furious that you'd left, so I sought a way to teach you not to try it again."

Amanda clutched the end of the railing. "You swore you'd never let anything harm me, yet you're telling me you deliberately slashed my head open?"

"That's right. A man has to keep his woman in her place."

"I am not your woman!"

"You are my woman! You will always be my woman! And no man is going to take you away from me! Do you understand that? I have been very patient until now!" He hit the heavy clothes tree in the front hall, and it crashed to the floor. "I've allowed you to have friends, and I've enjoyed watching you fight among yourselves. But now you've let them taint you. First the harlot, and now the drifter."

Amanda had covered her mouth and was staring at the fallen clothes tree. She couldn't stop her body from shaking. She couldn't bring herself to ask if he was responsible for the poor dog. "What about our horses?"

"I got rid of them. I assure you, so far I've been gentle." He smiled. "If you have anything more to do with Chance, I'll kill him. And if you try leaving, I'll kill all of you. Then I'll have you for eternity."

A strange coldness settled over Amanda. The only way Jack could hurt her was through Chance and Polly. "Is there really hidden gold, Jack?"

"Oh, yes. But you won't find it."

"You're not being fair."

"Fair? Who said I had to be fair? You just remember that their lives are in your hands. You've seen me kill once. You know I can do it again." His high-pitched laughter continued long after the vision of his body disappeared.

Amanda left the house, fear clutching at every fiber of her being. There was no way she could warn Chance and Polly of the danger they were in. Chance would never believe her, and Polly wouldn't leave on her own. She could try to talk them into leaving, but if they didn't, the next three weeks were going to be a living hell. The only way she could protect them was to have nothing to do with Chance. If she didn't, neither of them would ever leave town alive.

"Hello, sweetheart," Chance said when Amanda returned. "I thought you were going to change your clothes?"

Amanda had forgotten all about changing her clothes. "Oh... Well, I... The material is almost dry, and by the time I arrived at the house it seemed ridiculous to put something else on."

"You've only been gone a short time, and I was already missing you."

Amanda's heart swelled. It seemed as though she'd waited a lifetime to hear him say those words. She wanted to respond, but Jack had left her with no alternative. Whatever Chance was feeling toward her, she had to put a halt to it. "You shouldn't say such things around Polly," she bit out as she began helping Polly put the supper on the table.

Chance raised an eyebrow. What in hell's name had made Amanda turn so cold this time?

After the supper dishes were cleared away, the threesome sat at the table and mapped out the area. Each marked where he or she had already searched. It was decided to start at the northeast corner, outside of town.

Amanda rose and stretched. "I'm really tired, and since we'll be starting early in the morning, I'd best get some sleep."

Polly giggled. "I get the hint. I'll go to my bedroom. Besides, I'm tired, too."

"That won't be necessary," Amanda coldly stated. She still didn't like the idea of Polly and Chance living in the same house, but she couldn't afford to be jealous. Not now. "I'm quite capable of going home by myself."

"Why aren't you stayin' here with Chance?" Polly questioned.

Amanda evaded the question, saying only, "I'll see you both in the morning."

Chance slid his chair back and stood, his lips spread into a devilish grin. "I think Amanda is a little embarrassed, Polly."

"Why?"

"Probably because you're here."

Amanda jumped at the excuse Chance had given her. "It's true, I am embarrassed. I should never have done such a thing. But I did, so I'd like to leave it at that. It won't happen again."

"I'll be back shortly, Polly. I'm going to take Amanda to her house."

"I said I wanted to go alone!" She walked into the hallway and heard Chance's heavy boots behind her. Please, Lord, she prayed, don't let him follow me. I don't think I can stand to have another confrontation tonight.

When she walked out of the house, Amanda knew her prayers were not going to be answered. Chance was right behind her. "Just a minute!"

Amanda steeled herself and waited for him to catch up. Her heart was pounding. She had to bite the inside of her cheek to keep from reacting when he took hold of her arm. She jerked it away.

"What the hell is going on? When you left here to change your clothes, you couldn't stop smiling. Since you've returned, you've been as cold as ice. And don't tell me it's because you're embarrassed. I won't buy that."

"I said I wanted to walk alone. It's not my problem if you can't accept that. And if you think because we shared a few hours together I'm going to fall down on my knees and kiss your boots, you are in for a rude awakening!"

"Someday," he said in a hushed voice, "if it's not too much to ask, you really must tell me what goes on in that head of yours."

Amanda knew he was angry. He had every right to be. Unable to look at him, she stared at the moonlit road and shrugged her shoulders. "Maybe I will...someday. You're not making this easy for me."

"I didn't intend to."

"Don't you go thinking you own me."

"Are you just using me to satisfy a need?" he asked menacingly.

"Does that bother you? I'm sure you've done the same with more than one woman." Amanda forced herself to look up at him and smile, hoping to get her point across so that she'd never have to go through this again. It was killing her. "If you couldn't handle it, you should never have taught me the joys of the flesh."

Chance's eyes were as cold as a tombstone. He smiled back, but there was no warmth in it. "You're absolutely right. I have, and will probably do so in the future. Let me know when you're ready for another romp. It helps break the monotony."

His words hurt Amanda's very soul. She wanted to kiss him, wanted to beg him to say he didn't mean it, but that was impossible. She tilted her chin up and smiled sweetly. "I'm glad we have an understanding. It should make things easier." Amanda knew she couldn't hold back the tears much longer. "Now, if you don't mind, I want to get some sleep. I'll see you first thing in the morning." She walked away, and this time she didn't hear him following. By the time she reached the trees, she could no longer contain the flood of tears that were already rolling down her cheeks, or the anguished sobs.

When Amanda entered the house, she ran up the stairs and down the long hallway, and discovered Jack leaning against the wall next to her bedroom.

"See?" Jack crooned. "You only have me."

Amanda reached past him and turned the door handle. As soon as she was inside, she slammed the door behind her, then ran to the bed and fell on it, facedown. Trying to rid herself of the deep hurt and anger, she pounded her fists on the down pillow until she was exhausted. Her eyes blazing with hate, she turned her head and looked toward the door. Too bad Jack hadn't followed her in. She could have given him a piece of her mind. He's probably gloating, she thought, just before the sobs and tears returned.

Chance was glad Polly had gone to bed. He could sit in his chair and allow his anger to eat at him. Well, the next time Amanda wanted to make love, she was going to be in for a big shock. Let her find her satisfaction from someone else! He rubbed the back of his neck and rolled his head.

He should just look for the gold, then get the hell out of here. The problem was, he was tempted to take Amanda with him and... And what? Marry her? Not hardly. He'd be an even bigger fool than he was now. His gaze fell on the open diary lying on the mantel. Fortunately, Amanda hadn't seen it, and he'd discovered that Polly didn't know how to read. Maybe it would take his mind off his troubles. He went over and picked it up.

He'd left off where Emily had received a proposal of marriage from her father's mine superintendent.

Mother and Father are pleased about the proposal, but I have no feelings one way or the other. I know I will never again know the love I had for Billy.

After much thought last night, I have decided to marry Jeffery. Mother and Father will be happy to hear the news. Jeffery is a good man and will give me a good home. This is not a happy decision but a necessary one. I do not care to become an old maid and I desire children that I can raise and love.

Chapter Fourteen

After completing her toilette, Amanda hesitated before leaving the bedroom. Again she'd had a peaceful night's sleep with no nightmares. For some reason, she felt safe in this room. She knew she should hurry over to Chance's house so that they could begin their search, but she still tarried. It was quite early, and perhaps the others were still asleep.

Amanda picked up the large music box by the bed and examined it. The top was inlaid with mother-of-pearl in the design of a child holding an umbrella. The box itself was heavy and made of a dark wood that Amanda couldn't identify. Because of its size, she was surprised when she could find no way to open it. She turned it over, wound the key, then set it back on the bedside table. The tune was a lively piece that made Amanda smile. She danced a little jig over to the trunk sitting on the floor and opened the lid. She was about to pull out the beautiful green satin dress when she heard a click and the music stopped playing. At first she thought Jack had joined her, but she couldn't feel his presence.

Wanting to hear the tune once more before leaving, Amanda returned to the music box and made a discovery. A hidden drawer had popped out from the front of it.

Not believing her own eyes, she stared down at the jewelry inside. Carefully she removed the pieces, one at a time. There was a beautiful bloodred ruby pendant surrounded with diamonds; its bail was broken. There were diamond rings and bracelets of every description, but what really drew her attention was an emerald-and-diamond necklace that seemed to match her ring.

She held it up in the air and watched it glitter. When she realized the enormity of her find, paranoia immediately took over. Where could she hide it? It took a moment before deciding it was already in the safest place possible. She was about to put everything back when she saw a key in the drawer, shoved toward the back. Curious, she took it out, replaced the jewelry, then closed the drawer. Wondering what the key opened, she set it on the bedside table. Chance and Polly would be wondering what had happened to her by now.

The minute Amanda stepped out of the room, she was filled with a sense of uneasiness. As she hurried down the stairs, the uneasiness grew.

"Good morning, my love. I trust you had a good night's sleep." It was Jack.

"Yes, I did."

"You know, that bedroom is so small and far away, you should consider moving into one of the larger rooms."

Amanda ran her sweaty palms down her pant legs. "Is that a command?"

"Of course not. I was simply concerned about your comfort."

"Why do you always wear the same clothes and hat?"

"I don't exactly have a wardrobe to choose from."

"Open your shirt, Jack."

"Very well. Since we are always going to be together, I guess you should see my one flaw." He unbuttoned his shirt and held it open.

Amanda couldn't hide her horror at seeing the ugly red welt around his neck. He even tilted his chin so that she could have a better look. "I was right," she whispered. "You *were* hanged. Did you deserve it, or was it a mistake?"

"I was quite guilty," he replied. His lips twisted in an evil smile. "Maybe that's something you would be wise to remember." The smiled turned into one of amusement. "But there is nothing for you to worry about, as long as you remain faithful to me."

He came toward her, and Amanda couldn't keep a shiver from running through her body.

"Oh, my love, I've upset you," Jack said, with mock concern. He clasped the front of his coat. "Actually, I'm no longer amused with your friends. I'll be glad when they leave. Believe me, once they're gone, you'll settle down and find a happiness you would never believe possible. I may have to put you in your place occasionally, but you'll learn."

"I have to go. They're waiting for me."

"I hope you appreciate the little favor I'm granting you. I'm only letting them stay because that's what you want."

"Y-yes. I'm most grateful." She hated his grin. Most of all, she hated him for taking away her happiness. He'd done what he'd set out to do. She was terrified.

"Good. Now you go enjoy your day. Remember, I'll be keeping a close eye on you."

Resisting the urge to run, Amanda held her head high and walked away.

Once she was outside, Amanda no longer felt Jack's presence. She was angry with herself for letting him frighten her. If she stayed calm and did what he said, Chance and Polly wouldn't be harmed. And once they were gone, she didn't care what Jack did to her. But he had to have some kind of vulnerability. There had to be a way to thwart him, and it was up to her to find it.

When Amanda arrived at the house, she wasn't pleased to find out that Polly wouldn't be going with them.

"Like Chance said, I don't want to catch poison oak again," Polly said joyfully.

Amanda stood in the kitchen, holding a cup of coffee and watching Polly and Chance finish their breakfast. Had circumstances been different, she would have jumped at the opportunity to be alone with Chance. But now it only served to make her situation even more difficult. "I thought it was agreed that we could accomplish more if the three of us searched."

"But if I catch poison oak, I won't be able to help anyways," Polly insisted. "Amanda, are you sure you wouldn't like some breakfast? I swear you're gettin' thinner every day."

"No, thank you." Knowing she was fighting a losing battle, Amanda said no more. She took another sip of her coffee. If she couldn't budge Polly, maybe she could turn their thinking in a different direction. "There's something we haven't taken into consideration. What if the treasure is jewels instead of gold?"

"What made you think of that?" Polly asked.

Amanda looked at Chance. He hadn't said a word to her. "I found some more jewelry. I'm sure it's worth a fortune."

Polly jumped off her chair. "Did you bring it?"

"No, but I will. After all, we agreed to split everything three ways." She was surprised that Chance showed absolutely no interest.

"There's no doubt in my mind that at one time gold was hidden around here," Chance commented as he shoved his empty plate aside. "What I don't know is if someone else has already found it, or if the person it belonged to took it with him." He stood and looked at Amanda. "Shall we get started?" He picked up the knapsack sitting on the counter.

Amanda nodded and set her cup on the table. To place it on the counter would have put her too close to Chance, and she was already having difficulty just being in the same room with him. She had to keep her distance.

"Are you sure you wouldn't like me to get the jewelry while you're gone?" Polly inquired.

Amanda smiled. "I promise to bring it tomorrow."

When they'd left the house and were walking side by side toward the cliffs, Amanda knew she was going to have to confront Chance's silence. Though she couldn't see any future for them, she desperately wanted him at least to be her friend. "You're angry with me, aren't you?"

"To tell you the truth, at this moment I'm not sure what I feel."

"I'd like us to be friends."

"If I remember correctly, we've already tried that."

They continued on in silence. Amanda kept her eyes on the rocky cliffs ahead. Apparently Chance had a definite area in mind. There were more oak trees scattered about, and the walking wasn't difficult, until they came to a thick growth of bush that was taller than she was. Chance took the lead, and soon they were working their way through it. Amanda was sure that, because of his height, Chance could see where he was going. She couldn't. His long, sturdy legs carried him at a faster pace, and she soon lost sight of him. "Can you slow up?" she called.

"Just keep coming. About twenty more feet and you'll be out of there."

"Easy for him to say," Amanda mumbled. When she finally cleared the bushy area, she discovered they were in a small canyon surrounded by jagged rocks.

Chance set his knapsack on the ground. "We'll split up. That way, we can cut the time in half. Watch out for coyote holes." He pointed to a shaft directly ahead. "As you can see, there are mines scattered all about. Those holes are so deep we may never find you if you fall in. Men were lowered down them in buckets to work the mine. If you find one with an entrance, don't go inside. The bracing might be weak. Just try to see if they've been filled, or if they appear to have been worked. If you get thirsty, I have water in the knapsack, as well as food for later."

"Chance, can we take a moment to talk?"

Chance shoved his hat back and waited.

Amanda wondered why he hadn't shaved this morning. He looked lean and tough, and quite capable of taking care of himself. But she knew there were no defenses against Jack. "You asked earlier why I've been acting so strange. I think it's rather obvious that I'm physically attracted to you. But afterward, I get to worrying that you might want to make it something permanent." She looked down at the ground and began nudging a small rock with the toe of her boot. "Then I get angry at myself, because I'm assuming you might have feelings for me. When the three weeks are up, I want you to leave. But I'm not going with you."

"Are you planning on going to San Francisco?"

"No, I'm staying here."

"Why?"

"I like it here." She looked at the cliffs. "I like being by myself and not having any responsibilities. I'm not saying I'll remain here forever. When I feel the time is right, I'll leave."

"Why can't you look me in the eye?"

Amanda lifted her head, then immediately looked away. "I'm trying to be honest with you, but it isn't easy."

Chance knew she was lying. He could feel it in his gut. But for the life of him, he couldn't figure out why. Something was wrong. Something had been wrong for weeks, but try as he might, he couldn't put his finger on it. The only thing he kept coming up with was her ghost! And how the hell did a man fight something like that? "So what do you want from me?"

Amanda finally looked him in the eye. "I want you to tell me you're not angry with me. I meant it when I said I want us to be friends. You have no idea how important that is to me."

It was plain to see that this time she meant every word. It was as if she were pleading with him—something he had never thought he would see coming from Amanda Bradshaw. Last night, he'd decided that when he left she was going with him. Whether she liked it or not, he was taking her out of Springtown, and he wasn't going to wait any three weeks. He smiled warmly, deliberately misleading her. "You're right. I have become a bit enamored with you, but you have to remember, it's been a while since I've been with a woman as lovely as you."

Seeing sadness and anger in her eyes, he had the answer he was seeking. She was lying about not caring for him. But, for some reason, it was important to her that he believe her. He'd done the right thing by making sure Polly didn't accompany them. And, because he didn't necessarily believe what Amanda had said about the gold not being in town, he'd told Polly to continue searching the houses, or anything else she could find around town. "I would be pleased to call you my friend, Amanda. And what the hell—if we had stayed together, we'd probably have grown tired of each other."

Though Chance's words hurt, Amanda felt great relief at knowing she had accomplished what she'd set out to do. Nothing mattered more than his safety.

Chance gave her a brotherly pat on the back. "I'm glad we had this talk. Come on, partner, let's start looking for that gold."

The first mine she came to, she stuck her head in the entrance and screamed in frustration, knowing Chance wouldn't hear, and knowing she couldn't do it to his face. The nerve of the man! So it had been a long spell since he had been with a woman. Was she supposed to feel sorry for him? But by the time she reached the next mine, she wasn't feeling sorry for anyone but herself. The third mine was a hard climb, and by the time she reached it, she'd accepted the truth. It was all for the best, whether she liked it or not. Even so, she still thought Chance was a no-account, cheating— But what difference did it make? She loved him anyway.

By noon when they met up again, they were both hot and hungry. As they rested and ate the venison and bread Chance had brought, Amanda listened to him talk about his life in Texas. He told her about the good times he and his brother Ned had had, and how they had enjoyed their women. Though he'd never spoken of his past before, Amanda wasn't sure she wanted to hear any more. "Why are you telling me all this?" she finally asked, more than a little perturbed.

"What are friends for, if they can't share?"

"Well, yes, but—"

"You told me about your past. I only thought it right to share a little of mine." He climbed to his feet, then put a hand out to help her up. "Did you see any mines of interest?"

"One." She pointed to it.

"Let's go take a look, partner."

Amanda was getting damn tired of that word.

It was already turning dark by the time Amanda and Chance returned to the house. Amanda didn't realize how hungry she was until she inhaled the wonderful aroma of food being cooked.

"Did you find anything?" Polly called.

Chance and Amanda joined her in the kitchen.

"Not a thing," Amanda replied. "But we've only just started."

By the time Amanda was on her way back to her house, she could think of nothing she'd like more than to throttle Chance. Ever since they'd had their "talk," he'd seemed to be in the best of moods. Apparently she'd lifted a heavy burden from his shoulders when she'd told him she wasn't interested in any entanglements.

Amanda didn't hesitate to enter the house, and she didn't care if Jack was there. She lit the bayberry candle by the door and went upstairs. She didn't even bother to shut the bedroom door. She could see no purpose to it. After all, if Jack wanted to make an appearance, she certainly couldn't stop him.

She set the candle on the bedside table, then quickly stripped off her dirty jeans and shirt and tossed them on the back of the rocking chair. Her undergarments followed.

After taking a sponge bath, Amanda slipped a pink nightgown over her head, fluffed the down pillows and climbed into bed. Unfortunately, she wasn't sleepy. She considered going downstairs and taking a book from the library, but she was too restless. Was Chance already in bed? If only she could join him.

In an effort to distract her thoughts, she looked up at the candlelight reflection on the ceiling and tried to make pictures out of the light and shadows. "This is ridiculous," she said, frustrated.

She rolled over, and was about to blow out the candle when she saw the key. She'd forgotten all about it. Glad to find something to do, she eagerly jumped off the bed, then lit the lantern. As soon as she picked up the key, her eyes turned toward the armoire. The key looked to be the right size. Would there be more jewels inside? She raised the skirt of her nightgown and walked across the room. She was so excited about what she might discover that her hand shook as she slipped the key into the lock. It fit.

Slowly Amanda opened the heavy door. Her gaze started at the top and worked its way down. Suddenly she threw her hands up to her chest and backed away, gasping for breath. Sitting at the bottom of the armoire was a clothed skeleton. Amanda forced her arms down to her sides and tried to slow her breathing. She continued to back away, but couldn't tear her eyes from the sight of the woman's body. Blond hair partially covered what had once been a face. The material of her dress clung to her bones, crinkled and stiff. Amanda retreated until her legs touched the bed, and then she began to scream. She was still screaming when she ran out of the house.

Chance and Polly stood by the fresh grave, while Amanda leaned over and placed roses on top. Amanda stood up, then jiggled the cross Chance had made to be sure it was solidly in the ground. "You did a good job, Chance. Maybe now she'll rest in peace." Amanda glanced around the graveyard and slowly shook her head. There weren't many graves for a town supposedly infected by yellow fever. "What happened to all the people in Springtown?" she said, to no one in particular.

Chance placed an arm around both women's shoulders and led them away. Though he'd said nothing, seeing Emily in the armoire had affected him deeply. Somehow he'd pictured her alive, with a family and children. Not starving to death. He'd seen scratch marks on the inside of the door, where she'd tried to get out. What agonies she must have suffered. But something kept niggling at the back of his mind. He knew it was time to leave Springtown, but the town seemed to have a hold on him. As crazy as it seemed, he was becoming more and more driven to find out what had happened here.

For the next week, Amanda and Chance carried on their search, but each night they returned empty-handed. Chance continued giving Amanda bits and pieces of his past and treating her as his buddy. Amanda was getting sick and tired of it. During the day, she had to fight the desire to ask him to make love to her. And every night, when she climbed into bed, her hunger was unbearable. Her body became soaked with perspiration, and her need for him rang through every limb. Only her concern for Chance's safety gave her the courage to remain silent.

Despite her chilling discovery, Amanda hadn't changed bedrooms. The room still had a soothing effect, and for some reason, Jack never entered, something he'd had no qualms about when she was anywhere else. Amanda wasn't sure what that meant, but at least she'd finally found a flaw in Jack's armor.

As hopeless as she felt, she still thought that somehow she'd find a way to leave with Polly and Chance. Or maybe she just needed that belief because she knew that, when they left, her only companion would be Jack Quigley.

Chapter Fifteen

When Amanda entered the parlor of Chance's house, she found Polly standing by the window. To Amanda's surprise, Polly, too, had on britches and a shirt.

"I'm goin' to help search," Polly said proudly before Amanda had a chance to question her attire. "You said it was easier to move about in britches. I told Chance, and he got these things from the dry goods store." She stuck her hand in the waist. "The hips fit right good, but if it weren't for the suspenders, I think they'd fall off. They sure do feel funny."

"What about poison oak?"

"Chance also got some sweet oil to put on my skin. He said he'd make sure I didn't get around any bushes."

Amanda looked toward the window. "Where is Chance?"

"He's in town. Said somethin' about checkin' somethin' out. We're supposed to meet him by the well."

"Then I guess we'd better be on our way."

Polly slapped her hands against the sides of her legs. "Amanda, I gotta admit, I sent Chance on ahead."

"Why?"

"I thought you might want someone to talk to. I don't understand what's goin' on between you and Chance.

He's been actin' like an old bear, and you got dark circles under your eyes. If you care for each other, what's the problem? Is it Jack?''

Amanda brushed a tear from her cheek. "Jack said that if I have anything more to do with Chance, or if I try to leave Springtown, he'll kill us all."

"Can he do that?" Polly murmured.

Amanda bowed her head. "I shouldn't have told you."

"Amanda, you have to tell Chance. You owe it to him. Then we need to sit down and plan what we're goin' to do. We gotta get the hell out of here, that's for sure."

"I can't leave."

"What do you plan to do? Spend the rest of your life here?"

"We can't beat Jack. He's capable of anything." Then Amanda said thoughtfully, "I had a dream last night. I can't remember it now, but I know it showed how to trick him. I just know there is a way."

Polly took hold of Amanda's hand. "We're goin' to find Chance and tell him about this. I'll bet he can figure somethin' out."

"He thinks I'm making this all up."

"Then we're just going to have to convince him. Tell me one thing before we leave. Do you love Chance?"

"With all my heart."

"Then let's start doin' something about this mess. I have to tell you, I'm still scared as all get-out."

"So am I."

When they reached the well, Chance was nowhere in sight.

"Chance said something about taking a walk," Polly commented. "Let's just wait here. I'm sure he'll be arrivin' any minute." She sat on the stone lip of the well. "I hate waitin', but I hate standin' more."

Amanda walked to the other side of the well so that she could see down the road. She was worried about Chance. All morning she'd felt a strange premonition of doom. Her concern for Chance was growing with every second.

"Oh! That breeze is cold!" Polly said.

Fear sliced though Amanda as she snapped her head around to look at her. "No!" she screamed. Jack Quigley was walking toward the redhead. When she realized that Polly was frozen to the spot, Amanda tried to run around the well to reach her friend. Before she was halfway there, she saw Jack's evil smile, and then, as if in slow motion, he lifted Polly's feet and pushed her backward into the well. Amanda heard Polly scream—or maybe it was her own screams she heard. She stumbled, and then everything went black.

"Amanda! Amanda!"

Amanda could hear her name being called, and she opened her eyes to see Chance leaning over her, patting her hands. Amanda threw her arms around his neck and broke out in sobs. "Polly... Oh, sweet, Polly."

"What about Polly?"

"Jack...Jack killed her. He threw her down the well!" Amanda jerked away. "Maybe she isn't dead! You have to climb down the well!"

"Amanda, you've been dreaming." He brushed her hair from her face.

"Dreaming?" Amanda panicked. "No! I—" She suddenly realized she still had her nightgown on. She was in her bed.

Polly rushed into the room, panting. "Is she all right?"

"She's fine. She just had a bad dream."

Though tears were still streaming down Amanda's face, she was overwhelmed with relief. But in the next instant, she became very still. "Your clothes," she whispered.

"You said britches were easier to move around in, so Chance got these for me. We waited for you to come to the house, but when you were so late, Chance insisted we check to be sure you were all right. We had just come in downstairs when we heard you screaming. Chance went up those stairs a hell of a lot faster than I did."

"Are you feeling better?" Chance asked, his eyes mirroring his concern.

"I'm fine," Amanda reassured him. "I'll get dressed." But she wasn't fine. The dream had left her badly shaken, and seeing Polly dressed in men's clothing had her even more frightened. She wanted to force Polly and Chance to understand what Jack was doing. But they'd never believe her. Maybe she was losing her mind.

"If you don't feel like it," Chance consoled, "you can go out with us tomorrow."

"I have to go with you." Amanda rubbed her throbbing head. When Chance moved aside, she slid off the bed.

"I'll wait downstairs," Polly stated as she headed for the door.

"No!" Amanda practically yelled the word. If she kept Polly near, maybe her friend would be safe. Amanda snatched her jeans and shirt off the chair and started putting them on.

Polly glanced at Chance. He appeared to be just as confused as she was.

"All right, I'm ready." Amanda went to Polly and took hold of her arm, then guided her out of the room.

Chance followed, his concern for Amanda growing by leaps and bounds. Her dream had something to do with her ghost—and Polly—but he didn't question her. He knew she wouldn't give him any answers.

After a considerable climb, the small group arrived at the first mine they'd charted. While the women waited at the entrance, Chance lit the lantern and entered. After going only a few yards, he met a wall of tailings. Entering these mines was playing hell with him. His old fear of dark, musty places was always sitting in the back of his mind. If they did find one that was worth going into, he wasn't sure he could do it. On the other hand, how could he send the women in if they didn't know what to look for? Like it or not, he knew that somewhere down the road his mettle was going to be tested. It was obvious that at one time this area had been covered with men searching for the elusive ore. There were diggings everywhere.

"Well?" Polly asked when Chance came back out.

"If there's anything in there, we'll never get to it. Let's find the next one."

And so the day went. Sometimes all three would enter a mine, but they always went only a few feet. Either weak bracing or dead ends made them turn back. Chance had come prepared. Besides the lantern, he'd placed string, nails and a hammer inside the knapsack to let them mark their passage so that they wouldn't get lost. And he kept a close eye on Amanda. No matter what they did or where they went, she stayed by Polly's side, constantly cautioning her to be careful.

While Amanda worried about Polly, Chance worried about Amanda. He'd suggested several times that they give up the search and leave Springtown, but she adamantly refused. Her stubbornness made it tempting to pick her up and carry her off. He wondered what would penetrate her stubborn hide. He wanted to reach out to her, to console her and tell her everything would be all right if she'd just let him take care of her, but he didn't know how to approach her. She remained aloof, speaking to him only when it was necessary.

That night, Amanda insisted that Polly stay at her house. When she said they were going to sleep together, Polly was truly perplexed. Considering how Amanda had moved from room to room in the hotel when they had first arrived in Springtown, Polly found it impossible to understand why she insisted they sleep together when the house had so many bedrooms to choose from.

"Amanda, how can you sleep here after finding that skeleton?" Polly asked as she climbed into bed. Although, to tell the truth, she wasn't frightened. The room was strangely comforting.

Amanda finished tying the green bow on her nightgown. "I like this room. We're both safe here."

"What do you mean by that?"

"Nothing. I'm just being silly." She sat at the small dressing table and began brushing her long black hair.

Polly sat up. "Do you see Jack anymore?"

"Every now and then." Amanda placed the brush back on the table and forced a smile. "Well, in a little over a week you'll be leaving. Because I shall miss you, I'd like it if you'd stay here with me until it's time for you to go."

"I have to admit this bed is better than the one I've been sleeping on." Polly stuck a pillow behind her back. "Amanda, do you love Chance?"

"Polly, I—" Polly had asked that same question in her dream. Amanda clutched her hands together to keep Polly from seeing them shaking. Maybe if she could change the dream, everything would turn out all right. "I don't think so. I'm very attracted to him, but I doubt that it's love."

"I thought I loved him, but he's so smitten with you, he doesn't even see me."

Amanda bit the inside of her cheek, fighting the urge to express her emotions. She shifted her eyes away from Polly and saw the music box on the bedside stand. With everything that had happened, they'd all forgotten about the jewels! "Polly, why don't you wind up that music box. It has a very delightful tune."

Polly leaned over and picked up the box. After looking at it, she discovered the winding key and turned it until it stopped.

Hearing the lively music, Amanda's depression faded. She eagerly waited to see the expression on Polly's face when the drawer opened.

Polly was moving her head to the music, and her lips were spread in a happy grin. When the drawer clicked, she glanced down, astonished at what she'd found. "The jewels!" she exclaimed, her green eyes practically popping out of her head. She dumped everything in the lap of her nightgown, then began looking at each piece. "You said there were jewels," she said in awe, "but I had no idea you were talkin' about somethin' like this!" She examined a particularly large diamond ring, then tried to slide it on her finger. It was too small. "This necklace I've been wearin' is nothing compared to what's in this drawer."

Amanda went over to the trunk and lifted the lid. "I have more." She pulled out her saddlebag and reached in the pocket.

"I found this a while ago," Amanda said, joining Polly on the bed. She held the gold nugget out, then laughed when Polly reached out tentatively. "It's not going to bite you."

Polly took the nugget and kept turning it over in her hand. "Oh, Amanda, it's so beautiful! Were there any others?"

"No."

"This has to mean there really is hidden gold!"

Amanda became thoughtful. "I don't think so. I think it was dropped. Polly, do you realize that, with the exception of the items that were in that hidden drawer, everything we've found appears to have been dropped?"

"What do you mean?"

"That necklace you wear was by a partially packed reticule, my ring was found on the road, and now this nugget."

"I never thought about it."

"Sometimes I think the answer to why the people left Springtown is right under my nose, but... Maybe I'll figure it out one of these days. Here, put all that in the saddlebag. I keep the ring in there, too. In the morning, we'll take it to Chance's house. It'll come in handy when the two of you are out of this town."

"Amanda, why don't you come with us? Chance loves you."

"Did he tell you that?"

"He doesn't have to. Just the way he looks at you tells me everything."

Hope charged through Amanda like a welcoming beacon, then quickly faded. Jack had her in a stranglehold, and unless some miracle happened, she had no future with Chance. "It's getting late, Polly, and we need to get some sleep. We're going to have another hard day of searching tomorrow."

Polly began stuffing the jewelry in the saddlebag. "Don't you care that Chance loves you?"

"I care. That's why I'm staying in Springtown."

Polly looked at Amanda, who had lain down beside her. "What's that supposed to mean?"

"It means . . . it means he's better off if I end it here."

"But—"

"Polly, I don't want to talk about it anymore. If you're through, turn off the lamp."

Polly placed the saddlebag on the floor and extinguished the light. After climbing under the covers, she turned her back to Amanda.

Amanda stared into the darkness, tears trickling from the corners of her eyes. She hadn't dared to believe Chance loved her. Yet it seemed so obvious now. Even in her sadness, it warmed her heart. It gave her the courage to make sure he left. If she could just hold out a little longer from begging him to take her in his arms, he'd be safe.

To Polly's aggravation, for the following two days, Amanda was constantly by her side. She couldn't even go relieve herself without Amanda being there. Try as she might, Polly was unable to spend any time alone with Chance.

The third night, Chance sat in his parlor, feeling just as frustrated as Polly. There was no doubt in his mind that Amanda was protecting Polly. The question was, why? The only thing he could come up with was that Amanda was making sure she kept him and Polly apart. And the only understandable reason for that was jealousy. Yet at no time would Amanda even let him near herself, which made his reasoning collapse at the seams. He couldn't even get Polly alone to find out if she knew what was going on!

Chance took a bottle of whiskey over to his favorite chair and sat down. He was going to get drunk. He was angry at Amanda for not wanting to have anything to do with him, and angry at himself for wanting her so damn bad.

He took a long swig out of the bottle. He had to be the world's greatest sap, or he would have ended all this by getting his ass out of Springtown. Was he waiting for Amanda to tell him to go to hell? All she'd talked about lately was how much she loved this town, so what purpose would it serve to take her with him if she was only going to return? He took another drink. The truth of the matter was, he didn't know what to do, and that was the most frustrating of all.

Hearing a thud, Chance looked toward the fireplace. Emily's diary had fallen to the floor. He went over and picked it up. He was about to put it back on the mantel, but he decided to read a few more pages. He returned to his chair and stretched his legs out. When he opened the journal, just seeing her handwriting saddened him. He started to close it, but she was telling about Susan having a baby boy. Soon, he was engulfed in the story.

... they are a hard-looking bunch, though the man leading the group is really quite handsome. I feel terribly wicked at saying such a thing, since Jeffery and I are to wed next week. But try as I may, I can find no love in my heart for him. I no longer want this wedding, but Mother assures me that my feelings will pass once I'm married. I don't think so.

Chance turned the page to the next entry and read,

The men that rode into town yesterday have stayed at the saloon, but I overheard Jeffery telling Father that they've been drunk and rowdy. Jeffery is concerned.

He thinks the men mean trouble and are just making sure there isn't a traveling marshal due in town. As I left Father's shop, the leader of the men accidentally bumped into me. He was very much a gentleman and introduced himself as Jack Quigley. I was quite flattered by the interest I could see in his eyes, but of course I simply nodded my acknowledgment and hurried on my way.

Chance sat up and placed the bottle of whisky on the floor beside his chair. A hard knot was forming in his stomach. Jack Quigley was the name of Amanda's ghost. He quickly read on.

It is painful to write the words, but I must tell what has happened to me or go mad with the grief and fear. The gang of ruffians have taken over our once peaceful town. They have pillaged, murdered and raped. It is a bloodbath and I fear for my life. The demons captured Father and tortured him, trying to get him to reveal the location of the gold. He was not a young man and died from the pain. I found my mother dead in her bedroom. She had shot herself. She left a note asking me to forgive her, but she could not live without Father. I will not dally on the consuming grief I feel, not only for my loss but for the others as well. Jeffery ran off into the night. The coward didn't even try to take me with him, but I would not have gone anyway. Jack forced himself on me, claiming it was not rape because he loved me. I will never feel clean again, but I do not have my mother's bravery to take my life. May God forgive me, but if I kill anyone, it will be Jack if he dares to

come here again. I have tried to rally the people left
in town to fight back, but they are too frightened.

With my constant goading the townsfolk finally
took up arms. After a hard battle and the loss of even
more lives, we overpowered the gang. Jack Quigley
was the last to die. He cursed everyone and swore he
would return from the dead to wreak his vengeance.
He was laughing when he died. A big bonfire was
built to celebrate the hanging. I can't blame them for
their jubilation, but I feel no joy, only sadness for the
loved ones lost, and hate for the man who caused my
parents' death and soiled me.

Chance skimmed the entries until he found what he was
looking for, then read every word.

Who would have thought Jack would return? It
doesn't seem possible. Our town is cursed. Those that
caused his death have been killed. A sign was staked
out warning of yellow fever to scare off any unwary
travelers. Had they warned of a ghost, no one would
have believed it. The people who remain are leaving
with nothing more than the clothes on their back.
They are terrified and sneak out of town at night. I
do not know if any of them got away safely, but I
pray it is so. They will never return for fear of Jack's
vengence.

All others are gone from Springtown now. I am the
only one left. I will not leave, even though I know he
is coming after me. It is just a matter of time. Before
Father was taken away, he told me where the gold is
hidden, and I feel called upon to reveal its hiding
place, but first I must explain. From the beginning,
all gold from the area mines was tagged with the

owner's name and given to Father because he was an honest man. He in turn kept it safely hidden. The town fathers wanted the gold to remain a secret so that outlaws would not rob us, as has happened in other mining towns. They were planning a wagon train to take the load to Sacramento when Jack Quigley rode into town. The gold is in the old abandoned mine by the stream. There is a shaft on top, and when the sun is high, the bags of gold can be seen with the help of a mirror. This was Father's way of checking to see that all was well without having to enter. Though the mine looks as if it has been filled in, there is only a thin layer of rocks. Father had the rocks placed there shortly after the gang of men arrived. I am the only one left with this secret. All others are dead. I pray someone of a good heart will find the gold and it will bring them much happiness. I will then be at peace.

Chance knew the mine. It was one of the first he'd looked at, and also one of the largest. He had disregarded it because he'd thought it was filled in.

Jack is coming after me. He is knocking things over below, and soon will be ascending the stairs. I shall hide in my armoire as I did when I was a child. I do not believe . . .

The writing had stopped. Had Jack Quigley locked the armoire door, or had it accidentally latched shut? Chance would never know. He let the diary fall to the floor. Amanda had told the truth about the ghost, and he'd been too damn stubborn to believe her. He ran his fingers through his hair, trying to decide what he should do.

Feeling the need for the whiskey, he picked the bottle up and took a long drink. How the hell was he supposed to fight a ghost? Now that he understood more of what was going on, all of Amanda's actions were beginning to make sense. What if Amanda's lack of interest stemmed from a threat from Jack?

Chance stood and began pacing the floor. He stopped and stared down at the diary. He suddenly remembered how the blanket had slid off the trunk when he'd gone to fetch the second diary. And what about the glow he'd seen? Emily's ghost was still in that room! If he had to believe in ghosts, why not hers, as well? She'd made sure he found her diaries. As farfetched as it seemed, maybe finding the gold would make Jack go away. Emily had said that when the gold was gone she'd rest in peace. Why not Jack?

He rubbed the back of his neck as he resumed his pacing. Before he did anything, he was going to have to get Polly out of town. Getting Amanda out of town without Jack knowing might prove impossible. At least if he could get Polly away, there would be one less person to worry about. But how was he going to do that with Amanda constantly by Polly's side? He had a sudden, overwhelming sense of caution. He had to be careful. He couldn't let Amanda know of his plan. Somehow, he had to talk to Polly alone. He had to let her know of the danger. Once he had Polly out of the way, he'd take care of Amanda. A lopsided smile spread across his lips. No one was going to keep him from taking Amanda away from here, not even a ghost. And now there was no doubt in his mind that Amanda loved him. She was willing to trade her life for his.

Chapter Sixteen

As the threesome searched the latest area they'd mapped out, Chance was itching to get to the gold Emily had told of in her diary. Knowing they weren't even near it added to his impatience. But there were more important priorities. Somehow, he had to get Polly alone. But that was easier said than done. All day Amanda had remained at Polly's side. In another hour, they'd have to return to town.

The rocky region they were searching showed few signs of shafts. What visible diggings there were weren't very high up. Chance stood on the tangled growth that covered the ground and watched Polly and Amanda work their way up a short, rocky incline. "Watch out for snakes," he hollered.

Amanda turned to look down. "What did you say?"

Not watching where she was going, Amanda took a wrong step. Chance started running forward as she slid down the rocky hillside. She was sprawled at the bottom when he reached for her. "Are you all right?" he asked worriedly.

Still a bit stunned, Amanda answered, "I think so." She tried to stand, but the pain in her left foot caused her to sit down again.

"Don't move." As Chance pulled off her boot, he heard her grunt with pain. She had a minor ankle sprain, but apart from that she appeared to be all right. However, she had given him the opportunity he'd been searching for. "Looks like you're going to have to stay off that foot for a day or two." He gave her a devilish grin. "I also think your rear might have suffered a few bruises."

"Are you all right?" Polly asked as she joined them.

"She's sprained her ankle." Seeing the glint that came into her eyes, Chance had the distinct impression Polly, too, was pleased about Amanda's injury. He looked down at Amanda. "I'll carry you over to those trees so you can sit in the shade." He picked her up in his arms.

"But I'm sure it'll be fine," Amanda insisted.

"Chance is right," Polly added. "You can't be doin' any more climbin' today. Chance and I can take care of it."

"You have to stay with me, Polly!"

"Nonsense. She'll be just fine," Chance assured her.

Panic rose in Amanda's throat. "She might die! Damn it, Chance, put me back down!"

Chance looked into her whiskey-colored eyes. "What makes you think that?" he asked quietly.

"I had a dream and I saw Polly's death!"

"Amanda, it was only a dream. I'll watch after her."

"Polly, promise me you'll be careful."

"I promise."

"You wait here," Chance told Polly. "I'll be back in a minute, and we can continue our search."

Amanda could do nothing more. She couldn't walk, and she couldn't force Polly to stay with her. She could only pray Jack would leave them alone. Chance was right. She was losing touch with reality. She rested her head against Chance's shoulder and closed her eyes, enjoying the few moments she had to feel his arms around her. She inhaled the pleasing, earthy smell of his body, and listened to the beat of his heart. She wanted his kisses, she wanted him to take away the deep grief of knowing she would soon lose him. It would be so wonderful to once again feel his lips on her's.

Chance gently placed her on the ground. "Thank you," she muttered. "Will you look out for Polly?"

"I'll make sure she's all right." He could see the concern in Amanda's penetrating gaze, and he had to steel himself to keep from picking her up and walking away from everything that related to Springtown. But, after reading Emily's diary, he felt sure Jack Quigley was keeping a close eye on them. One wrong move could mean death for all of them. He wanted to tell Amanda that he was going to do everything in his power to get them all safely away, but he didn't dare. Even talking to Polly was going to be a gamble. He moved the knapsack to Amanda's side. "In case you get hungry or thirsty."

"You won't forget to watch after Polly?"

"No. I'll keep her by my side." Chance winked at her. "Cheer up, Amanda. Don't worry, things might not be as bad as you think."

Amanda stared at Chance's broad back as he walked away. Don't worry? She could do nothing but worry until he and Polly were safely away. She tried rotating her foot, but it was painful. One thing she didn't need was to be lame. Tomorrow, Polly and Chance were probably going to insist she be left behind, and there would be nothing she could do about it.

As soon as Chance joined her, Polly wanted to tell him about Amanda. "Chance, I—"

"Don't say anything," he whispered. "Just keep walking."

When they were out of Amanda's sight, Chance took hold of Polly's arm, then pulled her along beside him.

"Chance, I have to talk to you! Amanda said she's only stayin' in Springtown until she's sure you're out of her life. But I think—"

"I haven't time to explain." Chance leaned back and looked around to be sure Amanda had stayed put. "I'm already taking a big gamble that Jack isn't listening to what I'm saying."

"You believe there really is a ghost?" Polly gasped.

"Yes. Now listen to me. I want you to leave Springtown tonight."

"Tonight? Are you going with me?"

"No, I—"

"I can't walk all the way to Angels Camp." She brushed the dust from the seat of her britches. "Why can't you take me?"

"I have to get Amanda out of here, and I can't do it if I have to worry about you, as well. There is a town named Murphys not more than five miles from here."

"Why can't she leave, too?"

"Our friend may let us go, but he won't let Amanda go unless I can figure out a way to trick him." Chance became thoughtful. "If I can get the gold, I think he'll go away."

"I don't want to go alone!"

"You heard what Amanda said. Your life is in danger, so you have to get away from here." He had Polly's attention now.

"You mean Jack could kill me?"

"That's exactly what I'm saying."

"I don't want to die!"

"Then do as I say. Tonight, after Amanda has fallen asleep, I want you to steal out of the house. I'll be waiting. I'll take you halfway to Murphys. Then I'm coming back. Can you do that?''

"I'm scared."

"I know, but it's either that or stay here and constantly wonder when Jack is going to strike." He heard Polly suck in her breath.

"You'll be waiting?"

"I'll be waiting."

"All right, I'll do it."

Polly lay on the bed, listening to Amanda's even breathing. She'd tried to get up several times, but each time Amanda had awoken. "Are you all right?" she would whisper, but Polly would pretend to be asleep.

Carefully she moved one leg to the side of the bed, then the other. When Amanda didn't move, she slowly sat up, then slid off the bed. The moonlight coming in through the window allowed her enough light to see by. She grabbed her jeans, shirt and boots, then crept toward the door. At the last moment she thought to take a candle and a match. Fear was already permeating her senses. The door didn't creak when she opened it, or when she closed it.

It was a warm night, but the hallway was surprisingly chilly. Goose bumps rose on Polly's skin, and her teeth were starting to chatter. Amanda had said something shortly after they'd come to Springtown about the cold when the ghost appeared. Her hand shaking, Polly struck the match and lit the candle. The light made her feel somewhat better, but not much. She cupped her hand around the flame and started saying one prayer after another.

Polly was only halfway to the stairs when a sudden gust of wind blew out the candle. Everything became as dark

as pitch, and she had to bite back a scream. She didn't
know whether to go back to the bedroom or continue on.
Reaching to the side, she touched the wall and cautiously
moved forward. Finally she felt the rail. If there really was
a Jack Quigley, would he push her down the stairs?

Chance expelled a long breath when he saw Polly walk
out of the house. So far so good. Now he had to get her
away. He hurried to her. "Come on, Polly, let's get you
out of here."

"I have to put my clothes on."

"Your clothes can wait. Just slip your shoes on."

Instead of going through town, Chance headed toward
the back of the house. It was farther that way, but he intended to make a wide circle around Springtown. Polly
complained about him going too fast, but he continued to
push her on.

Chance didn't bring Polly to a halt until they were a
good mile away from Springtown.

Polly dropped to the ground, trying to catch her breath.
"Are . . . are we safe?"

"I'd say so."

"How much farther do we have to go?"

"*You* have about four more miles."

Polly brushed her hair out of her eyes. "Me? What do
you mean me?"

"I have to go back."

Polly scrambled to her feet. "You mean you're just
gonna leave me here in the middle of nowhere?" She tried
looking around, but it was too dark to see anything.

Chance pointed south. "Just keep going in that direction and you'll find Murphys."

"I'll get lost!"

Chance looked back toward Springtown. "Polly, you
know I can't go with you."

Polly sighed. "I know," she said finally. "You have to go back for Amanda."

"Would you have me do otherwise?"

"No. I love her, too." She slipped her shirt on. "Do you really think you can get her away from there?"

"I don't know, but I'm sure going to give it one hell of a try. Polly, I know where the gold is."

"You do?" Polly gasped. "You've seen it?"

"No, but I'm going to take a look at it come noon." He slung the saddlebags from his shoulder. "In here is a pouch and a half of gold that I found. I want you to stay at the Murphys Hotel for two weeks. If we don't show up by then, it's all yours. I want you to do me one favor. I've got my buckskin horse at the livery stable. Pay the boarding fee. He's yours if we don't return. I wouldn't advise you to try and ride him, but the blacksmith wants to buy him."

"Chance," Polly whispered worriedly, "you sound as if I'll never see you again. I won't run off with everything."

Chance chuckled. "You know, Polly, that's the one thing that never entered my mind. I know you'll wait. You're a good woman. I don't know if we'll be able to get the gold. Hell, I don't even know that someone hasn't already gotten their hands on the gold. But I do know there's enough in these saddlebags to get us all started again."

"Maybe we can open a saloon."

Chance shifted his weight to his other foot. "Polly, if you're smart, you won't go back to a saloon. Take your time and find yourself a good man to settle down with. I think that's what you really want. Now I have to go."

"Chance, you be careful."

"Believe me, I have no wish to die, but I'll be damned if I'm going to let some ghost take the woman I love." He leaned down and kissed her cheek. "I'll see you in a few days."

Polly took the saddlebags he handed her and watched him disappear into the night. "I found the right man," she whispered. "He just isn't available."

Amanda awoke to discover that it was late and Polly was gone. She jumped out of bed, but the sudden pain in her ankle made her sit down again. There was no need to rush. Polly and Chance would already have left for the day's search. It was doubtful she could find them, and her ankle was still too tender for her to trek over the rough terrain. Now all she could do was wait and worry.

She limped to the open window and stuck her head out. It was already nearing noon. At least she wouldn't have to wait all day.

Chance set the pick, grappling iron, rope and knapsack at the edge of the coyote hole. He grabbed the end of the rope and attached it to the grappling iron. The shaft appeared to be the first dig in the mine. All the riggings and timber were still in place, but the bucket to lower men down had been removed. How deep did the main tunnel go? Five, six hundred, a thousand feet? Two thousand? He took a deep breath. The hole was probably not more than twenty to forty feet deep, but even that held no appeal.

He took the mirror from the knapsack and glanced up at the sun, which was high overhead. Maybe now he'd finally find out if the gold was still there. Hopefully he could pull it out with the grappling iron instead of having to go down the shaft. The gold couldn't be just lying loose. It had to be in sacks or containers of some sort.

Chance moved to the wide lip of the shaft, then proceeded to adjust the mirror so that the sunlight reflected into the black hole. Leaning over, he looked down. Just as he caught a glimpse of what looked like gunnysacks, he felt the ground give way beneath his feet. He tired reaching out and throwing his body backward, but whatever it was he'd grab hold of slid into the black hole with him.

Chance hit the ground with a thud, but he was only dazed. He shook his head. The next instant he was consumed with terror. Sweat seeped out of his pores as he stared at the gaping hole some thirty feet overhead. He began to shake violently as the dank smell of damp earth violated his nostrils. Frantically he groped over the ground, looking for something, anything, that might help him escape. A steel spike jabbed his hand. He moved his hands over it, feeling it. It was the grappling iron! Holding the rope in one hand, he jumped to his feet. Time and time again he tried tossing the iron up to the top, only to have it fall back down, narrowly missing him. Breathing was becoming more and more difficult. His vision began to blur, and then everything went black.

When Chance came to, he realized he must have passed out. He needed to force himself to remain calm, but that was easier said than done. He could feel the panic once again trying to take hold. "Think, damn it, think! Think of Amanda. Are you going to let Jack Quigley win?"

Chance raised himself to a sitting position. As frantic as he'd been, it was no wonder he couldn't get the grappling iron to the top. He wiped the sweat from his face, refusing to give in to his fears. As long as he kept his mind busy, he would keep those fears under control. He began searching for the rope. His hand suddenly touched something familiar. The knapsack! He must have pulled it in with him when he fell. He dragged it to him and opened it with shaking hands. Feeling around inside, he located the candle he was searching for. Then he found a match and struck it, blessing the sweet glow when it burst into flame. He lit the candle and stood. The space he was in was quite large. He kept turning until he saw what he was seeking.

Not more than twenty feet away were the gunnysacks. He hurried over and began opening them. Finally he stepped back, unable to believe what he was seeing. Never had he seen so much gold! He raised the candle higher. The large room was three-quarters full of gold! He sat down on the ground and stared. He, Polly and Amanda were damn millionaires! His deep laughter echoed through the tunnels.

Not until Chance was able to contain his jubilation did reality set in. How was he going to get the gold out? He was also beginning to realize he was cold as hell.

Chance again looked up at the shaft opening, suddenly wondering if Jack Quigley had pushed him. A perfect way to get rid of him. Well, Jack hadn't beat him yet. Chance stood and began walking around the big room, taking a good look. There were tunnels branching off in every direction, most of them slanting downward to the hell below. But there were other things, too. Boxes of dynamite, as well as caps and wicks. Lanterns, picks... He chuckled when he saw a coat hanging on a spike that had been driven into the wall. He had two choices. Try to find his way out of here, or try the grappling iron again. The sun had long since passed over the hole, and that told him it was already late afternoon. He chose the grappling iron.

After numerous efforts, Chance knew he no longer had a choice. He had only twice managed to get the hook on the edge of the opening, and each time the ground had given way, sending dirt and grass down on top of him. Though he didn't relish having to find his way out, it suddenly occurred to him that his fear was gone. It had been replaced with dogged determination. He took the wool coat off the stake and put it on. The sleeves were way too short, and he couldn't close the front, but it was warm. He had no idea which direction to go in, but there were several things in his favor. He had light and he had a whole lot of string in his knapsack. And he knew a fair amount about mines. He piled everything he thought he might need in an old wheelbarrow. Knowing dynamite preferred warmer temperatures, he stuck a few sticks in his boot.

Amanda paced Chance's parlor floor, sick with worry. She'd limped here looking for him and Polly. Then she'd limped down to the saloon, and everywhere else she could think of, but they were nowhere to be found. It was now dark, and they should have returned hours ago. Something must have happened to them. Should she go searching for them? How could she? She'd never find them at night. She felt her skin prickle and stood still, waiting for Jack to appear. He was sitting in Chance's favorite chair, cleaning his fingernails.

"Is something wrong, my love?" Jack asked casually.

"Where are they, Jack?"

"They? Who is they?"

Amanda wanted to scream at him, throw something, do anything to rid his face of the look of pleasure. "Have you done something to them?"

"Of course not."

"Then where are they?" Amanda held her breath.

"They've left. They took all the jewels, and everything else they could get their hands on, and last night they sneaked away."

"I don't believe you," Amanda said.

Jack turned his gaze on her and laughed. "Did you honestly think a no-account drifter and a whore would stick around once they decided there was no gold? Shall I tell you about all the times they—"

"No!"

"But yes. I received a great deal of pleasure watching them."

Tears started falling down Amanda's cheeks.

"I told you I was the only one who really loved you, but you wouldn't listen. I only let them stay around so that you could find out for yourself. But they were clever and didn't show any affection for each other when you were around."

"I don't believe you!" She started to run toward the doorway, but he raised his hand and a strong gust of wind threw her to the floor.

Jack slowly rose from the chair, his face twisted with anger. "You will never try to leave when I'm talking to you! Do you understand?"

"What can you do? Kill me?"

"Oh, no. I would never do that. But I can maim you, bruise you, make your life a living hell. Believe me, I've done it many times before when I wanted a woman."

He was standing in front of her now. Amanda couldn't bear to look at his face. "Please, Jack. You say you love me. Let me go."

"Let you go? Are you begging me?"

"No. I won't beg."

"Good. I have never liked a weak woman. But I'm never going to let you go. I've waited too long for you to come into my town. We are destined to be together."

"I'll die first. I won't eat." His laughter made her think of cold steel being run up her spine.

"You'll live. Self-preservation is a marvelous thing to behold. Don't try to leave, Amanda. You won't escape me, and I assure you, when I'm through with you, you'll never try it again. And remember, though you can't see me, I can see you. I'm with you all the time, and I'm getting to know you very well."

When Jack disappeared, Amanda laid her head on the carpet and cried. Had he told the truth about Polly and Chance? No matter what he said, it didn't change her love for Chance. She'd known for some time that Jack would never allow them to have a future together, but she had her memories, and Jack couldn't take them away from her. And hadn't she prayed that Polly and Chance would get away safely? She sat up, angrily brushing her tears away. Why was she ready to believe Jack? He was always trying to manipulate her. And if Jack was lying, who was to say Chance wouldn't return? No, Chance couldn't return. There was no doubt in her mind that Jack would kill him if he did.

With each tunnel Chance tried he left pieces of string along the way. When he decided a tunnel was leading down, not up, or he came to a dead end, he'd retrace his steps, following the strings back. The fourth tunnel showed promise. He hadn't gone far when he found deep grooved tracks made by a small wagon. The tunnel was plenty wide enough to handle a mule and wagon. And the gold was far too heavy to have been carried. He had no idea what time it was, but he knew he must have been walking for hours, and it wasn't easy pushing the old wheelbarrow. Exhausted, and not knowing how long it would be before he found his way out, he stopped and sat down in the dirt. He rummaged through his knapsack and found some dried-out bread and hard venison.

After his small meal, he checked the lantern. He was hesitant to put out the flame, but he had to conserve the fuel. He had only three lanterns left. He might find some more in the tunnel, but he couldn't be sure. He reached over and extinguished the flame.

The minute he was engulfed in the darkness, Chance felt the old panic returning. To get his mind off his fear, he concentrated on Amanda. Just thinking about her warmed his heart. He smiled, remembering their times together, then frowned when he remembered how many times she'd tried to tell him about Jack. He lay down and closed his eyes, needing sleep. Suddenly, Chance's eyes flew open. If Jack had caused the dust devil and the storm, why hadn't he interfered when they'd made love on the boulder, or when he'd tackled Amanda at the lake. There was only one answer. And it had been right under their noses all along!

Chapter Seventeen

Amanda lay on the bed in Emily's room, watching as the afternoon breeze fluttered the lace curtains. Her lips were cracked, and her body was hot and sticky from the heat, but she refused to leave the room. She'd been there ever since her talk with Jack two nights before. If Chance were going to return, he would already have done so. As for Jack, as long as she stayed in this room, she was sure he couldn't touch her. Maybe Emily's spirit was what Jack feared and the reason he refused to enter.

"Amanda!"

Amanda jumped off her bed and stumbled. She hadn't realized how weak she'd become. Looking out the window, she watched Chance leave the trees, headed straight for the house. His clothes were filthy, and his jaw was dark with stubble. He looked haggard and angry. Then she saw the wind starting to move the leaves and branches, growing increasingly stronger. "Jack!" she whispered, heading for the door. "No!" she screamed as she ran down the hallway. She reached the landing and saw Jack standing at the bottom of the stairs with his back to her. "No!" she screamed again. As she started down the steps, she stumbled, but somehow she managed to grab the banister for support. When Jack turned to face her, her steps faltered. His face was contorted with hate and fury. "Please, don't kill him."

"Amanda!" Chance called. "Come out here. I want to talk to you."

"Are you begging me, Amanda?" Jack asked.

"Yes, I'm begging you." He turned his back to her again, and she could hear thunder, could hear the wind starting to howl. "I'll do anything you say!" Again he turned, his lips spread in a cold smile. Amanda took the last step and halted.

"Why should I save his miserable life? He is trying to take you away from me!"

His words seemed to bellow through the house. "Because if you do this I'll be your servant until my dying day."

He looked at her suspiciously. "You'll never go in that bedroom again?"

"Never."

"And you will do anything I tell you?"

"Yes, I promise."

He cocked his head. "Then I'll grant you this one last favor. But don't *ever* make me angry again. Get rid of him once and for all. I'll be watching, and if he doesn't leave, I'll kill him. I guarantee it won't be a pleasant death."

Amanda could hear the wind starting to die down. She went to the door and opened it. Chance hadn't moved, and she had no choice but to go to him. She forced herself to smile, praying that this time she could make him believe she never wanted to see him again.

Chance was well aware that he'd come damn close to meeting his maker, that somehow Amanda had managed to prevent it. He couldn't believe how much she had changed in such a short time. She was gaunt and had dark circles under her eyes. Her jeans and shirt looked as if she'd worn them for days. And from the way she walked, she was weak. Had she been sick, or was this Jack's doing? He had to force his body to relax so that neither Amanda or Jack would suspect the anger he was feeling, or what he was up to. As she drew closer, his anger intensified at the sight of the deep cracks on her beautiful lips.

"Chance," Amanda said brightly, "I thought you'd left. Where's Polly?"

"In a town called Murphys."

His blue-green eyes were assessing her, and Amanda had to lock her hands behind her back to prevent showing her nervousness. Even as filthy as he was, he was still the handsomest man she'd ever laid eyes on. God, how she loved him. "What happened? You look like you fell off a horse."

"As a matter of fact, I did. To tell you the truth, I got to feeling guilty about Polly and me just taking off. I had to come back to ask if you wanted us to leave any money at Murphys for you. Polly told me you were just waiting to get rid of me before leaving Springtown."

"You . . . you mean you're not angry with me?"

"Why should I be? We're both adults, and like I said before, whatever we shared wouldn't have lasted."

"And you have Polly when there's no one else around."

Chance was taking his cues as to what he should say from Amanda. Seeing the hurt in her large eyes made it all the more difficult to keep from drawing her into his arms. "Well, you know Polly. How long can a man resist?"

"Yes, how long indeed. I won't be needing any money. I assure you, I'm quite well taken care of."

Chance ran his fingers through his hair. "Just to prove you have no hard feelings, why don't you walk me to my horse?"

"Well, I . . ."

He gave her a smile. "Oh, come on. At least we can part as friends."

Amanda looked over her shoulder. Jack should be convinced by now that there was nothing between her and Chance. "Very well."

"So how long do you plan on staying in Springtown?" Chance asked as he guided her around to the back of the house. He kept talking as they walked farther and farther away.

Amanda suddenly stopped and looked around. "Where is your horse?"

Chance gently pulled her into his arms. "Amanda, I haven't got time to explain, but trust me. We're going to leave this place together."

"No!" Amanda tried to pull away from him. "Don't you understand? I hate you. You have to leave!"

"Amanda, listen to me," he said gently. "Jack can't harm you now."

"No! You're wrong. He—"

Chance leaned down and kissed her tenderly, not wanting to hurt her cracked lips. "I love you," he whispered, "and I wouldn't do anything that could jeopardize your life."

"But you said you and Polly—"

Chance smiled. "I lied. I couldn't tell the truth with Jack around."

"Chance, listen to me! Jack will kill us both. Please leave," Amanda pleaded, a quiver of fear running through her entire body.

Chance gently shook her. "No, you listen to me. I'm convinced Jack can't hurt us. Are you all right? You look awful."

Seeing the love in his eyes was all she had ever wanted. Chance really did love her. He had all along. "I'm fine now," she said softly.

Chance looked back toward the town. "I've had a lot of time to mull over our situation, and I think I know how to get rid of Jack once and for all."

Amanda pulled away. "It's impossible. He's not human. I know that even now he's watching us."

"Then why hasn't he done anything?"

"Well . . . I don't know."

"Where's the wind or storm?" Chance chuckled, feeling more sure of himself as the minutes ticked away. "While I was in the mine—"

"In what mine?"

"I'll tell you about it later. Right now we haven't much time. I got to wondering why Jack became so angry about you sleeping in my bed, yet he hadn't said or done anything when we were together at other times. Suddenly the answer came to me. He didn't know about the other times because we were out of town. Springtown is Jack's jail."

"But that's impossible. He said he was always watching me."

"I'm guessing that he was using your fear to control you. As long as he had you convinced he could see everything, then he had nothing to worry about."

Amanda rubbed her throbbing temples. "You're right. Now that I think about it, all kinds of things happened that he didn't know about. I even remember him once saying that he *thought* you were checking mines. We could have left at any time!"

"I have a plan, darling, but I have no idea whether or not it's going to work."

"What do you mean you have a plan?" Amanda gasped. "If you're right about him not being able to get to us, let's just get the hell out of here!"

Chance caressed her cheek. "Don't you see, we can't leave."

"Why not? We did it before. Chance, I can't bear the thought of him killing you."

"Yes, we left, but each of us had to return. Amanda, do you believe in destiny?"

"I doubt if there is anything I would question any more. Why do you ask?"

"Because I feel in my gut that you, Polly and I were destined to come here. You said we could have left at any time. I don't think so. We were meant to destroy Jack's evilness and we were meant to find the gold. And not until that was accomplished could we leave."

"And just maybe," she said softly, "we were meant for each other."

He looked down at her and smiled. "There's no doubt in my mind."

Amanda took a deep, shaky breath. Chance was right. If there was a way to get rid of Jack, it was up to them to do it. "What's your plan?"

"Can you walk or shall I carry you?"

Amanda was feeling stronger with each passing minute. She could do anything as long as Chance was beside her. "I can walk."

Holding Amanda's hand, Chance made a wide circle of the town. Finally he came to the spot where he'd left the loaded rifles.

"What's this?" Amanda asked worriedly. "You can't kill Jack!"

"I'm going to give it one hell of a try. I've planted dynamite all over town. All the time I was worried that Jack would see me, but for some reason, he didn't."

"He was too busy waiting for me to come out of Emily's room. What are you going to do?"

"I'm about to take the biggest gamble of my life. I'm going to try and blow up the town. But I won't do it without your agreement. Look at me, Amanda." He looked into her deep, warm eyes when she turned toward him. "Several things could go wrong. The biggest one is that if I do this, it might release Jack from the town. If that happens, you know he's going to come after us. Or, he may use his powers to prevent anything from happening to Springtown. Maybe he'll blow out the fires. I don't know what he'll do." He ran his fingers through his hair. "Like I said, the whole thing is a gamble, but I think we have to give it a try."

Amanda gazed at the town below them, bathed in sunlight, it looked like any other small, prosperous mining town. She glanced back at Chance. "Maybe you're right. Maybe we were destined to come here, because we both know there really wasn't any choice."

Chance nodded, picked up a rifle, and aiming it at one of the places he placed the dynamite, pulled the trigger.

Wood flew in every direction. As Chance continued to pick up the rifles and shoot at other spots, Amanda felt the earth trembling beneath her feet. Her body shook as unsorted emotions lodged in her throat. Fire burst forth, greedily jumping from one building to the other and licking up into the sky. The heat was overwhelming. The billowing smoke that drifted around them caused tears to run down her cheeks. She could smell it, taste it. By the time Chance stopped, the entire town was in flames. Amanda could have sworn she heard Jack calling to her.

She put her hands to her ears and was about to bury her head in Chance's shoulder when she saw him pick up one last rifle. Amanda watched him aim it at the beautiful big house standing alone. Frantic, she grabbed his arm. "You can't!" she screamed.

Chance gently pried her hand away. "It has to be every structure, Amanda, or Jack will live on. Besides, he isn't the only ghost that needs to be laid to rest. We owe it to Emily." He aimed the rifle again and pulled the trigger. One side of the house exploded, and flames began eating at the majestic structure. Amanda buried her head in Chance's chest, and he wrapped his arms around her.

"Amanda. Look."

Amanda turned her head. In the center of town, amid the flames, a thick black cloud was forming. There was a hard tightening in her chest as the cloud rose a short distance into the air and began moving toward them. She could see Jack's image, his face twisted with hate, fire glistening in his eyes. Then another figure rose up in the smoke, and Jack backed away.

"Emily!" Amanda whispered.

Emily covered Jack with what looked like some sort of a cloak, and the black smoke immediately sucked down into the ground. When it was gone, Amanda was engulfed in a freedom she hadn't felt in weeks. She looked up at Chance, smiled and said, "I'm so thirsty," then fainted.

They were on the creek bank. Amanda lay in Chance's arms staring up at the stars, and feeling as if the world were all hers. Chance had killed a rabbit and roasted it on a spit, she had all the water she could drink, she was a rich woman, and she had the love of the only man she'd ever wanted. "It's hard to believe that there really was gold hidden and you found it."

"You'll find it even harder to believe when we come back with a wagon and load it." Chance thought of Emily. Someday he would tell Amanda about the diaries. By then she would be sure enough of his love to understand the special place he had in his heart for that brave, gentle young woman.

"How many trips do you think it will take?"

"I have no idea. Amanda, have I asked you to marry me?"

"No."

"Well, will you?"

"Will I what?"

Chance broke out laughing and pulled her on top of him. "Do you have any idea how much I love you?"

"Prove it."

"It would be my pleasure, but are you sure you can—"

"Very sure." She ran her hand down his chest and kissed his lips.

"Oh, no," he said with mock sincerity. "I'm not the type who would share my body without a commitment of marriage."

Amanda laughed. "Then I guess you've left me with no alternative. I'll have to marry you."

He kissed her tenderly. "As soon as we get to Murphys?"

Amanda moaned with pleasure when his hand slid down her back and cupped her bottom. He moved her against him. She could feel his need. "Darling, do you know how many times I've wanted you to make love to me?" She raised her head so that he could nibble her neck.

"I can guess, 'cause I sure know the hell I've gone through from wanting you." He rolled her over on her back and began unbuttoning her shirt.

The bright sun was just peeking over the mountains when Amanda and Chance stepped to the edge of the boulder and looked down at what was once Springtown. Now there was nothing but smoldering wood and ashes. Thinking about all the people that had once lived there with their hopes and aspirations for the future caused a tear to trickle down Amanda's cheek.

"Come on, darling," Chance said gently, "we've got a five mile walk ahead of us, and Polly is waiting. She's in for one hell of a surprise."

Hand in hand, they turned and started walking.

"Chance, when we've collected all the gold, are we going to tell where it came from?"

"Nope. We'll just let people think it's from our own mine."

Amanda grinned. "Then the gold will become a legend."

Chance released a robust laugh. "It already is. Just think—years from now people will still be searching for the hidden treasure of Springtown."

As they headed toward Murphys, the warm mountain breeze picked up their laughter and carried it through the hills of eternity.

*   *   *   *   *